Through The Crystal Gate

Through The Crystal Gate

LG Rice

Disclaimer:

This book is a work of fiction. Any names, characters, events, and incidents are purely the product of the author's imagination or are used fictitiously. While this story may reference real locations and landmarks, these are included solely as a backdrop to the fictional narrative. Any resemblance to actual persons, living or dead, or real events is entirely coincidental.

Copyright © 2024 by LG Rice
All rights reserved. No part of this book may be reproduced in any manner whatsoever without written permission except in the case of brief quotations embodied in critical articles and reviews.
First Printing, 2024

In loving memory of my parents, Tracy and Christine Rice, whose boundless love and encouragement sparked my passion for books and reading. Your wisdom and stories live on in every word I write. This is for you.

1

Galen Valley was a place of whispered secrets and forgotten dreams, nestled between the arms of the Blue Ridge mountains and draped in a cloak of evergreen. In the heart of the valley stood Sage Manor, an ancient mansion with walls steeped in history and windows that seemed to gaze out like wise old eyes. Sage Manor was more than just a house; it was a sentinel of the past, guarding the memories of those who had walked its halls long before.

Gran Celia, as the children called her, was the matriarch of the manor, a woman as timeless as the stone walls themselves. Her silver hair flowed like moonlight down her back, and her eyes sparkled with the wisdom of someone who had seen the world in all its beauty and tragedy. She had been the caretaker of Sage Manor for as long as anyone could remember, but her role went far beyond that of a mere guardian.

She was the keeper of the valley's lore, the storyteller who wove together the threads of history and the supernatural that made Galen Valley so unique. Waverly and Lynx Beaumont, her grandchildren, were the latest in a long line of explorers who had roamed the grounds of Sage Manor. Waverly, at fifteen, was on the brink of discovering who she was, with a wild curiosity that often led her into the pages of old books or down paths in the woods of the Pisgah National Forest that served as the manor's backyard that no one else dared to tread. Lynx, only eleven, was a bundle of energy and imagination, always looking for the next adventure, with a mischievous grin that hinted at his next grand scheme.

The siblings loved Sage Manor, but they loved its grounds even more. The gardens were a wild expanse of roses, ivy, and ancient oaks that had stood for centuries. At the very center of the garden was the old pond, with water lilies floating lazily on the surface, their delicate pink and white petals catching the sunlight. In the middle of the pond stood a gazebo, weathered and worn, but still beautiful in its age.

One late afternoon with the rain pouring down relentlessly, turning the skies over the Pisgah National Forest into a dull canvas of gray, Waverly found herself drawn to the gazebo once more. With the roof above her offering shelter from the downpour, she nestled into one of the old wicker chairs, a book open in her lap, her attention rapt in its pages as the wind rustled the leaves around her.

The peaceful solitude was something Waverly cherished, especially on days like this when the outside world felt far away. Her fingers traced the edges of the worn pages, absorbing the words, escaping into an earlier century. It was quiet here, away from the bustle of the manor. Her thoughts wandered between the characters and the rainstorm, her mind floating in the comfort of this familiar routine.

Inside the manor, however, Lynx was less content. The steady rain had trapped him indoors, and boredom gnawed at him. He had already scoured the manor's library, poked through the kitchen for snacks, and even tried his hand at a few odd tasks around the house—none of them satisfying his restless energy.

Frustrated, he wandered upstairs, kicking his feet against the wooden floorboards. He had explored every room he could, but one place always seemed off-limits—the attic. His curiosity piqued, Lynx climbed the narrow staircase, the door creaking loudly as he pushed it open. Dust particles swirled in the air as he entered the darkened space, the only light coming from a small window at the far end.

The attic was filled with boxes and trunks of forgotten belongings—old family heirlooms, unused furniture, and objects long past their prime. Lynx felt like an intruder in a place suspended in time. As he pushed through the clutter, something caught his eye. There, in the far corner of the room, sit a very ornate box. It looked like a shiny pirate's treasure box.

I have to check that out, Lynx thought to himself. Moving other boxes from around it, he knelt down on the attic floor before the box to take a closer look. There were a lot of markings and symbols on this box that Lynx had never seen before. For that matter, the metal was not familiar to him either.

He reached out and flipped up the latch to open the box. Inside lay a strange, ornate device—circular, made of the same metal he still didn't recognize, with even more of the strange markings and symbols carved into it.

"What's this?" Lynx muttered to himself. He reached out, his fingers brushing the device. The moment he touched it, a strange warmth hummed beneath his fingertips, sending a shiver up his spine. Suddenly, the device came to life, the markings glowing faintly, a low rumble vibrating through the floorboards beneath him.

"Uh... what did I do?" Lynx said, wide-eyed, as he pulled his hand away in confusion.

The hum grew louder, pulsing with an almost mechanical rhythm. Without warning, a flash of light erupted from the attic walls, followed by a distant but unmistakable rumble—a sound so deep it seemed to come from the very earth itself. The energy crackled in the air, its force strong enough to shake the manor's foundation.

Down in the gazebo, Waverly heard it first—a tremor, subtle at first, but unmistakable. Her body tensed, a ripple of unease running through her as she snapped her gaze to the manor. Her heart thudded in her chest, a feeling of something off hanging in the air. Did we just have an earthquake?

Throwing the book from her hands, she stood, eyes scanning the surrounding trees, the gusts of wind swirling around her. The storm suddenlty felt strange—it was as if the air had become charged with electricity, a loud humming noise filled her ears drowning out the heavy rain.

Gran Celia, who had been inside the manor, felt it too. She stopped in her tracks, a frown forming on her face as she glanced toward the gazebo. The energy coming from the manor, the pulsing sensation—it was unlike anything she had felt in years.

Waverly ran toward the manor, her heart racing now with a mixture of concern and curiosity. She reached the door just as Lynx came barreling down the stairs, his eyes wide and full of panic.

"I didn't mean to! I swear!" he blurted, his voice high-pitched with nervous energy. "It just... it started glowing, and I touched it, and then—"

Before he could finish his explanation, Waverly's eyes narrowed. "Lynx, what did you touch?"

His words tumbled out in a rushed confession. "I found this device in the attic. I didn't know it was connected to anything, but then it—"

Gran Celia, arriving in the foyer, her gaze sharp and focused, hearing Lynx's last words. "Where is it?" she demanded.

Lynx led them to the attic, his face full of unease as he pointed to the now-dimmed device sitting in the box. Waverly and Gran Celia moved closer, both inspecting it with a mixture of curiosity and apprehension. The device was sleek and metallic, inscribed with intricate symbols. It looked like something ancient, and the way the energy from it still hummed in the air told them that whatever it was, it was far from ordinary.

Gran Celia knelt down, her fingers brushing the metal surface, feeling the vibrations still emanating from it. "This is no simple artifact. It's a piece of ancient technology, one tied to the portal."

"The portal?" Waverly repeated, her breath catching in her throat. "What... portal?"

Gran Celia turned to her, her face grave. "This device is a key. It activates the crystal gate—the very same one that's beneath the gazebo. It's been sealed for years, but it appears it's triggered again."

Waverly and Lynx looked at their grandmother with alarm and confusion showing on both their faces.

"Come with me," Gran Celia commanded as she turned and quickly made her way back down the stairs and out the door of the manor.

Waverly and Lynx, who scooped up the device before leaving the attic, followed right behind her as Gran Celia hurriedly walked to the gazebo mumbling under her breath the entire time. They had never seen their grandmother walk so quickly.

They crossed the earthen bridge leading to the gazebo in the middle of the manor's pond and joined Gran Celia in the middle of the gazebo, looking around the grounds as the storm contined, ignoring the fact that now all three of them were drenched from the rain.

Suddenly, there was a sharp grinding noise followed by a faint hum. All three of them turned in unison toward the old stone fireplace. It was shifting open, revealing a hidden doorway.

"What is that?" Lynx asked, his voice trembling slightly.

The light from the device in Lynx's hand flared once more, and with it, the chamber beneath the gazebo seemed to respond, the air thick with the unmistakable charge of ancient energy.

Waverly's heart pounded as she stepped closer to the opening. Her hands trembled as she reached out to touch the edge of the stone doorway, which now illuminated with an eerie light from below.

Gran Celia's face paled as she looked down at the device in Lynx's hand, now pulsing in sync with the energies coming from the opening. Her voice dropped to a whisper. "No... this can't be..."

Lynx, feeling the weight of the situation settle over him, held the device tighter in his hand. "What's happening, Gran?"

Gran Celia's voice was filled with both dread and awe. "This portal... it hasn't been activated in years. But now—now we must face what lies beneath. And we have no idea what it will bring."

Waverly and Lynx exchanged a look—one filled with both uncertainty and excitement. The unknown awaited them, and the adventure Lynx had unknowingly triggered had only just begun.

As the light from the chamber grew brighter, spilling out into the gazebo like a beacon from another world, Gran Celia stepped back, her expression one of profound realization. She looked down at the device in Lynx's hand, her fingers trembling as she clasped them together, trying to steady her breath.

"This changes everything," she murmured, her voice barely above a whisper, but the weight of her words hung heavily in the air. "For the family. For all of us. The portal is no longer sealed, and whatever lies beneath has now been awakened. I've always known that one day the gate would call us again... but I never imagined it would happen like this."

She looked up, her eyes locking onto Waverly and Lynx, both of them standing frozen before the opening, caught between fear and curiosity. "You two will be the ones to carry this family's legacy forward. It's now in your hands. And with it, the fate of not just our family, but the entire balance between worlds."

Waverly and Lynx exchanged a silent, stunned, uncertain glance. Everything they had known, all the quiet days spent in the sanctuary of Sage Manor, now a distant memory. The future loomed ahead of them, vast and unknown.

Gran Celia's eyes softened with both pride and sorrow. "Be ready, for this is just the beginning. What you have known has just changed forever."

As the light from the chamber bathed them in its glow, Waverly felt a surge of something deep within her—a pull toward the unknown. The light from the chamber grew brighter, spilling out into the gazebo as the three of them stood there, staring at the opening. What was hidden beneath Sage Manor was about to come to light.

As Gran Celia's gaze lingered on the device in Lynx's hand, she said, "This changes everything. I need to make a phone call."

She turned and headed back into Sage Manor, leaving Waverly and Lynx staring at the open doorway.

"Want to go take a closer look?" Lynx said to Waverly.

"Not without Gran," said Waverly, "Wait until she comes back."

"What's a portal?" asked Lynx, "What's a legacy?"

2

What seemed like the wait of a lifetime as they stared at the open door, finally ended when Gran Celia joined them again in the gazebo. Lynx, with the device still in his hand had been shifting from one foot to the other the entire time Gran Celia was gone to make her phone call. Waverly had been on full alert, sweeping the entire area of the gazebo with her eyes looking for anything unfamiliar but unsure of exactly what she was looking for. All she knew was that life had just changed in an instant.

"Gran," Lynx said, "you're finally back, who did you call?

"You will find out soon enough my dear," she said, "but for now we need to go look at the portal."

"Yes!" Lynx pumped his fist in the air excitedly.

Waverly felt massive anxiety, she loved exploring woods and caves but a portal was a different story, she felt like she had just been thrust into a fictional world, was dreaming and would soon wake up.

Together, they descended into the chamber with Gran Celia leading the way and Waverly bringing up the rear, the light from below glowing brighter with every step they took. The stone steps were worn smooth by time, and the air grew cooler as they went deeper into the earth underneath the gazebo.

The staircase was narrow, the rough stone walls damp and cool against their hands as they descended. Waverly's heart raced with each step. As they reached the bottom, they entered a low chamber that was surprisingly spacious, its ceiling arched high above them.

"Wow," Lynx breathed, eyes wide as he took in the sight. The walls seemed to shimmer and were adorned with intricate carvings of celestial bodies, all seemingly frozen in time. In the center of the chamber was a pedestal, and on it rested a glowing orb and an old, leather-bound book.

Waverly stepped forward, her hand trembling slightly as she reached out to touch the book. The leather was cracked with age, and the pages inside were yellowed and brittle. She opened it carefully, and as she did, a strange sensation washed over her, like a thousand voices whispering at once, just out of earshot.

"What is it?" Lynx asked, his eyes wide with curiosity as he peered over her shoulder. Waverly looked at the pages, but the writing was in a language she didn't understand. "I don't know," she admitted, "but I think we've just found something very important."

The chamber was silent, the only sound the faint dripping of water from somewhere deep within the stone walls. But Waverly and Lynx could feel it—an ancient power, hidden for centuries, now awakened by their discovery. As Waverly ran her fingers over the ancient text, a shiver ran down her spine. The book felt like a portal to another world, a link to the valley's hidden past.

The symbols, so intricate and mysterious, seemed to dance before her eyes, taunting her with their secrets. She traced the shapes, trying to commit them to memory, wondering what message they held. Lynx, ever the adventurous one, peered over her shoulder, his breath coming in short, excited bursts.

"What do you think it says?" he whispered, as if speaking too loudly might break the spell of the moment. "Is it a map to buried treasure?" His eyes sparkled with the same curiosity that drove Waverly, and together, they stood, captivated by their discovery.

The air grew heavier, and the silence deepened as they delved further into the mystery. It was as if the chamber itself held its breath, waiting to see what these explorers would uncover. The book, with its ancient knowledge, seemed to pulse with a life of its own, a silent guardian of Galen Valley's secrets, waiting patiently for someone to unlock its mysteries.

The siblings stood there, transfixed by the book, their curiosity burning brighter than ever. Waverly ran her fingers gently over the pages, as if the book were a sleeping creature that might stir at any moment. She felt a connection to this place, this valley, and its secrets.

Suddenly, Lynx gasped. "What's that?" He pointed to a gleaming object partially hidden in the shadows beside the pedestal.

Waverly turned to see a crystalline structure that pulsed with a soft, ethereal glow. It resembled a gate, arching high above them with intricate designs that matched the carvings on the walls and the device Lynx had discovered.

"It's a portal." Gran Celia said as she stepped from behind them and moved closer to it. The air around it seemed to hum with energy, sending tingles down their spines.

"Can we activate it?" Lynx's excitement bubbled over, and he moved closer to inspect the shimmering crystal.

Suddenly, a distant sound echoed from above—heavy footsteps approaching. Gran Celia and the siblings exchanged worried glances.

"Someone's coming!" Lynx hissed, his eyes wide with panic.

The rain had finally subsided by the time Ridge Beaumont's car pulled up the long, winding drive to Sage Manor. The tires crunched against the gravel, kicking up small stones as he hurriedly parked and exited the vehicle. His mind raced with every step. Gran Celia's urgent phone call had left him with a sense of dread. 'The portal has been found.' The words echoed in his mind as he hurried toward the gazebo.

Ridge was no stranger to the unusual happenings surrounding Sage Manor—after all, his family's connection to the mysterious crystal gate beneath the gazebo was well documented—but nothing had prepared him for what he was about to encounter. Seeing that doorway open in the gazebo was surreal.

Gran Celia, Waverly and Lynx looked extremely relieved when they saw him descending the stone stairs. "Ridge," Gran Celia said, her voice steady, "I'm glad you're here."

"I rushed over as fast as I could," Ridge replied, brushing the rain from his coat. He had come straight from the university, where he taught forestry and plant biology. The thought of leaving his research behind hadn't been easy, but the urgency in Gran Celia's voice had overridden everything else.

Gran Celia's face darkened, "It's worse than I thought. The portal... the seal is weakened. Now that the chamber has been reopened, it could activate at any second."

Ridge felt his pulse quicken. "The Abasimtrox," he murmured. "If the seal breaks... all the worlds could be at risk."

Gran Celia nodded gravely, her eyes distant as if trying to calculate the scope of the situation. "The Abasimtrox have been sealed away in a quarantine dimension for centuries. If they gain access to the portals again, they could unleash havoc across the entire universe."

"How do we stop it?" Ridge asked, his voice low with concern. He had always known there was a darker side to the power they guarded, but hearing it so plainly laid out was a different matter entirely.

"I'm not sure," Gran Celia admitted. "But there's something we can try. The book—the one we recovered years ago from the old library archives—could hold the answers. If we can decipher it, maybe it will guide us on how to reinforce the seal or even close the portal completely."

Ridge was about to respond when Waverly and Lynx, who had started looking around the portal suddenly were right in front of him, both looking shaken. Lynx's eyes were wide, and Waverly was gripping the old, ornate book with both hands, her face a mix of curiosity and anxiety.

"I thought you should see this," Waverly said, her voice full of urgency. "There are these doors—fancy, golden—and they seem like they should open, but... nothing we do works."

Lynx held up his hands as if to demonstrate. "I tried. The doorknobs vibrate in my hands, but they won't budge. It's like they're locked from the inside."

Gran Celia glanced at the two large doors flanking the portal, both adorned with intricate golden doorknobs that seemed to shimmer in the low light of the chamber. "I've seen these doors before," she said softly, a deep frown creasing her brow. "But we'll discuss that later. The more immediate issue is the portal itself."

Gran Celia motioned for them to follow her, leading them toward the stone staircase that led back toward the manor. "We'll take the book to the library. Perhaps there is something we missed—some piece of knowledge that can help us close the doorway and restore the seal."

Waverly and Lynx nodded in agreement, their faces taut with tension. As they started to make their way toward the exit, Ridge lingered for a moment, looking back at the glowing orb at the center of the chamber. The light from the portal seemed almost alive, thrumming with energy.

Gran Celia reached the entrance to the staircase and turned back to him. "We must leave the chamber now. We can't take any chances while the portal is active. We need to secure the manor and regroup."

Ridge nodded but hesitated. He had spent so many years of his life learning about nature, biology, and the delicate balance of ecosystems. But this... this was something entirely different. The feeling of ancient power filling the room was both overwhelming and unsettling.

As they began to leave, the chamber's atmosphere seemed to shift, the air growing heavier, charged with a strange energy. Waverly glanced over her shoulder, her heart racing. "Wait—look!"

At the center of the orb, a sudden pulse of bright light flared, more intense than before. The air vibrated, and the walls of the chamber seemed to hum with power. A holographic image began to form around the orb—a figure, shimmering with light and ghostly precision. It flickered and shimmered like a projection from another world.

Gran Celia froze, her eyes wide in both shock and recognition. "No... it can't be." She whispered to herself, but her voice was loud enough for Ridge and the others to hear.

Ridge's breath caught in his throat as the figure solidified into a recognizable form. It was a woman, cloaked in regal armor, her features soft yet commanding. Ridge had seen her before, in the history books and family stories—the image of the Arcmyrin leader, Elara, whom his family had once fought alongside during the cosmic battle.

"Gran Celia," Lynx asked, his voice filled with concern, "what's happening?"

Gran Celia's face went pale, her gaze fixed on the hologram. "This... this is Elara. She's been reaching out to us, through the portal. She must have activated the projection herself."

The image of Elara in the orb blinked once, her ethereal form shifting with a flash of light. Then, with a voice that echoed across the chamber, the image spoke.

"Beaumonts... you must come. The time has come for the realms to unite. The Abasimtrox are no longer confined. They will break free unless you act quickly. The power of the crystal gate is the key."

The image flickered again, and the pulse of light from the orb intensified, shaking the entire chamber. Waverly's hands trembled as she grasped Lynx's arm, both of them staring at the figure of Elara.

Gran Celia stepped forward, her voice barely above a whisper. "The gate is unstable. This is more than a call for help. The Abasimtrox are coming. And now... it seems they've found their way back."

Ridge looked down at the book in Waverly's hands, then back to the flickering image of Elara. "We need to act. We can't waste any more time."

Gran Celia looked at all of them, her face filled with determination, but also fear. "Yes, we will. But first, we must secure the manor. The portal is the only way between Earth and Arcmyrin, and if it stays open, it could bring chaos to both worlds. We'll need all our allies to stand against the Abasimtrox, but we can't let them reach us unprepared."

They all stared at the glowing orb for a moment, the presence of the hologram lingering in the air like a reminder of the dangerous road ahead. Finally, Gran Celia spoke, her voice resolute.

"We'll go to the library. We'll decode what's in the book. But first, we must close this doorway. For now, it's too dangerous to leave it open."

With the weight of their next steps pressing down on them, they turned to leave, knowing that the journey to stop the Abasimtrox—and possibly save all worlds—had just begun.

But as they turned to exit the chamber, the orb pulsed one final time, and the holographic image of Elara spoke again, her words cutting through the air.

"Do not let fear stop you. The fate of everything lies in your hands."

And with that, the chamber fell silent.

3

The library of Sage Manor was a vast chamber overflowing with ancient manuscripts stretching from the floor to the ceiling. Waverly and Lynx felt a sense of wonder and awe as they breathed in the musty air, a mixture of aged paper and ink. The silence was profound, broken only by the soft pad of their footsteps on the stone floor.

Waverly turned to her brother, her eyes shining with excitement, and whispered, "I always feel like I've stepped into a forgotten world when I come in here. It's like a treasure trove of secrets and stories, just waiting to be discovered."

Lynx nodded, his gaze fixed on the towering stacks. "Who knows what tales these manuscripts hold?", he murmured. As they ventured further into the room, the weight of the book they carried felt heavy, as if the library itself was beckoning them to return it to its rightful place.

Waverly placed the book on the large, aged wooden table in the center of the room, the same table where Gran Celia often sorted through her correspondence and managed the manor's accounts. The four gathered around, eyes fixed on the mysterious book.

The book itself felt like a portal to another world, and they were eager to uncover its secrets. As Waverly opened it, the pages crackled, and the scent of aged paper and ink filled their nostrils.

The text was unlike anything Waverly and Lynx had ever seen before.

It was written in a language that was unfamiliar to them, with intricate calligraphy that danced across the pages. They recognized the beauty and precision of the script, but the words themselves were a mystery.

Gran Celia's gaze softened as she looked at the book, and a faint smile played on her lips. Her eyes held a faraway look, as if she were remembering a long-forgotten melody. Waverly and Lynx exchanged a glance, their curiosity piqued. They knew that Gran Celia was well-versed in many languages and had an extensive collection of books from all over the world. Could it be that she understood the text?

Gran Celia's eyes sparkled with a mixture of emotions as she regarded the ancient book. With a gentle smile, she began to speak, her voice soft and filled with a sense of reverence. "This book is very special, indeed. It holds within its pages the centuries-old history of Galen Valley and our family's role in protecting it. You see, Waverly, Lynx, our family has been the guardians of this valley for generations, and this book has been passed down as a guide and a warning."

She paused, her gaze moving between the two siblings, ensuring they understood the weight of her words. "Within these pages lie the secrets to the valley's wonders and the dangers that lurk in the shadows. Our ancestors recorded their experiences and knowledge, so we might be prepared for any threat. It is a testament to the power and resilience of our family, and it has helped us maintain the peace and beauty of Galen Valley."

Her voice took on a faraway quality as she delved into the past, her eyes shining with a mixture of pride and sadness. Waverly and Lynx shared a glance, their fascination with the book deepening. They felt a sense of pride in their family's legacy and a newfound responsibility to uphold the traditions of Sage Manor and protect the valley that had been their ancestral home for centuries. As they listened to Gran Celia, the library seemed to transform into a sacred chamber, holding the keys to their family's past and, perhaps, their future.

Gran Celia's voice, soft and reverent, broke the silence of the library once more. "Now that you know about this book, it is important to understand your role as guardians." Waverly and Lynx, captivated by their grandmother's words, leaned forward, their eyes never leaving the ancient manuscript. "Your stewardship has been passed down through the generations, and with it, the responsibility to protect Galen Valley."

"This book must be returned to the chamber for safekeeping, but first, I want you to know what it means to be the caretakers of this knowledge." She paused, her gaze filled with a mixture of determination and warmth as she looked at her grandchildren. "The secrets within these pages are not just a record of our family's history but a guide to safeguarding the valley. Your ancestors' wisdom and experiences are woven into these texts, offering guidance and warning alike.

It is now your duty to carry this legacy forward and protect Sage Manor and all it encompasses."

"How about the portal?" Lynx asked.

"Ah, yes, the Crystal Gate," Gran Celia sighed, "we do need to discuss the portal. You see, it is supposed to be closed and for good reason. No one should be able to go through it right now from either side, however, seeing Elara has me worried about the Abasimtrox."

"Abasimtrox?" asked Waverly, "What is that? Never heard of it."

"An old enemy my dear, one I had hoped to never see again in my lifetime," said Gran Celia.

As Gran Celia spoke, Waverly and Lynx felt a sense of gravity settle upon them.

The aroma of roast beef filled the cozy dining room of Sage Manor as Lynx, Waverly and Ridge sat at the long, polished oak table with Gran Celia. The evening meal was a tradition, a time when the family would gather to share stories, both old and new. Tonight, however, they all were unusually quiet, their minds preoccupied with the discovery they had made.

Gran Celia, ever perceptive, noticed their distracted demeanor. She gently set down her fork and dabbed at the corners of her mouth with a napkin. "You three seem awfully quiet tonight," she remarked, her voice soft and knowing. "What's on your minds?"

Lynx leaned forward, his curiosity piqued. "Gran, what about the chamber under the gazebo?"

Gran Celia's expression grew more serious, and she looked at them both with a mixture of pride and concern. "Ah, the old chamber," she said softly, almost to herself. "I knew it would be discovered one day. The chamber, like the Crystal Gate, is part of Sage Manor's legacy, a place where the past and the present intertwine."

She stood and walked over to a large, intricately carved cabinet that stood against the wall. Opening it, she pulled out a small, velvet-covered box. When she returned to the table, she set the box down gently in front of Waverly and Lynx. "This has been passed down through the generations," Gran Celia said, her voice almost a whisper. "Always to the next caretaker of Sage Manor. It contains the key to understanding the secrets."

Waverly and Lynx exchanged eager, wide-eyed glances before Waverly slowly lifted the lid of the box. Inside was a small aged leather-bound journal, the cover adorned with swirling patterns that resembled the symbols they had seen carved into the walls of the chamber. It was embossed in gold with the intricate initials "V.H.B."

"This journal," Gran Celia explained, "unlocks knowledge and power. But you must be careful. With knowledge comes responsibility, and with power comes danger."

Waverly carefully picked up the journal, feeling its weight in her hand. It felt warm, almost as if it were alive, and she knew instinctively that this journal was important—perhaps even vital—to understanding what they had found today. She opened the cover and started skimming over the writings as she was carefully turning the pages.

"Who is V.H.B.?" Lynx asked, his voice barely above a whisper. Gran Celia smiled gently, placing a reassuring hand on his shoulder.

"Gran," Waverly said, her fingers tracing the faded gold lettering gently as she closed the journal. "Inside, it mentions Victoria Houston Beaumont. Who was she?"

Gran Celia's eyes softened, a touch of nostalgia coloring her tone as she began to weave the tale. "Victoria Houston Beaumont was your great-great-great-grandmother," she explained, her voice carrying a reverence that commanded the room's silence. "She was married to Galen Alexander Ridgely Beaumont, the patriarch of our family and the original builder of this very manor."

Waverly's eyes widened with interest, her gaze drifting around the room, imagining it in a bygone era. Gran Celia continued, "Victoria was not just the wife of a prominent man who introduced reforestation to Galen Valley and beyond; she was a formidable force in her own right. Intelligent, passionate about the arts, and deeply involved in the supernatural that led to the foundation of what Galen Valley is today."

Gran Celia paused, reaching over to gently take the journal from Waverly's hands. She opened it to a marked page, her finger pointing to an elegant script. "Here, Victoria writes about her vision for the valley—not just as a home, but as a sanctuary where the boundaries between the mundane and the supernatural were meant to blur."

Waverly listened, utterly captivated, as her great-great-great-grandmother's dreams and thoughts were voiced through Gran Celia's recollections. "Galen built this manor under her guidance, and together, they infused the land with protections that echo to this day. Much of what we discover are a result of their combined efforts and love for this valley."

"She sounds amazing... I wish I could have met her," Waverly murmured, a sense of connection to her ancestor stirring within her.

Gran Celia smiled warmly, closing the journal and handing it back to Waverly. "In a way, through this journal and the legacy they left behind, you can. Victoria was also a keeper of secrets. The gazebo was her private retreat, where she recorded her findings. Not much different from you, Waverly, except it's your reading escape."

"Is there more to find?" Waverly asked, her curiosity piqued as she clutched the journal a bit tighter.

"Oh, my dear," Gran Celia chuckled softly, "this manor is full of secrets waiting to be uncovered. Each corner, each stone holds a story, many of which began with Victoria and Galen. You are now part of that continuing story."

Waverly nodded, holding up the journal with excitement. "Just learning about our great-great-great-grandparents and their legacy. Turns out, there's a lot more to Sage Manor than meets the eye."

Lynx grinned, "Sounds like we have more exploring to do."

Gran Celia stood, her presence commanding yet comforting. "Indeed, you do. And with each discovery, you'll find not just tales of the past but lessons and powers that will help guide your future. But for tonight, I want you both to rest. The path ahead will require all of your strength and courage."

4

The next morning, after a hurried breakfast, Waverly and Lynx made their way to the library. Gran Celia and Ridge were already seated at the table with the book from the chamber sitting in front of them. Sliding into the chair beside Ridge, Waverly wasted no time in questioning Gran Celia, "Who are the Abasimtrox? The enemy you hoped to never see again?"

"Yea", said Lynx, "What is the seal about?"

Gran Celia sighed, taking a moment to collect her thoughts. "The seal was put in place to protect the Triad, to keep the Abasimtrox from returning. But over time, seals can weaken, and the signs are all around us—the Crystal Gate humming, the restless energy in the air, Elara's appearance..."

Lynx bit his lip, trying to process everything. "So, the Abasimtrox... they're back?"

Gran Celia reached across the table, placing a reassuring hand on each of theirs. "I don't know for certain, but the signs suggest that the seal is failing. That's why I've asked for help. This valley, this manor, this Earth, our sister planets have a long history, and there are those who know its secrets better than anyone. They're the ones who can help us protect it."

Waverly's mind raced. "Is there anything we can do, Gran? To help?"

Gran Celia smiled, though it was tinged with sadness. "You've already done so much, more than I could have asked for. But for now, we need to be patient. When the time comes, I'll need your help. But we must be cautious, and we must be ready for anything."

Ridge glanced at the children, then back to Gran Celia. "We'll figure it out," he said, his voice resolute. "We'll protect this valley and the manor, but let's talk through everything first."

Ridge took a sip of his coffee and then set the cup down, his eyes meeting Gran Celia's. "Mother, let's discuss more about the seal and the Crystal Gate. Start from the beginning about all you know, and don't leave anything out."

Gran Celia nodded. "The seal was created long ago by Origin to protect the Triad. The triad is the three planets of Earth, Arcmyrin and Tanzlora. Origin created the Universe that we all are part of including the Abasimtrox."

"Waverly, in the journal that you now have of your great-great-great grandmother Victoria, she wrote extensively about her visions and her studies. Those were not limited to our world or even our realm of existence. She spoke of three planets: Earth, which we call home; Arcmyrin; and Tanzlora. These planets were interconnected, not just spatially but supernaturally."

Waverly leaned in, absorbing every word. "What happened to these planets?" she asked, her brow furrowed with worry.

Gran Celia pulled the book from the chamber closer to her and turned to a page near the front, then pointed to a detailed sketch of a celestial arrangement. "According to our ancestors, there was a malevolent force known as the Abasimtrox. This force sought to conquer and destroy, driven by a dark desire to control the supernatural realms that flowed through these planets. The guardians understood this, and they knew that the Abasimtrox—creatures born from the darkest corners of the universe—would seek to control this power."

Lynx's hands clenched into fists, his sense of justice stirred by the story. "Did they... did they manage to?"

Gran Celia sighed, a trace of sadness crossing her features. "Arcmyrin and Tanzlora were nearly destroyed in a monumental galactic battle. The guardians of Earth, however, managed to protect our planet. They erected supernatural barriers of protection that were so potent, they've lasted through the centuries."

"The Abasimtrox," Waverly murmured, "They were sealed away, right? But now the seal is weakening? That's what Elara was saying?"

Gran Celia nodded gravely. "Yes, the seal has held for generations, but it was never meant to last forever. The guardians knew that one day, the seal would need to be renewed, but as time passed and the seal held, the knowledge of how to do so was lost. All that remains are fragments of information—old books, legends passed down through the ages, and, of course, the crystal portals."

Lynx leaned forward, his eyes wide. "But why now? Why is the seal weakening now?"

Gran Celia's face grew troubled. "I don't know, Lynx. But I have started having dreams that have been growing stronger, more vivid. They show me images of the valley in turmoil, the crystal portals flickering and dimming, and shadows creeping over the land. I've been doing my best to interpret them, but I fear time is running out."

Ridge, who had been listening intently, leaned back in his chair, his brow furrowed in thought. "We need to find out exactly how the seal was created, and more importantly, how it can be renewed. This book you found in the chamber holds some answers, but we'll need to study it carefully. And the crystals surrounding the gate—if they are part of the seal, they may be key to restoring it."

Waverly bit her lip, remembering the ancient symbols in the book, some of which had been too faded to decipher. "Uncle Ridge, do you know how to read the language in the book?"

Ridge gave her a reassuring smile. "I'm familiar with many ancient languages, Waverly, but unfortunately, I don't know this one."

The room fell into a contemplative silence, the weight of their conversation settling over them like a heavy blanket. Outside, the sun was beginning its slow descent, casting long shadows across the garden. The valley, so peaceful and beautiful, now seemed to hum with an undercurrent of tension.

Lynx broke the silence, his voice small but determined. "What do we do next?"

Ridge glanced at the children, his expression serious. "First, we'll study the book in more detail. Figure out a way to interpret it. We need to understand the symbols and the script used by the guardians. Then we'll examine the Crystal Gate closely. The crystals humming and glowing could be a sign, a way of communicating with us. And, we'll need to keep an eye on the valley itself—any changes, no matter how small, could be important."

Gran Celia nodded in agreement. "We must also be cautious. The Abasimtrox, if they sense the seal weakening, may try to escape. They thrive on fear and chaos, and they'll do everything they can to disrupt our efforts. We must stay strong, and stay united."

Waverly and Lynx exchanged a look. They had always been a team, but this was bigger than any adventure they had imagined. The fate of the valley—and perhaps more—rested on their shoulders. But with Gran Celia and Ridge by their side, they felt a renewed sense of purpose.

"Let's get started," Waverly said, her voice steady. "We don't have any time to lose."

5

The air inside Sage Manor's library was thick with the scent of old books and wood, the fire crackling softly in the hearth as Waverly and Lynx sat in front of their grandmother, Gran Celia, and Uncle Ridge. The large oak table between them was cluttered with books and notes, the pages covered in scribbled observations and theories as they tried to piece together the mystery that had unfolded beneath the gazebo.

Waverly shifted in her seat, her gaze flickering over to Lynx, who had been silent for the past few minutes, his mind clearly elsewhere. She could tell he was still thinking about the doors in the chamber—those strange, ornate doors flanking the crystal portal. The ones that had refused to open no matter how hard he'd tried.

Gran Celia noticed their lingering glances. "You're thinking about the doors, aren't you?"

Waverly nodded, her expression serious. "Yes. When we were in the chamber, there were two doors on either side of the portal, both with beautiful golden doorknobs. They vibrated in Lynx's hands, but they wouldn't open, even though they seemed...'alive'."

Lynx leaned forward, his elbows on the table, his eyes bright with curiosity. "I thought they were locked, but it was like there was some kind of energy preventing them from opening. The doorknobs felt warm, but nothing we did worked. I don't think it's just a physical lock. It's... something more."

Ridge, who had been quietly studying the notes in front of him, looked up at them both. His expression was thoughtful, his brow furrowed. "You think there's something significant behind them?"

Gran Celia let out a quiet sigh, her eyes narrowing as she thought. "Those doors have been a mystery for generations. They've been locked for a while, and not just anyone can get them open."

Lynx's frustration was evident. "But why? They seem so... purposeful. It doesn't make sense that they would be there and not be used. The chamber—everything around it—is so intricate, and then those doors are just... locked? It doesn't fit."

Gran Celia gave a slight nod, her gaze steady. "I agree. There is something special behind them. The portal itself is a conduit for more than just energy—it's a link between realms. But what those doors hold... I can't remember for sure until we try again."

"Try again?" Waverly asked, raising an eyebrow. "Do you think it's even safe to go back down there? What if it triggers something else? We barely have control of the portal as it is."

Gran Celia placed her hands flat on the table, her voice calm but resolute. "That's precisely why we need to understand everything in that chamber. The portal is unstable, yes, but there are more layers to this than we realize. The doors—what lies behind them—are key to stabilizing everything. If we can access those rooms, we may find answers. Answers that could help us control the power of the gate and keep the Abasimtrox from breaking free."

Ridge leaned back in his chair, rubbing his chin thoughtfully. "The Abasimtrox's influence has always been tied to the gate, even when they were sealed away. If Gran Celia's right, then whatever is behind those doors could be crucial in keeping that darkness contained. It's worth the risk."

Waverly glanced over at Lynx, her eyes flickering with concern. "But how do we even approach this? What if it's too dangerous to open?"

Lynx, always eager to solve a mystery, didn't hesitate. "We have to try. We can't just sit here and wonder about it forever. Gran said that what's there is linked to the portal, and if it's what we need to keep the balance, then we have to get them open."

Gran Celia nodded in agreement. "Exactly. The longer we wait, the more unstable things could become. We don't have the luxury of time. But we must be cautious. When we go back, we'll need to be prepared for anything."

Ridge stood, a determined look crossing his face. "Let's go back to the chamber then. We need to get those doors open. Mother, do you remember what's behind those doors?"

"Not completely," Celia said, "a lot of changes were made to the chamber before it was closed up so I can't be confident of what lies behind each door."

Waverly stood up as well, her eyes meeting Lynx's. "Alright, we'll go. But we need to stay alert. No heroics, no rushing ahead. We do this together."

Gran Celia, already standing, gave a soft smile. "Remember, every step we take from here on out could have far-reaching consequences."

The group moved toward the door, and as they left the library and made their way back down the hall, Waverly couldn't shake the weight of the moment. The uncertainty of what lay beneath Sage Manor, hidden in the chamber, felt like an undeniable call—a force pulling them toward a future they could barely comprehend. There was something about the doors, about the secret they held, that felt both ancient and modern, as if it had always been waiting for them to return.

By the time they reached the gazebo, the air around them felt thick with anticipation. The portal below seemed to hum with a low, almost mournful resonance as they descended toward the stone steps leading into the hidden chamber.

Lynx's hand hovered near the golden doorknobs on the ornate doors. His fingers trembled with frustration. "I really thought it would open this time."

Gran Celia stepped forward, her eyes tracing the intricate carvings on the doors, her hands clasped in front of her as if in prayer. "The key isn't in the doors themselves," she said softly. "It's in the context of what's behind them. We need to understand the supernatural powers at play here. The portal and its gatekeepers. The power is ancient, and it reacts to intention. The doors will open when we're ready to face what they conceal."

Waverly stood a few steps behind her, feeling the weight of Gran Celia's words settle over her like a mantle. "Then how do we get to that point?" she asked, her voice tinged with anxiety.

Gran Celia looked back at them, her eyes both filled with wisdom and concern. "The book. It may hold the final piece of the puzzle. But first, we must explore these doors again. Together."

As they gathered around the golden doorknobs, ready to face the unknown, Gran Celia's voice broke through the silence. "But know this—whatever is behind these doors is not just a door to another room. It is the doorway to something that could change everything. The balance of power between our worlds hangs in the balance, and this knowledge could be the key to controlling it."

Before they could proceed, a low hum filled the room, the ground vibrating slightly beneath their feet. The orb in the center of the chamber pulsed brighter, a soft golden light beginning to shine from its core.

"What's happening now?" Waverly asked, alarm creeping into her voice.

Gran Celia's face turned pale. "The portal is reacting to something. We need to be careful."

Suddenly, the light from the orb grew brighter, flickering faster, and the room filled with a deep, resonant hum. The holographic projection of Elara's form began to reappear around the orb, flickering like a candle flame in the wind.

Gran Celia's expression hardened. "Stay close," she warned. "We're not alone down here anymore."

6

The orb's light pulsed, growing brighter and more intense by the second, filling the chamber with a warm, golden glow that seemed to penetrate to the very core of everyone present. Waverly's pulse quickened as she instinctively stepped closer to Gran Celia and Lynx, feeling an electrifying charge in the air that made the hairs on the back of her neck stand up.

And then, as if summoned by the rising energy, a faint shimmer formed within the orb. It was subtle at first, like a mist gathering in the light, but then the image solidified—Elara.

Her figure emerged from the swirling glow, a holographic projection that hovered in the center of the room. Her armor shimmered with faint cosmic energy, and her piercing eyes locked onto Ridge, Waverly, and Lynx as if she had been expecting them. Her presence, despite being an ethereal projection, seemed to fill the room with a power that made even the stone walls hum with purpose.

"Waverly, Lynx, Ridge, Gran Celia," Elara's voice rang out, clear and resonant. It seemed to echo from every corner of the chamber, bouncing off the walls with an urgent cadence. "I have called upon you once again, for a time of great peril."

Waverly stepped forward, her heart pounding in her chest. "Elara, we—what's happening? Why are you appearing now? What has happened on Arcmyrin?"

Elara's image flickered momentarily, as though fighting against the interference of the powerful forces within the chamber. "The portal has awoken, and with it, the seal that has kept the Abasimtrox locked in quarantine is weakening," Elara's voice was steady, but it carried a depth

| 29 |

of concern. "I can feel it—the dark forces stir, preparing to break free. Our worlds are in danger. Your worlds are in danger."

Ridge, who had been silent up until this point, took a step forward. His expression was one of quiet resolve, but his voice trembled with the weight of the responsibility. "How can we help? What do we need to do?"

Elara's hologram shimmered, her eyes locking with Ridge's in a moment of silent understanding. "The portal must be sealed once more, but it is not simply a matter of closing it. The Abasimtrox are no ordinary foes. They are ancient beings, older than even the portals themselves. If the seal is broken, they will flood into your world, and no force on Earth or Arcmyrin will be able to stop them."

Gran Celia stepped forward, her voice tinged with worry. "We've always known the threat of the Abasimtrox, but we never thought the seal would weaken so quickly. The portal should have been secure for centuries."

"The powers within the portal are ancient and strong," Elara explained, her form flickering slightly as though adjusting to the intensity of the energy in the room. "But nothing lasts forever. The forces of the Abasimtrox are not mere creatures—they are chaos incarnate. The portals that bind your world to Arcmyrin must be maintained. If they are left unchecked, the balance will shatter."

Waverly's mind raced, absorbing the gravity of Elara's words. She had felt the strange energy surging through the chamber when the orb first activated. There was something more at play here—something far larger than anything she had ever imagined.

"What can we do?" Lynx asked, his voice determined. "How do we stop the Abasimtrox from getting out?"

Elara's holographic form flickered once again, but this time, her gaze softened slightly as she looked at the siblings. "The answer lies not just in the portal, but in what lies behind the doors you found. You must gain access to those rooms. The knowledge to reinforce the seal is hidden there. The power to stop the Abasimtrox from escaping is locked away."

Ridge's brow furrowed. "What's behind those doors? We tried to open them, but it's like something's blocking us. The doorknobs vibrate, but nothing moves."

"The doors will not open until the time is right," Elara replied, her tone somber. "The supernatural powers that protects them are woven into the very fabric of the portal itself. Only when you understand the true nature of the seal will those doors yield. The answers you seek are there, but you must unlock them first."

Gran Celia's expression darkened, and she glanced at the golden doorknobs, her gaze heavy with recognition. "The doors are tied to the balance of the worlds," she murmured. "It is powerful but to understand it, we need more information—something we haven't uncovered yet."

"Gran Celia," Waverly asked, her voice filled with urgency, "how do we balance the powers of three worlds? How do we get behind those doors?"

Elara's holographic figure pulsed with light as she began to speak. "There is an ancient text that will guide you. The book you recovered contains fragments of knowledge passed down through generations of guardians. You must study it—it may hold the final key to understanding the power to balance the worlds and how it relates to the seal."

Waverly glanced at Lynx, then at Gran Celia, feeling the weight of the situation settle upon her shoulders. "The book..." she echoed. "We thought it was just history—just stories—but it's more than that."

Gran Celia nodded slowly. "Yes. The book has always been important, but we never fully understood its significance. It was kept hidden for a reason. But now, we have no choice. We must go back to the library and study it."

Lynx turned to Elara's image, his voice full of determination. "We'll do whatever it takes. We won't let the Abasimtrox get out. We'll seal the portal, no matter the cost."

Elara's image flickered one final time, her voice filled with both urgency and gratitude. "You must hurry. Time is running out, and the forces of darkness grow stronger by the minute. The future of your world—and ours—rests in your hands."

As the hologram began to fade, Gran Celia turned to Ridge, Waverly, and Lynx. "We need to leave the chamber now. We can't risk the portal's power growing any stronger. We'll gather everything we need in the library and continue our research."

Waverly nodded, her heart pounding with a mixture of fear and excitement. The stakes had never been higher.

They turned to leave, but just as they crossed the threshold of the chamber, the orb pulsed one last time, and Elara's voice rang out one final time.

"Remember," she said, her voice strong but distant, "the seal is not just a barrier—it's a bond. If it breaks, the darkness will consume everything. You must protect it. Protect all worlds."

With that, her image disappeared, leaving only the fading glow of the orb in the center of the room.

Gran Celia motioned for them to move quickly. "Let's go," she said. "We'll need every ounce of our strength and wisdom to solve this. The battle for the balance of all worlds has begun."

7

Gran Celia said, "Let's start assembling a team. We'll need experts in ancient languages and portal technology. This is going to require all hands on deck."

"I agree," Ridge said, "I can make some inquiries at the university to see if there are any experts close by. I do know a couple in Germany that have expertise in interplanetary technologies and extraterrestrial environments. Not sure how quickly they can get over here."

"Very well," Gran Celia said, "I do know someone that may know about the ancient language and symbols in the book but I will need to go to her. She is a bit of a recluse and does not use any communication devices."

"What?" Lynx was perplexed, "Are you saying she has no phones? How can someone live like that?"

"Probably very peacefully," said Ridge chuckling.

"Waverly dear, you can go with me later this afternoon and we can pay her a visit to see if she would be willing to help us," said Gran Celia, "Ridge, you make your phone calls to see who you can round up. Remember, time is of the essence."

"What do I do?" asked Lynx

"Stay out of the attic," said Waverly, "that's what got all this started."

The air was thick with the scent of rain as Gran Celia and Waverly made their way up the winding, tree-lined path toward the Birkinridge house. The estate loomed ahead, an imposing, dark silhouette against the stormy sky. From the outside, it looked every bit the part of a haunted mansion—weathered stone walls covered in creeping ivy, tall, narrow windows, and a sagging roof that seemed to have borne the weight of too many years.

"Gran Celia, are you sure this is the right place?" asked Waverly, "this is the Birkinridge house, it's haunted and all the school kids avoid it at all costs."

"Just looks that way," Gran Celia said, "on purpose I might add, that way Francis is not bothered by anyone, exactly the way she likes it."

"Whoa...you mean to tell me someone has been living here the whole time?" Waverly exclaimed. " I have believed it to be deserted and haunted my whole life!"

"Yes," Gran Celia said, "Francis has lived here over 40 years and it has looked like this the entire time. I think the only other person allowed to see her in person besides myself is her priest."

"How do you know her so well?"

"She was the first person I met when I arrived in Galen Valley after I married your grandfather," Gran Celia replied, "at that time, she worked as an assistant librarian and was married. We became close bonding over books. She was very eccentric and a lot of people could not relate to her. I understood her eccentricities and she felt comfortable with me."

Gran Celia continued, "After a few years of meeting over tea every week to discuss the latest books we had read, her husband passed away unexpectedly and she did not handle the grieving process well at all. I tried to help her as best I could but she shut herself off and would not communicate."

Gran Celia glanced at her granddaughter, her expression thoughtful. "Francis may be a recluse, but she is also one of the most brilliant minds I've ever known. Her expertise in ancient languages and symbols is unparalleled. I've known her for years, and if anyone can interpret the book we found in the chamber, it's her."

Ridge paced back and forth in his office, phone in hand, as he dialed the number that would connect him to an old friend and colleague halfway across the world. He waited with bated breath as the rings echoed in his ear, each tone heightening his anticipation. When the line finally clicked, and a familiar voice answered, he felt a rush of relief.

"Marshall, it's Ridge Beaumont. I hope I'm not calling at a bad time," Ridge began, his voice tinged with urgency.

Dr. Marshall Stern, a renowned expert in portal technology and quantum physics based in Germany, responded with a warm, albeit curious tone, "Ridge! It's been too long. What brings you to call? It must be important."

"It is," Ridge affirmed. "I need your help, and possibly Madre's as well. We've stumbled upon something... extraordinary. It involves portal technology and potentially intergalactic communication."

There was a brief pause as Marshall processed the information. "That does sound extraordinary. Tell me more."

Ridge quickly outlined the recent discoveries at Sage Manor—the mysterious portal, the doors that would not open, and the urgent need to communicate with another planet. He also explained the critical situation that Elara had warned them about through holographic imagery via the orb.

Marshall listened intently, his interest piqued. "This is indeed beyond the usual scope of any project we've worked on before. Madre and I would be very interested in seeing this firsthand and contributing to your efforts."

Relief washed over Ridge. "Thank you, Marshall. Your expertise could make a real difference here."

"We'll arrange to fly out to Sage Manor as soon as possible," Marshall assured him. "Give us a day or two to sort things out here, and we'll be on our way."

After a few more details were exchanged, Ridge hung up the phone, a weight lifted off his shoulders.

As they reached the front door of the Birkinridge house, Gran Celia gave a firm knock, the sound echoing through the cold air. They waited for a moment before the door creaked open slightly, revealing Francis's pale face framed by graying hair. Her deep blue eyes, sharp with intelligence but softened with years of grief, locked onto Gran Celia's.

"Gran Celia," Francis said, her voice quiet but welcoming. "It's been too long."

"Francis," Gran Celia replied warmly, her tone kind. "I'm sorry to intrude, but I need your help. There's something we've uncovered—something that only you can help us with."

Francis stepped aside, motioning for them to enter. "Come in, both of you. I'm not used to visitors, but if you've come for something important, then I won't keep you out in the rain."

Waverly followed Gran Celia inside, and as they entered the dimly lit foyer, the heavy silence of the house seemed to envelop them. Dust motes danced in the air, illuminated by the faint light that seeped through the heavy curtains. The house was beautiful in its own way, with antique furniture and bookshelves filled with volumes that looked ancient and well-read.

Francis led them into a sitting room, where a fire crackled softly in the hearth. The room felt warmer and more inviting than the rest of the house, with comfortable armchairs and a low table covered in an array of scattered books and papers. There was something about the space that felt like it had been abandoned by time, as if the world outside hadn't touched it in years.

Gran Celia sat in one of the chairs, settling herself with a sense of purpose. Waverly stood near the window, glancing out at the storm. She couldn't shake the sense that the Birkinridge house, despite its oppressive exterior, had a way of drawing you in, of making you feel both protected and suffocated at once.

Francis, who had been standing by the fire, turned and walked over to the table where a stack of old manuscripts and journals sat. She picked up a small, weathered book, glancing at Gran Celia with a raised eyebrow. "What is it that you've found this time?"

Gran Celia looked at her intently. "We need your expertise, Francis. There's a book we've uncovered—one tied to an ancient portal beneath Sage Manor. We believe it holds the key to understanding how to activate and stabilize the portal. And... there are also two rooms behind doors in the chamber. We need to know what's behind them, and how we can access them."

The mention of the portal seemed to stir something within Francis. Her eyes, which had been half-lidded with the weariness of age, now sharpened with interest. "A portal, you say?" She set the book down and crossed her arms, her gaze intense. "This is much more than just an old artifact, isn't it? And the rooms—there must be something hidden there. Something important."

Gran Celia nodded solemnly. "Yes. We believe the portal is linked to interplanetary travel. There's more to it than just a doorway—it's a bridge between worlds. But the power it holds could be dangerous. We need to understand it fully before it's too late."

Waverly, who had been standing by the window, turned toward them, her face pale. "You'll help us, won't you? We need you here, at Sage Manor, for a few days to help us decipher it. You're the only one who can make sense of the symbols in the book."

Francis turned to her, her expression unreadable. She studied Waverly for a long moment, as if weighing the situation. Finally, she gave a small sigh. "I've spent too many years alone, trying to bury myself in books and solitude. But the truth is, I don't think I can ignore this. Not when the world might be in danger."

Gran Celia's face softened. "Thank you, Francis. We're glad to have you."

Francis gave a small, almost imperceptible nod. "I'll come. But only for a week. I'm not ready to fully re-enter the world, but I will help you. After all, this isn't just your problem—it's one we must face together."

Gran Celia stood, a hint of a smile on her lips. "Can you come first thing tomorrow morning? The sooner we can begin, the better."

Waverly's relief was palpable, though the weight of their task still hung heavily over her. The truth was, even with Francis's help, they were venturing into uncharted territory. The book was no ordinary text, and the portal was no mere doorway. There was so much they didn't understand, so much that was still unknown.

As Gran Celia and Francis continued to discuss the details of the plan, Waverly stepped over to the fireplace, her gaze flickering to the flames. The crackling sound of the fire was soothing, but she couldn't escape the unease growing in the pit of her stomach. Something about all of this felt like they were walking a fine line—on the brink of something that could either save them all... or destroy everything they knew.

"Tomorrow," she whispered to herself. "Tomorrow, everything changes."

8

The arrival of Francis Roller at Sage Manor was met with a mixture of anticipation and nervous excitement. The rain had returned, soft but persistent, as Francis Roller's old sedan crunched along the long gravel drive toward Sage Manor.

The car was an oddity—vintage, with rust creeping up the sides and a muffled engine that spoke of its many years spent traveling forgotten roads. It looked out of place on the well-manicured grounds of the manor, yet it carried with it a woman whose knowledge was invaluable to the Beaumont family.

Waverly stood by the front window, watching as Francis pulled up. She stepped out of the car with a practiced grace, her posture straight, her expression unreadable behind the small glasses perched on her nose. Francis was a woman of few words, but her presence was commanding—she had the kind of knowledge that could unlock ancient secrets and protect entire worlds.

Gran Celia was already waiting at the door, and the two women exchanged a warm, quiet greeting as Francis entered the manor. Waverly followed them into the grand hallway, her heart pounding with anticipation. They had so much to learn, and time was running out. The portal was still unstable, its pulse growing stronger with each passing hour, and the mystery of the two locked doors beneath the gazebo weighed heavily on their minds.

"Everything is ready in the library," Gran Celia said, turning to Francis with a look of quiet determination. "We've already gathered the texts and the book you requested. There's a great deal to decipher."

Francis nodded, her sharp eyes scanning the room before her gaze settled on the tall bookshelf at the far end of the hallway. "Lead the way," she replied, her voice calm and steady. "Let's begin."

Waverly followed them into the library, a vast room filled with towering shelves of books, their spines worn from decades of use. The room smelled of aged paper and wood, a fragrance that Waverly found oddly comforting. At the center of the room, the large stone fireplace crackled, filling the space with warmth. A low hum emanated from the direction of the gazebo, where the portal still pulsed, but Waverly forced herself to push that thought aside. There was too much to focus on right now.

Francis settled herself at the large wooden table, pushing aside papers and laying down the ancient book. The cover was cracked and faded, the leather binding softened with age. Gran Celia watched her carefully, waiting for any sign of recognition, while Waverly moved closer, eager to learn.

Francis opened the book with careful hands, revealing pages filled with symbols Waverly couldn't begin to understand. They were alien to her, as if they belonged to a language not meant for Earth. Francis's fingers traced the symbols, her brow furrowed in concentration.

"This is older than I thought," Francis murmured. "A combination of several ancient languages—some of which haven't been used for millennia. It's not just a record; it's a guide. A map of sorts."

Waverly leaned over, her eyes scanning the pages. "A guide to what?"

"A guide to controlling the portal," Francis said, her voice quiet but certain. "And to understanding what powers it. The power within this portal is tied to the very fabric of space itself. If we don't stabilize it, there is no telling what could happen."

Gran Celia nodded solemnly, her gaze unwavering. "We've been working under the assumption that the portal could be used for interplanetary travel, but the seal… we've always known it was fragile."

Francis closed the book gently, her eyes reflecting the weight of its contents. "It is. And it's tied to the two rooms behind the doors in the chamber below. Whatever lies beyond them is critical to keeping the

Abasimtrox contained. But it's clear now that you can't simply force the doors open. They won't yield to brute force or willpower. We'll need to decipher the exact meaning of the symbols in this book if we want to understand how to activate the portal properly—and keep it safe."

Waverly, her brow furrowed, glanced over at Lynx, who had been quietly observing from the corner. "So... if we open the doors, we might find a way to strengthen the seal?"

"Exactly," Francis said, her eyes alight with understanding. "The doors protect more than just a room. They guard something that, if accessed, will give you the knowledge you need. But I'm afraid you can't open them unless you know exactly what you're dealing with."

Gran Celia stepped closer, her face serious. "Then let's start. We don't have time to waste."

Francis opened the book again and began to translate the symbols on the pages, her eyes darting over the lines of text with practiced ease. Her hands moved swiftly as she made notes, cross-referencing other texts and manuscripts that lay scattered across the table. Waverly sat down beside her, trying to keep up with the complexities of the language and its deep, layered meanings.

For hours, they worked, the ticking of the old clock on the wall the only sound breaking the silence. As the light outside began to fade, Francis made an exhale of frustration. "It's here. The key to unlocking the doors, but it's buried within these symbols. This book speaks of an activation sequence—something that will allow you to engage the power of the portal and access the rooms behind the doors."

Gran Celia leaned forward, her hands resting on the table. "What does the sequence entail? How do we start?"

Francis ran her finger down the page, her expression growing more focused as she traced the hidden instructions. "The key lies in understanding the emotional resonance of the portal. You'll need to align your intent with the essence of the supernatural power—the right emotional energy will unlock the doors."

Waverly raised an eyebrow. "Emotional energy?"

Francis nodded. "Yes. The portal, like all powerful supernatural constructs, responds not just to physical actions but to the energy you channel into it. You must approach it with clarity—of heart, of mind. The doors won't open for you if you act out of fear or uncertainty. You have to approach them with calm, with resolve."

Lynx stepped forward, his face full of determination. "That makes sense. It's like we're connecting with it, not just trying to force it open."

Gran Celia's eyes softened. "We'll need to do this together, then. All of us. To ensure we approach it with the right intent."

As Waverly stood to gather the notes from the table, her gaze turned to the library's doorway. She felt the familiar tug of something 'calling' her, the hum of the portal still faintly vibrating through the walls. The time had come.

"Let's go," Gran Celia said, her voice calm but filled with urgency. "We have the key, and now we must act before the portal grows unstable."

The group made their way to the chamber beneath the gazebo, the air feeling heavier as they descended the stairs. Waverly's heart pounded in her chest as they reached the portal, the doors on either side of it glowing faintly in the low light. Francis moved to the center of the room, where the orb pulsed gently with a soft, golden light.

"You must focus," she said quietly. "Align your emotions with the purpose of this moment. Channel your energy into the portal."

Waverly stood with her hand resting lightly on the orb, feeling the gentle vibration beneath her fingertips. She closed her eyes, allowing the world around her to fall away, focusing only on the purpose of this moment—to stabilize the portal, to ensure it would not slip into chaos. She felt a warmth grow within her chest, a surge of energy that spread outward as if she were connecting with something vast, something ancient.

When she opened her eyes, the doors to the chamber—the two that had remained locked for so long—began to hum. Slowly, imperceptibly at first, they shifted. Then, with a sudden burst of energy, the golden doorknobs turned. The doors creaked open, revealing an unknown space beyond.

9

The air in the chamber was thick with an almost tangible sense of discovery as Waverly, Lynx, Gran Celia, and Francis stepped through the newly opened door. The moment the heavy wooden doors creaked open, a burst of golden light poured into the room, revealing a space unlike anything any of them had ever seen before. It was vast and quiet, with a feeling of ancient, purposeful stillness hanging in the air.

The room stretched out in front of them, its stone walls lined with shelves that were stacked high with hundreds—no, thousands—of small glass vials and jars. Some of them were open, and others were sealed tightly, their contents unclear. But what caught Waverly's attention immediately was the sheer quantity of them—seeds, carefully stored and preserved, filling the space like a vast vault.

"It's a... a seed vault?" Waverly whispered, stepping closer to one of the shelves. Her fingers brushed over a jar filled with seeds that shimmered faintly in the light, each one slightly different in shape and size, their colors ranging from pale ivory to deep green.

Gran Celia moved forward, her expression one of quiet amazement. "These aren't just any seeds," she said softly, lifting one of the jars to examine its contents. "These look like they've been preserved for something... far beyond the scope of any ordinary botanical study."

Lynx leaned in closer, eyes wide with curiosity. "There are so many of them! Why would they need so many different seeds?"

Francis stepped forward, her sharp eyes scanning the shelves with growing intensity. She had been silent since they'd entered, but now, her mind seemed to be whirring with the implications. "This isn't just a storage room. This is a place of experimentation—a lab, perhaps. The

| 45 |

jars are organized in a way that suggests more than just preservation. These seeds have been cultivated, perhaps even engineered."

Waverly walked down one of the aisles, noticing the small glass vials resting on the counters next to carefully labeled files. The files seemed to contain notes, diagrams, and sketches, most of which she couldn't make out, but the title on one caught her attention: 'Interplanetary Germination and Plant Growth.'

"What is this place?" Waverly asked, her voice almost a whisper, as if she were in a temple of lost knowledge. "These seeds... they were meant for something more than just planting."

Francis's expression deepened. "They were meant to travel between worlds. These seeds aren't simply for Earth's ecosystems. The markings, the research—it's clear now. They've been studying ways to adapt plant life to survive across different planets."

Gran Celia took a long breath, her face pale as the pieces began to come together. "Interplanetary travel... with botanical life? Is this how the portal was designed? To move plants between worlds?"

"Yes," Francis said, her voice heavy with the weight of her understanding. "And not just to move plants, but to cultivate life on other worlds. To terraform planets, perhaps. Or to create something that could help restore balance on planets that have lost their ecosystems."

Lynx, who had been carefully inspecting the shelves, turned back to them with wide eyes. "So this is all about bringing life to other planets... using plants?" He paused for a moment, his mind racing with the possibilities. "Wait... so is the portal supposed to help 'us' travel between planets, too?"

Francis's face darkened. "That's the most disturbing part. The portal was likely designed not just for transportation—but for the transfer of life. Not just plants... but the potential for far greater consequences. It was meant to bridge the divide between Earth and other worlds, allowing not just resources, but entire ecosystems to travel."

The implications of her words hung heavy in the room. The idea of moving life from planet to planet was nothing short of monumental.

But the questions began to rise: Why was this system left behind? And more importantly—'who' had designed it?

"We have to understand more," Gran Celia said, her voice firm. "We need to know exactly what they were trying to do. The key to controlling the portal may be in this room."

Francis turned to one of the workstations at the back of the room, where various pieces of equipment had been set up in a small laboratory. Glass vials containing liquid were arranged on a shelf beside what appeared to be a germination chamber—an elaborate setup designed to nurture seeds into life, with temperature and humidity controls carefully monitored. She reached over, her fingers tracing over the small metal mechanisms in front of her. "This isn't just botany. It's biotechnology. They were genetically altering plants to survive in different environments—different atmospheres, gravities, perhaps even different light spectrums. This is far beyond Earth-bound gardening."

Gran Celia took a deep breath. "We need to move on. We'll study these findings later. There's another room we must explore."

Francis didn't argue. The gravity of the discovery weighed on her as she moved toward the second door, a massive, arching structure at the far end of the room. The ornate golden doorknobs, still undisturbed, caught the light as they approached.

"Do you think this room will hold more answers?" Waverly asked, her voice filled with wonder and fear as she followed Francis toward the entrance.

"I'm afraid it holds more than answers," Francis replied grimly. "This is the control room. If I'm correct, it will reveal what they truly intended the portal to be used for."

Gran Celia stepped forward, her hands resting lightly on the door's surface. "Let's see."

With a click and a deep sigh of air, the doors creaked open slowly. They stepped into a large oval-shaped room, its design completely different from the first. The walls were lined with sleek, metallic surfaces, and a large pedestal table stood at the center of the room, surrounded by four chairs. Each chair was equipped with advanced-looking restraints and controls, almost reminiscent of astronaut seating. Waverly's heart pounded as she approached the table, taking in its peculiar design.

"The table... it's built for something. Someone." Waverly whispered, her gaze falling to the indentations in front of each chair. They were round, large enough to fit a person's hands, and smooth—like they were meant to be activated in some way. But for what purpose? Waverly's mind whirred.

Francis circled the table, her fingers brushing against the surfaces of the chairs. "These... these look like they were meant for space travel," she said thoughtfully. "They're ergonomic, designed for long durations in zero gravity or under extreme pressure. But why were they placed here?"

"The portal?" Waverly suggested, stepping closer.

Gran Celia moved around the room, scanning the walls. "These curved screens... they show the elements. Earth, water, air, fire," she murmured. "They're not just decorative."

Waverly turned to look at them, seeing that each screen was displaying one of the four elements, the images swirling and shifting. The image of air swirled with gusts and clouds, water rippled across the screen, while fire flickered and danced.

"They're representations of the basic forces of nature," Francis said slowly, her voice filled with realization. "They're connected to the power of the portal. Each element corresponds to a key aspect of what this portal is designed to do."

"But what do they have to do with the seal?" Waverly asked. "And why does it matter that the four of us are here?"

Francis stood still for a moment, absorbing the information. Then she turned to them, her face a mask of understanding. "This is it. The portal is powered by the elements. Not just plants or energy—it's the balance of the four elements working in unison. And in order to stabilize the seal, you need all four elements to be present at once."

Gran Celia furrowed her brow. "You mean, the four of us—'us'—have to somehow channel these elements to stabilize the portal?"

Francis nodded. "Yes. I believe it's not just about controlling the portal, but about aligning it with the elemental spirits—forces of nature that can strengthen the seal. But this can only be done if all four of you are present, using your own energy to balance the forces. This is why the table has four chairs, each connected to the elements."

Waverly's mind spun as she processed the implications. "We're supposed to—what? Become the vessels for these elements?"

Francis's gaze grew serious. "Yes. And if you don't act together, the seal will weaken. If the portal is activated improperly, the Abasimtrox will break through."

Gran Celia looked between Francis and Waverly, then to Lynx. "How do we even begin to perform something like this? And what does it mean for the future of the portal?"

Francis's eyes were filled with the weight of the responsibility. "I'm not entirely sure, but I believe the symbols in the book will guide us. The activation of the portal is not just about opening it—it's about channeling the elemental forces in balance. It's about ensuring that each element is aligned with the others, working together."

Waverly felt a chill run through her. "And if we don't?"

"Then the balance will be shattered," Francis said softly. "And the Abasimtrox will be free."

10

The chamber beneath Sage Manor was silent, the only sound the faint hum of energy that seemed to reverberate through the stone walls. The golden light from the portal shimmered softly, casting long shadows across the oval room where Ridge, Gran Celia, Waverly, and Lynx now stood. Their footsteps were heavy with the weight of what had been revealed in the last few days, and the urgency of their task pressed on them like a physical force.

Francis had already led them through the discoveries she'd made in the Elemental Room, but now it was time for Ridge to see for himself. The rest of the family had gathered here, knowing they couldn't afford to waste any more time. The room, with its four advanced astronaut-like chairs surrounding a pedestal table, was at the heart of the mystery. Each chair seemed to call out to the four of them, almost as if the room was anticipating their arrival.

"I can't believe this room is so... intact," Ridge said, his voice low as he stepped toward the table. His eyes scanned the array of curved screens showing the four elements—air, water, fire, and earth—each one flickering as if alive, reacting to the very presence of the group.

Gran Celia took a deep breath, her hand brushing lightly over the surface of the pedestal. "This room... it's a nexus for the elemental forces. The portal, the seal... all of it is tied to these elements. It's more than just a gateway; it's the balance of nature itself."

Waverly nodded, her heart still pounding from the discoveries they'd made earlier. "And if we're able to connect with these forces, we may be able to strengthen the seal and stop the Abasimtrox. But we've only just begun to understand how."

Lynx stepped up to one of the chairs, eyeing it with a mix of curiosity and apprehension. "So, we sit down, place our hands where the indentations are, and see what happens?"

Gran Celia turned toward them, her face a mask of concentration. "Exactly. The chairs are designed to connect us with the elements. But there's something else, something we don't fully understand yet."

The family took their places in the chairs, and Ridge sat in the one closest to the pedestal, his eyes fixed on the screens around him. Waverly and Lynx followed suit, their hands resting in the indentations at the front of the chairs.

For a moment, nothing happened. The room remained eerily still, as if holding its breath. Then, slowly, the first chair flickered to life—the one Waverly sat in. She gasped as the air around her seemed to shift. The screen depicting the element of air swirled in front of her, the image alive with gusts and shifting clouds. She felt a sudden surge of energy, a connection to the elemental force of air itself.

Lynx's chair hummed to life next, the image of fire flickering before him. He stared in awe as the flames on the screen danced in time with the pulsing energy around him. He felt warmth, a strange power running through him, filling him with vitality.

But then, Gran Celia's chair remained still. There was no vibration, no hum of energy. Her screen, the one depicting water, remained dark, unmoving.

Gran Celia's brow furrowed in confusion. She tried to adjust her position, but still, nothing happened. No energy surged through her. The realization hit her all at once, a sudden epiphany that stopped her cold.

"What is it, Gran Celia?" Waverly asked, sensing the shift in her grandmother's demeanor.

Gran Celia slowly lifted her hands from the indentation, her eyes wide with understanding. She turned to Ridge, her voice barely above a whisper. "It's not just about the elements. It's... 'bloodline'. Only Beaumonts can connect to the elemental spirits to secure the seal. That's why my chair won't activate. It's because I'm not... not a direct blood descendant. I'm not connected the way you are."

Ridge looked at her, his face growing pale. "What are you saying?"

Gran Celia's gaze softened, filled with both sorrow and acceptance. "The power to stabilize the seal—to activate it fully and keep the Abasimtrox quarantined—it lies with you, Ridge. And with you, Waverly, and Lynx. The three of you, as direct descendants of the Beaumont bloodline, are the key to connecting the elements. I can help guide you, but I can't directly interact with the spirits of the elements the way you can. You three must be the ones to perform the sealing."

Ridge's heart sank, a heavy weight pressing on his chest. "So... it's us. We're the ones who have to fix it. We have to stabilize the portal."

Gran Celia nodded slowly, her eyes full of understanding. "Yes, Ridge. You and the grandchildren. Only the blood of the Beaumonts can restore the balance and seal the portal."

The realization settled over the group like a cold mist. The responsibility of it was staggering. They had known the portal held great power, but now they understood just how intertwined their family's bloodline was with its workings.

"We need to talk," Gran Celia said, her voice sharp with resolve. "In the sitting room. Let's leave the chamber and discuss this as a family. There are things we must decide now."

Before they reached the stairs, a sudden presence filled the chamber, the familiar hum of energy vibrating through the air. The temperature shifted, and Elara appeared once more, her ethereal form shimmering in front of the group. Her voice, both distant and urgent, filled the room.

"Time is running out," Elara said, her holographic form flickering with an intensity that matched the desperation in her voice. "You must hurry. Parts of Arcmyrin are being corrupted. Waterfalls are drying up, trees are dying, plants are withering... the lifeforce of our planet is ebbing away. You need to act now, or we will lose everything."

Waverly's breath caught in her throat as the weight of Elara's words hit them all. The urgency was undeniable. Arcmyrin's very lifeblood was fading, and their time to act was quickly slipping away.

Elara's image flickered again, her voice growing more strained. "We cannot wait any longer. The longer the seal remains weakened, the more damage the Abasimtrox will cause. If you don't act now, the balance will be shattered, and Arcmyrin will fall."

Gran Celia turned to Ridge, Waverly, and Lynx, her eyes filled with determination. "We must be ready. The time to perform the sealing is now."

Ridge stood, his hands clenched at his sides. "Then we'll do it. We'll fix the portal, we'll restore the balance. For Arcmyrin. For Earth. And for our family."

With those words, the family stood united, knowing that their task was clear—but the path ahead would be anything but easy. The portal was theirs to control, and the fate of both worlds rested on their shoulders.

As Elara's image began to fade, she left them with one final command: "Hurry."

The group moved quickly, their minds racing with the weight of all they had just learned. As they exited the chamber and made their way toward the sitting room next to Gran Celia's bedroom, the air around them seemed to grow heavier with every step.

The sitting room was warm, lit by the fire crackling in the hearth. Gran Celia settled into one of the armchairs, her hands resting in her lap as she gazed at her family. Ridge, Waverly, and Lynx sat across from her, the silence between them thick with unspoken thoughts.

Gran Celia spoke first. "Ridge, Waverly, Lynx... what we've learned is that the power to close the portal and seal the Abasimtrox is tied to the Beaumont bloodline. You must be the ones to perform the sealing. But how you do this, and when, is still unclear."

Ridge's voice was steady but filled with uncertainty. "We've always known there was something about the portal, but this—this is too much. How can we activate something that connects to the elements? How can we control the portal and the forces behind it?"

Gran Celia sighed deeply, her eyes filled with both concern and hope. "I don't know, but I do know that we can't wait any longer. The seal weakens with every passing moment, and the Abasimtrox grow more restless. You'll need to connect with the elemental spirits, utilize their power to stabilize the seal, and hold it steady. That means confronting the elements themselves."

Lynx looked up from where he sat fidgeting his hands, his voice laced with a nervous energy. "But what if we're not ready? What if we can't control the power?"

Gran Celia reached out, her hand resting gently on his. "You've always been ready. The Beaumont legacy is part of you, and the portal won't activate for anyone else. You have the power, even if you don't understand it yet. You must trust in yourselves."

11

The quiet of the sitting room was broken by a gentle knock on the door. Gran Celia, who had been pacing thoughtfully, stopped and looked toward the door.

"Come in," she called, her voice steady.

Francis entered, her expression neutral but alert. She stepped into the room, her eyes meeting Gran Celia's with a sense of urgency. "Gran Celia, I just wanted to inform you that Dr. Stern and Dr. Walsh have arrived from Germany."

Gran Celia's brow furrowed slightly in surprise.

Ridge said, "Ah, yes. I forgot to mention I had reached out to them. Dr. Marshall Stern and his wife, Dr. Madre Walsh have been involved in interplanetary technologies and extraterrestrial studies for years—they may hold the answers we need to understand the full scope of the portal's capabilities."

Gran Celia nodded, a hint of relief washing over her. "Good timing," she said. "They'll be a welcome addition. We've all been grappling with the enormity of what we've uncovered so far, we need their expertise to move forward."

Waverly, who had been quietly sitting near the window, turned to her uncle. "So, you were able to get them to come quickly? That's great news."

"Yes, it wasn't easy," Ridge replied, his tone more serious now. "But with everything that's been happening, I knew we needed the best. Dr. Stern's and Dr. Walsh's work with extraterrestrial environments and interplanetary travel is exactly what we need. They may be the key to understanding how to stabilize the portal and use it safely."

Gran Celia nodded, her face thoughtful. "Good. Let's meet them in the library and bring them up to date. There's much they need to know."

As they left the sitting room and made their way down the grand hallway, Gran Celia's mind wandered back to the revelation they had made in the Elemental Room. Her heart was heavy with the weight of it all. Only the Beaumont bloodline could control the portal's power, but there was still so much they didn't understand. The knowledge they had just uncovered was only the beginning. The sealing of the portal would require not only their physical presence but also their connection to the elemental forces—and the cost of that knowledge was becoming clearer with each passing moment.

In the library, the group was soon joined by Dr. Stern and his wife, Dr. Madre Walsh, both of whom were in their early fifties. Dr. Stern had a sharp, scholarly appearance, with graying hair and wire-rimmed glasses that seemed to always be perched at the edge of his nose. His wife, Madre, was a stoic presence, with a calm demeanor that contrasted with her husband's more animated energy. Both of them exuded an aura of intelligence, but there was a quiet sadness behind their eyes as if they had seen things—had studied things—that most people couldn't begin to understand.

"Gran Celia, Ridge," Dr. Stern greeted, offering a handshake to both. "I'm glad to be here. Though, I must admit, I've never been so intrigued and perplexed by a project in all my years of research."

Dr. Walsh offered a smile, though it was faint. "It's not often we're called upon for something as... 'extraordinary' as this," she said, her German accent light but distinct. "But we are eager to help. Tell us everything."

Ridge gestured for them to sit, and they quickly got to work, explaining everything that had happened since Francis's arrival. The family recounted their discoveries in the Elemental Room, the activation of the three chairs by Waverly, Lynx, and Ridge, and the troubling realization that Gran Celia could not connect to the elemental spirits the way the direct Beaumont descendants could.

"There's still so much we don't understand," Ridge said, leaning forward. "But we know now that the elemental forces—the air, fire, earth, and water—are connected to the portal's power. The three of us—Waverly, Lynx, and I—can connect to the elements, but only because we're direct descendants of the Beaumont bloodline."

Dr. Stern, who had been listening intently, adjusted his glasses. "This is… fascinating," he murmured. "The portal is more than just a means of interplanetary travel—it's a conduit for the elemental forces themselves?"

Gran Celia nodded gravely. "Yes. And we believe that only those with Beaumont blood in their veins can truly control the portal and stabilize it. The chairs that activated… they are part of a process to connect to the elements."

"Yes," Waverly replied, her eyes filled with uncertainty. "But there's still one question we haven't answered: Who will be able to activate the water element?"

Lynx's voice was filled with doubt. "I'm wondering that too. We don't have any cousins or other family members. I don't know anyone else who can connect with it."

Gran Celia's face grew even more somber as the pieces of the puzzle began to fall into place. "There's only one answer to that, Lynx. It would take your father, Lincoln."

Waverly's breath caught in her throat. "But… that's impossible. Our parents are dead." Her voice was a mixture of disbelief and grief, the weight of her words hanging in the air like an unspoken truth.

Ridge, who had been watching the siblings intently, exhaled slowly. His face was pale as he met their gazes. "That's not exactly true."

The room fell silent as everyone stared at Ridge, all of them confused and shocked by his statement except for Gran Celia. Waverly looked at him in disbelief. "What are you talking about, Ridge? You can't possibly mean…"

Ridge's voice was steady, but there was a raw edge to it. "I'm telling you, they're not dead. Lincoln is alive. He's been alive all this time, but he's been hidden—protected from those who would use him."

Waverly felt a cold wave of shock crash over her, her heart pounding in her chest. "But why didn't you tell us? How could you keep something like that from us?"

Gran Celia's expression was one of quiet understanding, though there was sadness in her eyes. "It wasn't something we could reveal until now, Waverly. Lincoln's safety was paramount. There were forces out there—dark forces—that were trying to find him. For years, we kept him hidden, to protect the family and the legacy of the Beaumonts."

Lynx's eyes widened as he turned to Ridge. "You mean… Dad is out there? He's been alive all this time?"

Ridge nodded slowly. "Yes. And now, with everything that's happening, we need him more than ever."

The weight of the revelation hit them all like a ton of bricks. Waverly's mind reeled. Her parents—'her father'—hadn't been killed in a car accident. They had been alive all this time, hidden away, protected from a world that didn't understand the legacy of the Beaumonts.

And now, they would have to find them.

The room seemed to hold its breath, the implications of this revelation settling over them like a dark cloud. Waverly stood up, her heart racing. "Where is he? How do we find him?"

Gran Celia stood as well, her face filled with both determination and sorrow. "We will find him, Waverly. But first, we have to prepare. The portal, the elemental spirits—everything depends on us being ready."

12

The chamber beneath Sage Manor was quiet except for the distant hum of the orb, which pulsed with a soft, rhythmic glow. Ridge and Gran Celia stood in front of it, their faces solemn as they prepared to make contact. It had been a long time since they had tried to reach Keelee on Tanzlora, and with the revelations of the last few days, they knew they needed to connect with him.

Gran Celia stepped forward, her fingers brushing the cool surface of the orb. "We need to connect with Keelee," she said, her voice filled with quiet determination. "He's the one who can tell us what's happening with Lincoln. We have to reach them, Ridge. We need Lincoln back on Earth."

Ridge nodded, his eyes narrowing as he stepped closer to the orb. "I know. We've got to act quickly. The Abasimtrox are getting closer to breaking free, and the seal is weakening. I just hope Keelee can get through. It's been so long since we made contact."

Gran Celia's fingers hovered over the orb's surface, and with a deep breath, she began speaking aloud. "Keelee of Tanzlora, this is Gran Celia and Ridge Beaumont from Earth. We need to speak with you. It's urgent."

For a long moment, the orb remained still, its surface reflecting the dim light of the chamber. Gran Celia and Ridge exchanged a tense glance, both of them knowing how delicate this connection could be. The portal system, after all, had been closed for physical travel for years, and even holographic appearances were only allowed at limited frequencies. They didn't know if they could reach Keelee at all.

Suddenly, a faint flicker of light began to form at the center of the orb, growing stronger by the second. The air in the chamber grew thick with energy, and the orb's hum turned into a steady vibration. A figure began to emerge, but it was faint—too faint to be fully visible.

"Gran Celia? Ridge?" came a voice, distant and ethereal, like a whisper carried across a great distance. It was Keelee, but his voice was strained, weak.

Gran Celia stepped closer to the orb, her voice urgent. "Keelee, can you hear us? It's Gran Celia. We need your help. Please, if you can, respond. It's about Lincoln."

The figure of Keelee flickered again, and for a moment, it seemed like he might fade completely. But then, his image solidified just enough to be seen. His face was blurry, the energy surrounding him causing the details to shift like a mirage. He looked tired, his expression worn, but his eyes—those familiar, intelligent eyes—met theirs.

"I hear you, Gran Celia. Ridge," Keelee's voice crackled, a faint distortion in the signal. "It's... it's been so long since we've been able to speak like this. What's happening?"

Ridge's heart raced as he stepped forward, his eyes fixed on the holographic image of Keelee. "Keelee, we've discovered something terrible. We need Lincoln's help. He's on Tanzlora, isn't he?"

Keelee's expression softened, a flicker of relief crossing his features despite the weak signal. "Yes, Lincoln is here. He's been safe, doing well with Bethany. Why do you need his help?"

Gran Celia's voice trembled slightly as she spoke. "The portal system has become unstable. The seal is weakening, and we're on the verge of losing control of the interplanetary gates. The Abasimtrox are close to breaking free from their quarantine, and if that happens, it could mean the end of Earth and all the worlds connected to the portal system."

Keelee's image flickered again, a slight distortion in his form, as though the connection was straining under the weight of the message. "The seal... weakened?" he repeated. "This is... grave. But I can't do much to help from here. The portal system has been closed for physical travel, Gran Celia. Only holographic appearances are allowed, and even those are at a low frequency. That's why my connection is so faint."

Ridge's face darkened. "We've been doing everything we can on Earth, but we need Lincoln here. He's the fourth bloodline family member, and we can't complete the elemental sealing without him."

Gran Celia leaned closer to the orb, her voice pleading. "We need Lincoln here, Keelee. The longer the seal remains unstable, the more dangerous the situation becomes. The Abasimtrox will escape, and all the worlds will fall into chaos."

Keelee seemed to hesitate, his image wavering as though he was battling against something unseen. "I will consult with the elders of Tanzlora. We have kept the portals closed for many reasons, but this... this is different. If Lincoln is truly needed, then we will find a way to bring him back. But the process will take time."

Ridge clenched his fists, frustration mounting in his chest. "Time is something we don't have, Keelee. The longer we wait, the worse it gets. We need him now."

"I understand," Keelee's voice faltered, his image flickering again. "But there's only so much we can do from here. The elders are the only ones who can authorize the physical connection. We have to be patient. But know this, Ridge, Gran Celia—if Lincoln is to return, it will take all of us to ensure the portal is properly protected during travel."

Gran Celia took a deep breath, her fingers clenched tightly around the edge of the table. "Then we wait. We can't risk the Abasimtrox escaping."

The energy in the orb shifted once more, and Keelee's image became more faint, his voice growing even more strained. "I'll make sure the elders understand. But until then, you must do everything you can to prepare. The elemental spirits—everything—is linked. If the portal is to be stabilized, it must be done properly."

And then, just as quickly as he had appeared, Keelee's image began to fade, the light from the orb dimming in the room. His final words echoed in the air, barely audible.

"Be safe. We are doing everything we can."

The connection cut out completely, leaving only the soft hum of the orb in the silence of the chamber. Gran Celia let out a long, steadying breath, her eyes closing briefly as the weight of Keelee's words settled in.

"We have to wait," Ridge said quietly, his voice low and filled with frustration. "We have to trust that Keelee and the elders can bring Lincoln back. But in the meantime... we continue. We make sure everything is ready."

Gran Celia nodded, though her face was tight with the knowledge of what was to come. "We'll prepare. But we must be ready for anything. Arcmyrin's survival depends on it. The balance of the worlds depends on it."

Waverly, who had been standing silently at the bottom of the stone stairs, walked over to them. "What now?" she asked softly.

Gran Celia's expression was firm, yet tinged with sorrow. "Now, we prepare ourselves. We must ensure that when Lincoln returns, we are ready. But there's more at stake than we realize. We can't let the Abasimtrox break through."

Ridge looked at his family, his resolve hardening. "Then we fight. We fight for the future of every world connected to this portal."

As they left the chamber, the quiet tension between them was palpable. They had no choice but to wait for Keelee's word, and for Lincoln's return. The portal's instability was growing by the day, and the threat of the Abasimtrox was closer than ever.

13

The grand parlor of Sage Manor, with its rich tapestries and historical portraits, had witnessed many crucial family discussions over the centuries, but perhaps none as momentous as this. The soft crackling of the fireplace filled the room with a comforting warmth as the Beaumont family gathered to discuss the implications of the journey through the crystal gate.

Gran Celia sat in her high-backed chair, a dignified figure who, despite her age, held the commanding presence that had guided her family through numerous challenges. Ridge, Waverly, and Lynx gathered around her, each wearing expressions of concern mixed with resolve.

Dr. Marshall Stern and his wife, Dr. Madre Walsh, shared the findings of their latest assessments. "The preparations for the trip include consuming specific beverages and herbs that enhance physical and mental resilience. These are potent and tailored for individuals in prime physical condition." Dr. Stern explained.

Dr. Walsh, with apprehension in her eyes, stated, "This is not just a journey; it's a mission that carries significant risks."

Waverly, always the adventurous one, felt a surge of both excitement and fear. "I'm ready to take this responsibility," she said, her voice firm. "I've learned about our family's legacy, and I believe I can do this—not just for us, but for the sake of Arcmyrin."

Lynx, who was equally courageous, added, "And I'll be right there beside her to get those Abasimtrox sealed back in!"

Gran Celia reached out, taking a hand of each of her grandchildren. "I am proud of both of you. This decision isn't taken lightly, but I know our family's legacy and the safety of another world are in capable hands."

Ridge, feeling a fatherly type of protective instinct, spoke up. "We'll spend the next few days preparing. We'll review all the protocols and ensure we are fully prepared." Turning to look at Gran Celia, he asked, "Mother, how did the portal work back then? Back during the intergalactic war. How did father and Lincoln manage to travel to Arcmyrin and Tanzlora so frequently to help fight the Abasimtrox?"

Gran Celia, who had been staring into the fire, turned slowly to face him. Her eyes were filled with a quiet sorrow, but also a deep well of wisdom. She had lived through so much—seen her family fight battles both on Earth and beyond—and the stories she held were more than just memories; they were pieces of history.

"It wasn't as simple as just walking through a door," she began, her voice distant at first, as if remembering something long buried. "When Jameson, your father, and Lincoln traveled through the crystal gate during the war, they weren't just crossing space. They were crossing realms—and the portal was much more than a passage. It was a gateway to something far greater."

She paused, her hands resting in her lap. Ridge could see the weight of her words sinking in, the gravity of the past taking hold. "The portal was connected to both Arcmyrin and Tanzlora through a very ancient network of energy, an energy tied to the elemental forces themselves. The gate was attuned to these elements, just like it is now, but back then, it was much more stable. We had access to resources, knowledge from both planets, and were able to stabilize the portal with their help."

Ridge leaned forward. "But how did they manage the travel itself? I know the portals had their dangers, but how did Lincoln and father manage the transition to other worlds without facing the risks we now know exist?"

Gran Celia's eyes grew darker, and she let out a small sigh. "They were fortunate. Back then, we had more control over the portal. The link was strong, and the gateway didn't just connect us to the realms physically—it also connected us to the life forces of Arcmyrin and Tanzlora. We had their support, their energy. But there were precautions.

The portal itself was a living entity, with its own ways of testing those who entered."

"Precautions?" Ridge asked, a hint of confusion crossing his face.

Gran Celia's face softened as she spoke. "When you traveled through the crystal gate, you didn't just walk through a door. You were linked to the very essence of the world you were traveling to. The atmosphere, the gravity, the life force itself—you had to adapt to it. Arcmyrin and Tanzlora were both powerful, but not without their dangers. For them to survive, we took special measures."

She leaned back in her chair, her hands still folded neatly in her lap. "In the seed room... in the lab beneath the gazebo, we had access to special herbs and concoctions—ones that were cultivated on both Arcmyrin and Tanzlora. These were mixed with special botanical brews to help travelers adapt to the different environments. Without them, your father and brother would've never been able to withstand the harsh atmospheres, the varying gravitational fields, or the unpredictable energy surges from the portal itself. Dr. Stern and Dr. Walsh knows this from their research but what they don't know until right now, is that all that research was based on the travels of Jameson and Lincoln."

Ridge's eyes widened slightly. "So... the seed room? It wasn't just for storage?"

"No," Gran Celia replied, shaking her head. "It was much more than that. The herbs and plants we used weren't just for physical survival. They were tied to the very lifeforce of the planets themselves. Special brews were made to help strengthen the body and spirit, to make the transition between worlds safer. It protected them, allowed them to breathe the air of those worlds, allowed their bodies to adapt."

Ridge glanced down, trying to process the enormity of what his mother was saying. "And these brews... were they connected to the elements as well?"

Gran Celia nodded. "Yes. Water, earth, fire, air—each brew was linked to one of the elemental forces. For example, a water-based concoction would help Lincoln adjust to Arcmyrin's sometimes harsh weather systems and water-based energies. The fire-based brews helped Jameson endure Tanzlora's more volatile climate, which often had extreme temperature shifts. They had to be careful with the amount they consumed—too much, and they could overwhelm their systems—but just the right amount kept them safe."

Ridge looked back up at her. "So this is why the seed room is so important. These concoctions, these brews—they could help us now. Could they help us stabilize the portal again?"

Gran Celia hesitated, her gaze turning inward as she considered his question. "Possibly. If we could make use of the plants we still have and recreate the brews, it might help us in the short term. But the real solution lies in the elemental spirits. You have to align the elements—each of you, with your own connection to the elemental forces. This is what will stabilize the portal long-term, not just brews and herbs."

Ridge absorbed her words, but his mind was still racing with possibilities. "So if Lincoln and Jameson were able to travel safely because of the herbs, could we use them now to help us get through the portal?"

14

Dr. Marshall Stern, a man of methodical precision, was pacing near the fireplace in the parlor of Sage Manor, his glasses perched on the tip of his nose as he considered their options. He stopped pacing after Ridge's question and looked at the group assembled in the parlor.

"That's an interesting question," he said slowly, his fingers tapping together thoughtfully. "I imagine the herbs could play a role in stabilizing your body's ability to withstand the stresses of interplanetary travel. But it's not just about the herbs themselves. It's the entire system—the portal's power, the elements, and the energy flow through the gate. The herbs were designed to allow you to adapt to the environments of other worlds, yes, but the portal itself is far more volatile now."

Gran Celia nodded in agreement. "That's true. The herbs may provide short-term benefits, but they can't stabilize the portal itself. They were never meant to. The power behind the portal comes from the elemental forces, and that's where the real solution lies."

Ridge sighed, the frustration building again. "So, no shortcut. We're still left with the elemental forces, which means we need Lincoln back to fully stabilize everything. But what if we could use the herbs just to make sure we can travel safely once we get through the portal? Could we risk it?"

Dr. Stern hesitated, clearly uncomfortable with the idea of taking such a risk. "It's hard to say. The portal was designed with the intention of moving life between planets, yes, but not for a scenario like this, where the seal is weakening. We're dealing with a much more delicate situation. The herbs might help with physical adaptation, but I wouldn't trust them to control the portal's supernatural powers, especially given its instability."

Dr. Walsh, who had been quietly reviewing some notes, looked up with an expression of realization. "Actually, there may be something else," she said. "While researching the history of the portal in the upper section of the library, I came across an ancient text. It looks like it could be a guide to the botanical concoctions, but... it's not like anything I've seen before."

Ridge's attention snapped to her. "You found a book that might help?"

"Yes," Dr. Walsh confirmed, her voice growing more animated. "It's an old manuscript, buried among other forgotten texts. It contains diagrams and recipes for brews that seem to be designed specifically for interplanetary travel. But there's a catch—most of the symbols and writings are unreadable. Some appear to be ancient language, mixed with botanical terminology I haven't seen before."

Gran Celia leaned forward, her interest piqued. "Where did you find this text?"

"In the archives, in the upper part of the library," Dr. Walsh replied, her tone laced with excitement. "It was buried beneath a pile of old manuscripts. I don't know how it went unnoticed for so long, but it's definitely important. The problem is that I can't decipher all the symbols. They're unlike anything I've encountered."

Gran Celia's gaze shifted to Ridge, her brow furrowing. "This may be the breakthrough we need. If those recipes are tied to the portal's energy flow and the elemental forces, then we need to understand them. But Dr. Walsh... if you can't decipher them, I believe we have someone who can."

Ridge glanced at Gran Celia, his mind racing. "Francis," he said.

Gran Celia nodded. "Yes, Ridge. If Francis can help us translate this, we might be able to understand the full scope of the botanical concoctions and their relation to the portal. It could provide the missing link we need."

Dr. Walsh's face lit up at the suggestion. "That's true. I've tried every method I know, but if Francis has the expertise to interpret these symbols, she could uncover things we've missed. And it would be crucial for understanding how these herbs and brews could be used safely in the context of the portal."

Gran Celia turned to Ridge. "I'll consult with Francis immediately. She'll need to examine the text and if it's truly a guide to the botanical brews we're seeking, it could help us stabilize the portal temporarily while we work on the long-term solution."

Ridge stood up, his hands clasped behind his back as he thought about the task at hand. "If Francis can help us unlock this information, then we'll have one less thing to worry about while we wait for Lincoln."

Gran Celia left the parlor, her footsteps echoing down the hall as she made her way to find Francis. The weight of their mission hung heavily in the air. The portal's instability, the Abasimtrox threat, and the logistics of Lincoln's return—everything was converging, and they had no more time to waste.

As Gran Celia made her way toward the back of the manor, she couldn't help but feel the pressure of everything that lay ahead. They had a chance, but only if they could decipher the past and use its secrets to protect the future.

It was a race against time—and the Beaumonts were running out of it.

Francis had kept to herself over the past few days, retreating to her quarters when not needed for discussions or research. The weight of everything they had uncovered, combined with the pressure of what lay ahead, seemed to have taken a toll on her. Gran Celia knew that Francis, for all her sharp mind and formidable expertise, carried her own burdens—burdens she often kept hidden from others. But now, as the need for answers grew more urgent, Gran Celia couldn't afford to wait.

She reached Francis's door and knocked gently, the sound muffled by the thick wood.

"Francis?" Gran Celia called softly. "It's Gran Celia. Can we talk for a moment?"

There was a pause, a rustle of movement from inside, before the door creaked open. Francis stood in the doorway, her expression neutral but tired. Her hair was slightly disheveled, and her usually impeccable attire was a little more relaxed than usual, as if she had been lost in her thoughts.

"Gran Celia," Francis greeted her with a faint smile. "What can I do for you?"

Gran Celia studied her for a moment, her gaze softening. "I know you've been... secluding yourself away, Francis. You've had much to think about, and I understand that. But there's something important we need you for."

Francis raised an eyebrow, her curiosity piqued. "What's happened now?"

Gran Celia didn't mince words. "Dr. Walsh has found an ancient text in the library—one that seems to be a guide to the botanical concoctions used for safe interplanetary travel. It contains a series of symbols and writings that she could not decipher. I was hoping you might be able to make sense of it. It could hold the key to understanding how to stabilize the portal and make safe passage through it."

Francis's eyes narrowed, her attention now fully captured by Gran Celia's words. "Another ancient text?" She stepped aside, gesturing for Gran Celia to enter. "And you think it's connected to the herbs and brews from the seed room?"

Gran Celia nodded. "Yes. The symbols seem to be tied to the same language we've seen before in the portal's chamber."

Francis took a deep breath, then looked back at Gran Celia, her expression no longer as distant as it had been. "If this text can help us figure out how to make the portal stable again, then I'll help."

Gran Celia smiled faintly, relieved. "Thank you, Francis. I knew we could count on you."

15

The ancient book was lying on the table in the library when Gran Celia and Francis walked in, Dr. Walsh must have optimistically laid it there on their way out of the parlor in the hopes that Francis said yes.

"The text," Gran Celia prompted.

Francis walked over to the table, pulled up a chair and gently slid the old manuscript in front of her. It looked aged, the pages fragile and worn. She handled it very carefully, already immersed in its symbols and barely noticing Gran Celia taking a seat across from her.

Francis ran her fingers along the edges of the book. "This looks like something from the early days of the portal system. The design of the symbols... they're familiar, but not entirely. It's like a hybrid of several languages."

Gran Celia leaned forward, her voice quiet but insistent. "Do you think you can decipher it?"

Francis gave a small, rueful smile. "I don't know. Some of these symbols are based on ancient Arcmirian glyphs, while others seem to be local to Earth. It'll take time, but I can try."

Gran Celia nodded, her eyes full of understanding. "Time is something we're running short on. The portal is unstable, and the elements are at risk. If we don't stabilize it soon, the Abasimtrox will break free. But this," she said, placing her hand gently on the manuscript, "this may be our only shot at securing it."

Francis's eyes softened as she regarded Gran Celia. "I know. I won't let you down."

Gran Celia stood up, her shoulders straightening with resolve. "I'll leave you to it then. We'll be ready to move forward as soon as you've cracked the code. In the meantime, I'll check on the others."

Francis gave a brief nod, already lost in thought as she opened the book to the first page. "I'll get started right away. It may take a while to get through, but I'll make sure we have something useful soon."

Gran Celia turned to leave the library, but just as her hand touched the door, she paused and glanced back. "Francis?"

She looked up from the book. "Yes?"

"Thank you," Gran Celia said softly, her voice filled with gratitude. "I know this is hard for you... but we're relying on you. The future of the portal, of Earth, of Arcmyrin and Tanzlora—it all depends on us working together."

Francis gave a faint smile, her eyes already focused on the page in front of her. "I know. And I'll do everything I can."

Gran Celia left the room, closing the door behind her. She walked down the hallway with purpose, her mind full of everything they still needed to do. As she passed the foyer, she glanced out the front door toward the gazebo, thinking of the chamber and its crystal gate. The weight of the task ahead was heavy, but now there was a renewed sense of urgency. They couldn't afford to waste time.

When Gran Celia entered the parlor again, the scent of freshly brewed tea filled the air, mingling with the sweet aroma of pastries set out on the table. It was a welcome respite from the heavy burden of their discoveries, a momentary pause before the weight of their mission pressed back in.

Gran Celia took a seat beside Ridge, who nodded briefly at her but said nothing. The conversation had slowed to a lull as everyone seemed to be lost in their own thoughts. Waverly, who had been absentmindedly stirring her tea, broke the silence.

"Gran Celia," Waverly began, her voice quiet but firm, "there's something Lynx and I don't understand. You've told us about how our parents had to stay hidden on Tanzlora... but why? Why was it necessary for them to be kept away?"

Gran Celia's heart clenched at the question. She had known this moment would come, but it didn't make it any easier to answer. The history behind Lincoln and Bethany's decision to remain on Tanzlora was complicated, filled with secrets and hard truths that she had tried to protect her grandchildren from for years.

She set her tea down, her hands steady as she met Waverly and Lynx's eyes. "Your parents were never just ordinary people. The Beaumonts are tied to something much bigger than any of us ever realized, and Lincoln's bloodline was always going to be a target. That's why we had to keep him—and Bethany—safe."

Lynx leaned forward, his eyes wide with curiosity and confusion. "But why couldn't they just fight, Gran Celia? Why hide? Dad was always so strong, so confident. It doesn't make sense."

Gran Celia sighed, her mind wandering back to the days when the decision was first made. "It wasn't about strength, Lynx. It was about survival. When the intergalactic war broke out, the Abasimtrox became a bigger threat than we could have imagined. And the truth is, they were after Lincoln. His connection to the portal and the elemental forces... they knew how important he was, how crucial his role would be. Keeping him hidden, keeping him safe on Tanzlora—away from the Abasimtrox's reach—was the only way to ensure the family legacy could continue."

Waverly's brow furrowed as she processed Gran Celia's words. "But... why didn't they just tell us, Gran Celia? Why didn't they tell us that they were alive? That they were on another planet?"

Gran Celia's gaze softened with the weight of the burden she had carried all these years. "The truth, Waverly, is that the risk of your parents returning to Earth was too great. There were too many enemies, too many forces seeking to destroy everything the Beaumonts had worked for. Your father knew this better than anyone. And Bethany, she—well, she insisted that it was for the best. She believed their being hidden would give you and Lynx the chance to grow up in peace, without the constant threat of being caught in the middle of a war."

"But they could have helped, right?" Lynx's voice trembled slightly as he spoke. "They could have helped stop the Abasimtrox before any of this happened."

Gran Celia nodded slowly, her fingers tightening around her teacup. "Yes, they could have. But the Abasimtrox knew too much. If they had returned, they would have been marked, and everything would have been lost. There were too many powerful forces at play, and your father and Bethany made the hardest decision they could—one that would keep you safe. They wanted you to live a normal life, free from the horrors of the war."

Ridge, who had been silently listening, finally spoke up. "It wasn't easy on them, either. Lincoln... he never wanted to leave, but he understood why it had to be done. And it wasn't just about the family's safety. It was about protecting Earth, protecting the worlds tied to the portal."

Gran Celia looked up at Ridge, her eyes filled with years of unspoken history. "Yes. Lincoln had a responsibility—a burden he couldn't share with you until the time was right. The Beaumonts have always had a connection to the portal. And your father understood that connection. But the war wasn't just about protecting the family. It was about securing the balance of the worlds, keeping the Abasimtrox in quarantine, and ensuring the portal wasn't misused."

The weight of her words hung in the air, and the silence that followed was thick. Waverly and Lynx sat quietly, trying to process everything Gran Celia had shared. It was a lot to take in—so many questions, so many truths that had remained hidden for so long. The enormity of their family's legacy was beginning to reveal itself, piece by piece.

Waverly was the first to speak, her voice soft yet resolute. "So, all of this... everything we're facing now, with the portal, with the

Abasimtrox—it's all been building up to this moment. We're the ones who have to finish what was started."

Gran Celia nodded, her eyes heavy with the weight of responsibility. "Yes. It's been a long time coming. The pieces are all in place now, and the only way to stop the Abasimtrox is for you—Ridge, Waverly, and Lynx along with Lincoln—to unite the elements and stabilize the portal."

Lynx shook his head, still trying to make sense of it all. "I don't get it. If they were so important—if our parents were the key to all this—why wasn't I told sooner? Why did they have to stay hidden?"

Gran Celia's expression softened with a sadness that was almost tangible. "I understand your frustration, Lynx. But sometimes, protecting you meant keeping you in the dark. Lincoln and Bethany made a choice to keep you safe, to let you grow up without the threat of danger hanging over your heads. And they thought that if they stayed hidden, you could have a life without the weight of the portal on your shoulders. A normal life. But now, things have changed. The portal is weakening, and the Abasimtrox are stirring. Lincoln's return is necessary to complete the sealing process."

Ridge stood, moving to the window as he looked out at the sprawling grounds. His mind was racing, taking in all the pieces of the puzzle that were falling into place. "So now we wait for Lincoln to come back," he said, his voice low. "And once he's here, we can stop the Abasimtrox for good."

Gran Celia turned to face him, her eyes full of both resolve and regret. "We don't have the luxury of time, Ridge. The seal is weakening with every passing day. Arcmyrin, our sister planet, is in danger, its life force slowly dying. We must act quickly, before it's too late."

Waverly placed her teacup down and stood as well, her expression firm. "We'll be ready. We'll do whatever it takes."

Lynx looked between his family, his face a mixture of determination and lingering confusion. "And when dad comes back, we'll have the chance to fix everything? To stop the Abasimtrox for good?"

Gran Celia nodded, her voice unwavering. "Yes. But it will require all of us—together. We must unite the elements and seal the portal before the Abasimtrox can completely break free."

16

The heavy, worn door to the parlor creaked as Ridge, Gran Celia, Waverly, and Lynx stepped out into the hallway. The air in the manor felt still, as if the old house was holding its breath, waiting for something to shift. Ridge's mind was racing with questions, but the task ahead was clear: they needed to reach Keelee and the Tanzloran elders to get their input on Lincoln's return. They had already discovered that Lincoln's bloodline was key to the portal's stabilization, and now they had to find a way to bring him back safely—without triggering an even greater catastrophe.

Gran Celia led the way to the gazebo, her pace deliberate, her thoughts clearly focused on the task ahead. Ridge followed, his steps purposeful, but he could feel the weight of the moment bearing down on him. Waverly and Lynx walked closely behind, both of them quiet, knowing that their family was about to face yet another pivotal moment in their long, intertwined history with the crystal gate.

"I still don't understand why the Tanzloran elders are so hesitant," Waverly murmured as they walked. "Why can't mom and dad just return to Earth? What's the problem with them traveling again?"

Gran Celia's voice was steady but filled with a quiet frustration. "The Tanzlorans are careful. They know how dangerous it is to open the portal. The connection between all three worlds is delicate.

Upon arriving at the gazebo, Ridge reached for the door, pushing it open, and they descended into the chamber. The air surrounding them was cool as they approached the crystal orb. The soft hum of energy filled the space, and Ridge's pulse quickened in anticipation. As Gran

Celia stepped forward to connect with the orb, Waverly and Lynx took their places nearby, both of them eager for news from Keelee.

Gran Celia's hands hovered above the orb, and she spoke clearly. "Keelee, this is Gran Celia, Ridge, Waverly, and Lynx Beaumont from Earth. We need to discuss the plan for Lincoln and Bethany's return. Have you got an answer from the Tanzloran elders?"

For a long moment, the orb remained still, the energy inside it pulsing faintly. Then, as if answering their call, Keelee's holographic form began to emerge, shimmering with faint blue light. His figure was ghostly at first, but as his image solidified, his face appeared with a mixture of solemnity and caution.

"I hear you, Gran Celia," Keelee's voice came through, distant but clear. "The Tanzloran elders have discussed the matter. We are all aware of the risks involved. But the plan they've suggested is the only one that may work without compromising the balance of the portal."

Ridge stepped forward, speaking with urgency. "What is their plan?"

Keelee's holographic figure flickered slightly as if adjusting to the strain of their communication. "It will require precision but they suggest only opening the portal once on all three planets at the same time. They fear if Lincoln were to travel back to Earth, the portal would have to be opened twice—once to allow him to return to Earth, and once for him to travel to Arcmyrin. That could cause an instability we're not prepared for.

Gran Celia spoke up, "I understand that fear and I share that same one, what do they suggest instead?"

Keelee's faint figure flickered again trying to come through strong enough to relay the plan to them. "If the portal is opened simultaneously on all three planets—Earth, Tanzlora, and Arcmyrin—the energy will be distributed evenly. The elemental forces will work together, and the portal's stability will be secured. But this can only happen if we are all aligned. If the connection between the worlds is broken at any point, the portal will become unstable."

Ridge stated, "So let me see if I am understanding this correctly, the elders want Lincoln, Bethany, Waverly, Lynx and myself to go through the portal system to Arcmyrin at the same time?"

"Yes," replied Keelee, "it requires the portal only being activated once instead of twice and the elders feel that is the safest option, our only option."

Gran Celia's gaze was steady, her voice filled with determination. "And you're certain the Tanzloran elders are ready to facilitate this? They'll need to ensure that their part of the portal system is activated as well."

Keelee nodded, his image solidifying further. "Yes. The Tanzlorans are prepared. But it is up to you, the humans, to agree to this plan. Once you do, we will begin the necessary preparations."

Just as Keelee's figure began to shimmer again, a new presence emerged in the chamber. The air seemed to shift, and with a brilliant flash of light, Elara appeared before them, her ethereal form appearing beside Keelee. Her appearance was sudden but expected, as Gran Celia had hoped to hear from the Arcmyrin leaders as well.

"Elara," Gran Celia greeted her, her tone calm yet filled with respect. "I'm glad you've joined us. We need your insight on the Tanzloran plan."

Elara's voice rang out, clear and resolute. "I agree with Keelee. The plan is sound. My fellow Arcmyrians are prepared to defend the portal from our side once it is opened. We will ensure that the balance is maintained and that no external forces can take advantage of the portal's instability."

Waverly, who had been standing quietly, now stepped forward, her voice filled with quiet urgency. "So, if we agree to the plan, we'll open the portal simultaneously on Earth, Tanzlora, and Arcmyrin. Mom and Dad will return to Earth, and we'll travel with them to Arcmyrin, where the real work of stabilizing the portal will begin?"

Elara said, "No. You will join together on Arcmyrin. Lincoln and Bethany will travel from Tanzlora directly to Arcmyrin while you, Ridge and Lynx will come here directly from Earth.

You must understand, the moment the portal opens, the risk will be high. The Abasimtrox will sense the energy surge. Once the portal is activated, you must be ready to move quickly. Your task is to stabilize the portal, protect the worlds, and hold the line against the Abasimtrox. We are ready on our end to support you."

Keelee's image flickered again, his voice calm but filled with an undercurrent of urgency. "The Tanzloran elders agree with the plan. If the humans are agreeable, we will proceed with the preparations. But the balance of all the worlds depends on you—on your ability to activate the elements and stabilize the portal once it's opened."

Gran Celia's heart quickened with the realization of how critical this moment was. She looked at Ridge, Waverly, and Lynx, who were all standing together, their faces filled with determination.

"We agree," Gran Celia said firmly. "We understand the risks, but we will do whatever it takes. Let's proceed with the plan."

Keelee's face brightened with approval. "Very well. We will begin coordinating with the Tanzloran elders and the Arcmyrian forces. Once we have confirmation, we'll move forward. Be ready."

With that, both Keelee and Elara's figures flickered one final time before disappearing, leaving the room in quiet anticipation. The weight of their decision settled over them like a heavy cloak, but there was no turning back now.

Gran Celia turned to Ridge, Waverly, and Lynx, her voice resolute. "We need to speak with Dr. Stern, Dr. Walsh, and Francis. They need to know what we've just agreed to. Time is of the essence."

The four of them left the chamber. The plan was set in motion, but there was still much to prepare for.

17

The grand library of Sage Manor was the heart of the Beaumont legacy—a place where knowledge and secrets had been passed down through the generations. Now, it was filled with a sense of purpose, the air heavy with the weight of everything they had learned. Ridge, Gran Celia, Waverly, and Lynx stood together near the large oak table at the center of the room, the familiar shelves of books lining the walls surrounding them. Across from them, Dr. Stern, Dr. Walsh, and Francis were seated, their faces attentive, ready to hear the next crucial piece of the puzzle.

Gran Celia cleared her throat, her voice steady but filled with the gravity of their current predicament. "We've made a decision. The Tanzloran elders have proposed a plan. If we agree, the portal will open simultaneously on all three planets—Earth, Tanzlora, and Arcmyrin—allowing Lincoln, Bethany, Ridge, Waverly and Lynx to join together on Arcmyrin. It will be a one-time opening, but it's the only way to stabilize the portal and keep the Abasimtrox from escaping."

The group sat in silence for a moment, each person processing the enormity of what had been proposed. Francis, who had been sitting quietly off to the side, glanced up from the pile of books and notes she had been reviewing, her brow furrowed with concentration. The weight of the plan and what it meant for the Beaumont family and their allies was clear.

"That's a dangerous plan," Dr. Stern said, his voice calm but filled with concern. "Opening the portal once, with all three planets aligned… there are risks. It could trigger instability across all worlds if something goes wrong."

Gran Celia nodded, her expression resolute. "We know. But it's the only option we have. The portal is weakening. If we don't act quickly, the Abasimtrox will escape, and nothing will be able to stop them."

Ridge crossed his arms, his jaw clenched. "There's still one question. How do we survive the journey? What about the risks to our bodies when traveling through the portal?"

Francis looked up at that, her eyes sharp with clarity. She had been quiet for most of the conversation, but now she stood up from her chair, her energy shifting from contemplative to focused.

"I think I can answer that," she said. "I've been studying the ancient text that Dr. Walsh found. It's not easy to decipher, but I've made some progress. The symbols in the text correspond to the botanical concoctions and herbal mixtures needed for each species to acclimate to the different environments of the sister planets. The book provides detailed instructions on how to create these mixtures, specifically tailored to Earth, Arcmyrin, and Tanzlora."

She continued, "The herbs have specific properties that protect the body from the shock of traveling through the portal and adapting to the atmospheric and environmental conditions of each planet. The plants have been carefully cultivated for this purpose, and they're meant to help travelers from each world adjust to the unique conditions of the others."

Waverly leaned forward, her curiosity piqued. "And what about the Tanzlorans and Arcmyrians? Do they need something similar when traveling to Earth?"

Francis nodded again. "Yes, they do. In fact, the text I'm currently deciphering also includes mixtures for the Tanzlorans and Arcmyrians to survive on Earth. Their environments are so different from ours—Arcmyrin's intense gravity, Tanzlora's unstable atmosphere—so the herbs and concoctions were designed to help them adapt to our planet's conditions. For example, Arcmyrians would need a mixture to withstand Earth's lower gravity and the different atmospheric pressure. Tanzlorans, on the other hand, would require a brew to protect them from our oxygen-rich atmosphere."

Ridge's mind was racing. "So, these brews... they're key to our success. They'll allow us to travel safely between planets, and they'll allow the Tanzlorans and Arcmyrians to come to Earth without endangering themselves?"

"That's correct," Francis said, her voice firm with the certainty of someone who had unlocked a crucial piece of the puzzle. "But there's more. I've just reached the section of the text that explains the connection between the Beaumont bloodline and the elemental forces."

Ridge raised an eyebrow, intrigued by the shift in topic. "What do you mean, the connection between the bloodline and the elements?"

Francis turned the pages carefully, her fingers tracing over the delicate text. "The ancient text speaks of Origin, creator deity—an ancient, powerful force that gave the Beaumont bloodline its gifts. The text explains that these gifts are passed down from one generation to the next, from one bloodline descendant to the other. The four elemental powers—air, fire, earth, and water—are granted to the descendants, and each one possesses an affinity for one of these elements."

Gran Celia's expression softened as she absorbed this new piece of information. "The powers are passed down..."

Francis's voice dropped slightly, her eyes glinting with the weight of what she was about to say. "The text explains that the elemental powers are linked to the balance of the world. When the Abasimtrox first arrived, it was the Beaumont bloodline that was tasked with protecting the elemental forces, ensuring they were in balance. The gift of Origin is a legacy—the bloodline must always have four descendants alive at the same time in order to counteract the evil of the Abasimtrox."

Ridge's face went pale as the implication of Francis's words settled over him. "So, if there are not four bloodline descendants alive at the same time, the balance is thrown off? The Abasimtrox can take advantage of that?"

Francis nodded solemnly. "Exactly. The Beaumont bloodline is integral to keeping the elemental forces in check. If the elements aren't properly aligned, the portal becomes unstable, and the Abasimtrox grow stronger."

Waverly's voice was soft but filled with awe. "So, it's not just about the elements. It's about keeping the balance of the entire universe. We're the ones who are supposed to hold that balance."

Gran Celia stood up, her hand pressing against the table as she processed the weight of Francis's words. "Yes. And now, with Lincoln's return, the four of you—Ridge, Waverly, Lynx, and Lincoln—must work together to ensure the balance is restored. The elemental spirits will guide you, but you are the key to keeping the Abasimtrox at bay."

Dr. Stern, who had been quietly listening, cleared his throat and leaned forward. "This is all… quite extraordinary. But we still have a lot to prepare for. We need to make sure the portal is stabilized, the herbs are ready, and that all the logistics are in place. Time is running out."

Gran Celia nodded gravely. "We don't have the luxury of waiting any longer. The Tanzloran and Arcmyrian forces are ready. The brews need to be prepared. Now, it's up to us to bring everything together."

Ridge turned to his family, his expression one of quiet resolve. "Then we'll do it."

Waverly and Lynx exchanged a look, both of them filled with a quiet sense of determination. They were ready. They had no choice but to be ready.

Gran Celia turned to Dr. Stern and Dr. Walsh. "The time has come. We'll need your expertise in preparing the herbs and ensuring everything is in order for the portal's activation. Francis will continue her work on the ancient text, and once it's ready, we'll begin the preparations."

18

The air in the seed room was cool and earthy, filled with the scent of herbs, roots, and plants carefully cultivated for centuries. The stone walls, lined with shelves and glass vials, seemed to hum with quiet energy, as if the very plants themselves were aware of their sacred purpose. Francis, Gran Celia, and Dr. Madre Walsh moved with purpose through the room, selecting the herbs and ingredients they would need for the mixtures that would ensure Ridge, Waverly, and Lynx could survive the journey through the portal.

Gran Celia carefully sifted through a row of vials, inspecting the labels. "We'll need the root of the arcus plant for this mixture," she murmured, her voice filled with reverence for the task at hand. "It will help stabilize their bodies during the initial phase of the portal transition."

Francis nodded, her fingers brushing lightly against a cluster of delicate flowers on the nearby shelf. "And the silvershade leaves will be crucial for adapting to Arcmyrin's atmosphere," she added, her eyes scanning the rows of plants as she selected the leaves. "This will help prevent dizziness and nausea once they step into the new environment."

Dr. Walsh, who had been studying the plants with a keen eye, stepped forward with a small vial of a shimmering powder. "This compound," she explained, "is a mix of Tanzloran herbs. It will help protect their respiratory systems from the strain of Arcmyrin's air, which has a different oxygen density than Earth's."

Gran Celia carefully measured out the ingredients, making sure each component was precisely prepared. "Each world's atmosphere, gravity, and environmental conditions are so different," she said, her hands steady as she worked. "But with these brews, they'll have the best chance of surviving the portal's effects."

Francis placed the final vial into a small pouch and tied it securely. "The herbs alone won't be enough. The brews will need to be consumed just before they enter the portal. But they're also only temporary solutions. Once they reach Arcmyrin, the key will be acclimating to the world's gravity, weather systems, and elemental forces."

Gran Celia turned to face her. "We've all seen what happens when the elements aren't in balance. This is a delicate task we're preparing them for. Once they're on Arcmyrin, they'll have to be prepared for the unknown. But these brews will keep them from being overwhelmed by the transition."

Dr. Walsh stepped back, admiring the meticulous work Gran Celia and Francis had done in preparing the brews. "I think we have everything ready," she said, a note of satisfaction in her voice. "These mixtures will provide them with what they need to survive the journey. But we should still be ready for anything."

Gran Celia nodded. "Indeed. There's no telling what might happen once they enter the portal."

Meanwhile, in the chamber with the pedestal table and curved screens, Dr. Marshall Stern prepared to explain to Ridge, Waverly and Lynx what they could expect once the portal opened. They had gathered around the large table, each seated in one of the chairs, their hands resting on the smooth, curved indentations in the table. The air around them was still, but the hum of the orb outside the room and the screens displayed in front of them filled the space with a quiet, expectant energy.

Dr. Stern's expression was serious, his gaze focused on each of them as he spoke.

"The portal, as you already know, is not simply a doorway between worlds," he began, his voice low and measured. "It is a conduit—a bridge that connects different planes of existence. But crossing through it is not like walking through a door. The portal itself is not just a space—it's a force. And when you enter, it will take you not just through space, but through time and energy."

Ridge shifted slightly in his seat, his mind racing. "What do you mean, time and energy?"

Dr. Stern nodded. "The portal doesn't just transport you to another world. It alters the fabric of your being, and you will feel that change physically and mentally. You'll experience a shift in perception as your body adjusts to the different gravitational forces, atmospheric conditions, and even the elemental energies of the new world. For a brief moment, it will feel as though your body is being stretched—pulled through space and time. You may experience a feeling of vertigo or dizziness. The sensation will be disorienting."

Waverly frowned, her grip tightening on the chair as she listened intently. "So, you're saying we'll feel the change in our bodies immediately? Like, we won't be able to control it?"

"Correct," Dr. Stern confirmed. "But that's where the brews come in. They will help you adjust more quickly to the new environment. They'll counteract the initial shock of the portal's transition. The herbs and compounds will ease the process, allowing your body to gradually adapt to the new gravitational field, atmospheric pressure, and elemental energies of Arcmyrin."

Lynx looked up, his expression uncertain. "And how long will it take for our bodies to fully adjust? Will we be able to function normally once we arrive?"

Dr. Stern gave a thoughtful pause before responding. "That depends. The adjustment period is different for each individual, and it also depends on how your body interacts with the elements of Arcmyrin. The brews will protect you, but you'll still need time to acclimate. Some of you might feel more fatigued than others, especially in the first few hours after arrival. The air on Arcmyrin, for example, is thicker, with higher levels of certain gases that Earth's atmosphere doesn't have. It's not toxic, but it will require time for your respiratory systems to adjust."

Waverly nodded, her mind already racing through the possible challenges they would face. "What about gravity? Will it be hard to walk?"

"Arcmyrin has a higher gravity than Earth," Dr. Stern explained. "So, expect to feel heavier, especially at first. It will be like walking in an environment where you're carrying a significant weight. But that's where the brews will help you. They'll fortify your body's strength and make the transition smoother."

Lynx shifted in his chair, his mind working through the implications of everything Dr. Stern had said. "And how will we know when we're safe—when we've fully adjusted?"

Dr. Stern paused, his gaze steady as he met each of their eyes. "You'll know. Your senses will recalibrate. Your body will adjust to the gravitational pull, and the discomfort will ease. But there is no exact time frame. For some, it could take a few minutes, for others, it could take longer. That's why it's important to stay calm and focused during the transition. Trust in the brews, and trust in yourselves."

Ridge took a deep breath, the weight of what they were about to undertake settling over him. "What else should we expect once we arrive? Will there be dangers waiting for us?"

Dr. Stern's eyes softened, and he seemed to hesitate before speaking. "The most immediate danger, as I mentioned before, is the Abasimtrox. Once the portal is opened, they'll feel the surge of energy. You must be ready to protect the portal and the elements at all costs. There are forces at play here that none of us can fully predict. Once you're on Arcmyrin, you'll have the support of their forces, but the responsibility to stabilize the portal will lie with you, the Beaumonts."

Waverly, her voice steady but filled with concern, asked, "And what if we can't stabilize it? What happens if the portal collapses or the balance is lost?"

Dr. Stern's expression hardened. "If the portal collapses, it could tear the very fabric of the universes together. It could lead to a catastrophic chain reaction. That's why we need to make sure everything is in place before you go through. The elemental forces must be aligned, and the brews must be prepared. Only with all of these things in place can you safely travel and ensure the portal's stability."

Ridge, who had been listening intently, spoke up with quiet resolve. "We will be ready. Waverly and Lynx have the strength and the power to see this through as do I."

The room fell silent as the weight of their task pressed down on them. Ridge, Waverly, and Lynx exchanged determined glances. They were ready, but they knew that the journey ahead would be fraught with unknown dangers. Still, they had no choice but to move forward. The balance of their worlds—and the fate of the portal—rested on their shoulders.

Gran Celia entered the room, her voice resolute as she addressed the group. "We have the mixtures ready. The Tanzloran and Arcmyrian forces are waiting. We'll contact them once you three are ready. But the most important part is that you—Ridge, Waverly and Lynx—must trust in the power that's within you. Together, you'll make this work."

As the conversation turned to the final preparations, the sense of urgency in the room grew stronger. The portal was about to open, and the time for waiting had passed. The Beaumonts, united with their allies, would face whatever came next—together.

19

The chamber beneath the gazebo was tense with anticipation. The orb in the center of the room hummed quietly, its soft glow casting an eerie light against the stone walls. Ridge and Lynx stood near the entrance to the crystal gate, but their gazes were focused on the stone stairway. The air seemed to thrum with the promise of something monumental about to happen, and yet one crucial element was still missing: Waverly.

Gran Celia stood with her arms folded, her eyes cast toward the entrance, her brow furrowed in concern. "What is taking her so long?" she muttered under her breath. "She knows what's at stake. We can't waste any more time."

Lynx, who was standing near Ridge, gave a small grin and shrugged, clearly trying to lighten the mood. "She's probably stuck in her closet, trying to figure out what to wear for an interplanetary trip," he said with a wink.

Ridge snorted a laugh, the tension in his shoulders easing just slightly. "Ah, that's wisdom I can get behind, Lynx. You've learned a lot about women for someone your age," he said, shaking his head in mock amazement.

Lynx grinned, clearly pleased with himself. "You'd be surprised how much I've learned from watching Gran Celia and Waverly."

Ridge chuckled, ruffling his nephew's hair. "Well, in that case, you're ready for anything. But seriously, Waverly knows we can't afford delays. She'll be here."

Gran Celia gave a small sigh, her gaze shifting toward the chamber stairs once again. "I just worry about her," she said softly, more to herself than anyone else. "There's so much riding on this, and I don't know if she's ready for the weight of it all."

Lynx glanced over at his grandmother, his tone softening. "I was kidding Gran, she'll be fine. She'll be here."

Ridge nodded in agreement. "Waverly is tougher than she lets on. She'll be here soon. She knows how important this is."

As the minutes ticked by, Gran Celia couldn't shake the worry gnawing at her. Waverly had always carried the weight of responsibility with a quiet grace, but this time was different. This mission, this journey—she was about to step into the unknown, and Gran Celia knew that the fear of failure was something that could weigh down even the strongest of hearts.

Upstairs, in the privacy of her room, Waverly sat curled up on the edge of her bed, her knees drawn to her chest. She was clutching a pillow tightly to her, her hands trembling ever so slightly. The soft light filtering in through the curtains did nothing to ease the growing sense of unease inside her. Her mind raced with a million thoughts, none of them able to quiet the storm swirling within her.

What if she couldn't do this? What if she failed? The weight of the mission, the responsibility of being one of the bloodline descendants, it was too much to bear at times. And then there was the looming thought of seeing her parents again. After all these years, what would it be like?

The thought of failing them, of not being able to live up to their legacy, felt like an elephant lodged in her chest, weighing her down with its crushing pressure.

She wanted to be brave. She had to be brave. But in this moment, on the cusp of a journey that could change everything, all Waverly felt was fear.

Her hands clenched the pillow tighter, her breath hitching as she fought to keep her emotions in check. It was no use. The dam finally broke, and hot tears spilled down her cheeks. She buried her face in the pillow, muffling her sobs, feeling the deep ache of fear and uncertainty wash over her like a wave.

Gran Celia, feeling the pull of worry, couldn't stand it any longer. She moved briskly toward the stairs, her resolve firm. "I'm going to check on her," she said quietly to Ridge and Lynx. "I can't wait any longer."

Ridge nodded. "Go. We'll be here."

Gran Celia left the chamber, quickly making her way back up to the manor. The sound of her footsteps echoed in the hallway as she ascended to the upper floors. The door to Waverly's room was closed, and she paused for a moment before gently knocking.

"Waverly?" Gran Celia called softly. "It's me. Can I come in?"

There was a long pause, and then Waverly's quiet voice came through, muffled by the door. "Gran Celia... I—I don't know if I can do this. I'm not ready."

Gran Celia's heart clenched as she stepped into the room, her gaze immediately falling on her granddaughter sitting on the edge of the bed, clutching the pillow as though it could shield her from everything she feared. Waverly's face was pale, her eyes red from the tears she had been crying.

"Waverly," Gran Celia said softly, crossing the room to sit beside her. "It's okay. I know you're scared. This isn't easy. But you are ready."

Waverly shook her head, her tears still fresh on her cheeks. "I don't think I am. What if I fail? What if I can't do what's expected of me? What if... what if I'm not enough?"

Gran Celia reached out and placed a hand gently on her granddaughter's shoulder, her voice soft but firm. "Waverly, you've always been more than enough. You've shown strength and wisdom that most people only dream of having. You are more than capable of facing this journey, and you will succeed, because you carry within you the bloodline of those who've fought before you."

"But... my parents," Waverly whispered, her voice breaking. "What if they don't think I'm strong enough? What if they're disappointed in me?"

Gran Celia's heart tightened at the mention of Waverly's parents. She knew the pain of missing them, of having them hidden away for so long. She also knew the longing in Waverly's heart to see them again, to have them by her side. But it was more than that. Waverly feared failing the very legacy her family had built.

"Waverly," Gran Celia said, her voice a little stronger now, "your parents are not disappointed in you. They've never been disappointed. They've always believed in you, just like I do. The fact that you're here now, preparing to face the portal, to stand by your family and protect all the worlds... that is the greatest honor they could ever ask for."

Waverly wiped her eyes, her breathing still shaky. "I just want to make them proud."

Gran Celia gave her a warm, reassuring smile. "You already have. You already are."

After a long pause, Waverly took a deep breath, her shoulders relaxing just a little as the weight of her fear began to ease. She slowly stood up, her eyes meeting her grandmother's with a renewed sense of resolve. "Okay. I'm ready."

Gran Celia nodded and gave her a gentle hug, pulling her granddaughter close. "Let's go. They're waiting for you."

The two women left the room, and together they made their way back down to the chamber beneath the gazebo. Ridge and Lynx were still standing near the entrance to the crystal gate, their eyes watching expectantly as they saw Gran Celia and Waverly coming down the stairs.

"We're ready now," Waverly said quietly, her voice filled with a sense of calm that hadn't been there before. She was ready for the journey ahead.

Gran Celia smiled, her heart swelling with pride. "Then let's do this."

20

The chamber beneath Sage Manor was quiet, save for the soft hum of the crystal orb at the center of the room. Gran Celia stood with a calm but determined presence, her hands raised above the orb as she prepared to initiate the connection. The room, heavy with anticipation, felt charged with energy. Ridge, Waverly, and Lynx stood at the entrance to the crystal gate, their gazes fixed on the glowing orb.

Gran Celia had known this moment would come—when the portal would be opened, and they would all be called to their fates. The preparations were complete, and the time had finally arrived. But even with everything set in motion, there was a sense of unease in the air, the gravity of the task ahead weighing heavily on them all.

"We're ready," Gran Celia said softly, her eyes meeting those of her grandchildren. "The journey begins now. We've prepared as much as we can. It's time to reach out."

Her hands moved gently over the surface of the orb, and with a quiet command, the air around them seemed to shimmer. The light from the orb intensified, casting intricate shadows on the stone walls as the energy inside it pulsed in response to her summons. The group stood in still silence as they waited for the familiar figures to emerge from the orb.

After a few moments, the soft glow of the orb gave way to a holographic form, and Keelee's image appeared before them. His form flickered and shimmered, becoming more solid as the energy flowed into him. Beside him, Elara materialized, her elegant form filled with the quiet strength and grace that marked her as one of Arcmyrin's leaders. Both were ghostly and luminous, their forms not entirely solid but clear enough to convey their resolve.

Gran Celia stepped forward, her voice steady despite the anticipation that gripped her. "Keelee, Elara, glad to see you again. Waverly, Lynx, and Ridge are ready to enter the portal. But we need to know—are Lincoln and Bethany ready?"

Keelee's expression remained calm, but there was a deep sadness in his eyes. "Lincoln will be traveling alone, Gran Celia. The elders have decided that Bethany must remain on Tanzlora for now, for her safety."

Gran Celia's heart skipped a beat at the mention of Bethany's absence. She had hoped—perhaps foolishly—that Bethany would be with them, reunited with her family, but the weight of the decision was clear in Keelee's voice. "Why is Bethany staying behind?" she asked, her voice tight with concern.

Keelee's gaze softened. "The elders have determined that, with the portal's instability and the immense danger that is at stake, only those who are directly connected to the elemental forces should travel. The four bloodline descendants—Ridge, Waverly, Lynx, and Lincoln. The connection between those four and the elements is crucial to the success of this mission. Bethany, despite her strength, does not have the same elemental connection. The elders fear that her presence would disrupt the energies and frequencies needed for a successful transport."

Elara's voice came through, calm and reassuring, as she stepped closer, her figure glowing faintly in the dim light of the chamber. "The decision was not made lightly. The elders understand your family's desire for reunification. But Arcmyrin's safety, as well as the stability of the portal, depends on this delicate balance. The elemental powers you and your family carry are not easily disrupted. Bethany, without the same spiritual connection to the elements, could unintentionally throw off the frequencies and jeopardize everything we're working to protect."

Gran Celia understood, even though the decision felt painful. She could see the weight of it in Keelee and Elara's demeanors. They were doing what they thought was best, not just for the Beaumonts but for the safety of every world tied to the portal. "I see," Gran Celia said quietly, her voice filled with both acceptance and a hint of regret. "So, Lincoln will travel alone, and Bethany will remain on Tanzlora for the time being. But we are still united in this mission."

Keelee nodded solemnly. "Exactly. Lincoln will come through the portal and join you on Arcmyrin. But for now, we must trust that this decision will ensure a successful transport."

Ridge clenched his jaw, the weight of the decision settling heavily on him. He had longed to see his brother again, but the absence of Bethany left an emptiness he hadn't expected. Still, he understood. The mission had to come first. "Understood. We will go forward with this. Safety is what matters."

Elara's tone shifted slightly, becoming more purposeful. "We are ready on Arcmyrin to receive you. The Arcmyrians are prepared to help you acclimate to the planet once you arrive. Our people will be there to guide you through the adjustments necessary to survive on Arcmyrin, especially with the gravitational and atmospheric differences. Once you arrive, your work will begin."

Waverly looked toward Elara, her eyes filled with determination despite the lingering sadness. "We're ready to do whatever it takes. We will do this together."

Lynx nodded beside her. "Yeah. We've prepared and we're ready."

Gran Celia smiled, though her heart was heavy. "Then let's not waste any more time. The future of all three worlds depends on us. We are the ones who will restore balance."

Elara's form flickered once more as her voice rang out with finality. "You will succeed. You carry the strength of the Beaumont legacy. Gran Celia, I must ask you and your guests to vacate the chamber now. It is too dangerous for you to remain here when the portal opens."

Gran Celia's brow furrowed in confusion. "What do you mean, too dangerous?"

Elara's eyes were filled with a mix of urgency and resolve. "The portal is an unstable force, and once it opens, the energies inside the chamber will reach critical levels. It is not safe for anyone who is not directly involved in the transport to remain. I'm afraid you must leave, Gran Celia, for your own safety and the safety of those around you."

Gran Celia's heart sank, but she understood. The portal had always been a powerful and unpredictable force, and she could feel the weight of its impending opening in the very air. She nodded, a calm determination settling over her.

"I understand," she said quietly, turning to her family. "Ridge, Waverly, Lynx, this is it. Your mission begins now. I'll see you when you return, and I wish you all a safe and successful journey."

Waverly stepped forward, her voice firm, though the fear in her eyes was unmistakable. "We won't fail, Gran Celia. We'll do what needs to be done."

Lynx, ever the brave one, nodded with a quiet smile. "We've got this. Just make sure to keep things safe here."

Ridge placed a hand on his mother's shoulder, giving it a reassuring squeeze. "We'll make it back. You've raised us well, Mother. We know what we have to do."

Gran Celia smiled through the ache in her heart, her eyes filled with love and pride. "You're ready. All of you. I'll be waiting for you when you return. Go, and remember that the fate of the worlds is in your hands."

With one last glance at her family, Gran Celia turned and made her way to the stone stairway. As she ascended the stairs and moved through the gazebo towards Sage Manor, she felt the weight of the moment. Her heart swelled with pride for her sons and grandchildren, but also with a quiet, unspoken fear. There was no turning back now.

As Gran Celia entered the parlor, followed closely behind by Francis, Dr. Stern, and Dr. Walsh, she motioned for all of them to sit.

"We've done all we can," she said, her voice steady despite the storm of emotions swirling inside her. "Now, we wait."

21

Back in the chamber, Ridge, Waverly and Lynx stood united once more, surrounded by the pulsing energy of the orb. They could feel the air thickening around them, the sense of something ancient and powerful awakening. They stood side by side, their eyes locked on the orb as it began to flicker more intensely. The time had come. The portal was opening.

Elara's voice rang out, clear and filled with purpose. "It's time. The portal is about to open. You must step through together, all at the same time. As soon as the portal is fully open and you can see the two planets, you must walk forward."

Keelee's voice followed, firm and commanding. "Do not look away. Do not hesitate. When you step into the portal, you must focus. Focus on Arcmyrin—nothing else. Think only of Arcmyrin. You must visualize the planet in your mind, over and over. Your connection to the elemental forces will guide you, and the portal will transport you to the planet you focus on."

Waverly's heart raced, her mind already focused on the task ahead. "Arcmyrin," she whispered, though the word felt strange on her tongue. She could feel the power of the portal pulling at her, but she knew what had to be done. She had to concentrate, to hold on to the vision of the planet they were headed to.

Lynx stood beside her, his gaze unwavering. "Arcmyrin," he echoed, his voice steady. He had always been the one to jump into action first, but even now, he could feel the gravity of what they were about to do. The unknown stretched out before them like a vast ocean, and they were about to dive in.

Ridge, the ever-determined leader, stepped forward. "We're doing this together," he said, his voice calm but filled with the fierce love of an uncle and protector. "We focus on Arcmyrin. We step in, and we stay focused. We'll get through this."

Elara nodded, her voice filled with quiet reassurance. "When you step through, the portal will take you to Arcmyrin. We will be waiting for you on the other side. Lincoln will be there, and we will help you adjust to the planet's gravity and atmosphere. But remember, this journey is just the beginning. You are the ones who must stabilize the portal, restore the balance, and protect all the worlds."

The chamber seemed to hum with anticipation as the portal's energy reached its peak. The orb glowed brighter, its light stretching and expanding, creating a swirling vortex in front of them. Ridge, Waverly, and Lynx stood ready, their hearts beating as one.

"Remember," Keelee said, his tone insistent. "Think only of Arcmyrin. The portal will take you there, and you must be focused when you step through. The portal will sense your thoughts, and it will guide you to the planet you are mentally focused on."

Gran Celia's voice echoed in the back of their minds as they took their final steps. "Be brave, my children. You are ready. Go now."

And with those final words, the three of them stepped forward, their bodies disappearing into the swirling vortex of light.

As the portal engulfed them, Elara and Keelee faded away.

The moment Ridge, Waverly, and Lynx stepped through the swirling vortex of the portal, everything around them changed. The air grew thick with energy, and the sensation of being pulled through space and time overwhelmed their senses. For a moment, it felt as though their bodies were being stretched in every direction, their minds swimming with strange, unexplainable images and flashes of distant worlds.

Then, just as quickly as it had started, the feeling of disorientation faded, and they found themselves moving through the dark void of the portal. The distant glow of planets on the other side came into focus, but before they could even process their surroundings fully, something else appeared—something dark.

Ridge's heart raced as he sensed the shift in the air. A shadow passed over them, and then, out of nowhere, the space around them seemed to crackle with dark energy. Glowing red eyes blinked into existence, and the form of the Abasimtrox—dark, twisted figures, cloaked in shadows—materialized in the void around them. Their bodies flickered like shadows cast under a flickering flame, their eyes glowing a fierce and unnatural red.

"Abasimtrox!" Ridge shouted, realizing what they were facing.

The dark beings lunged at them with terrifying speed, their clawed hands reaching out, their mouths open in snarls of fury. Ridge quickly raised his arm, but the energy was pulling them forward too quickly to react. The Abasimtrox closed in on them, their figures warping and shifting as if they were made of nothing but darkness itself.

"Stay focused!" Waverly shouted, trying to summon the elemental energy within her, but before she could even make a move, one of the Abasimtrox surged toward her, claws slashing through the air. A dark force knocked her back, sending her tumbling through the swirling chaos of the portal's interior.

"Waverly!" Ridge shouted, his eyes wide with panic. He reached out for her, but the portal was like a swirling storm, and she was being pulled away from him.

Lynx, ever the quick thinker, took in the situation, his heart pounding in his chest. "We need to fight back!" he yelled, his voice shaking with the urgency of the moment.

Just as the Abasimtrox closed in, ready to strike with their deadly force, something extraordinary happened. Out of the corner of his eye, Lynx noticed a glimmer of movement. The Tanzloran warriors—their tall, blue-violet skin shimmering with an otherworldly energy—had appeared, their dark blue indigo eyes glowing fiercely. They were tall, their bodies lithe but powerful, and they stepped into the void around them with confidence, weapons drawn.

In the same moment, the Arcmyrin warriors arrived—large beings with olive skin that shimmered in a golden hue, their eyes a brilliant gold that seemed to glow like the sun. Their arrival was like a sudden burst of light against the dark chaos of the Abasimtrox.

The battle began immediately.

The Tanzlorans clashed with the Abasimtrox with ferocious speed, their long, glowing weapons striking through the dark figures of the enemies. Their movements were fluid, almost graceful, yet filled with immense strength. The Arcmyrins, equally powerful, wielded massive, energy-infused blades, their golden eyes flashing as they engaged the dark beings with unmatched precision. They moved as one, cutting down the Abasimtrox with strength that seemed to emanate from the very core of their beings.

But despite the warriors' strength and skill, the Abasimtrox kept coming, relentless and powerful, their dark energy wrapping around the warriors, forcing them back. The forces of light were struggling, barely able to hold their ground against the overwhelming might of the Abasimtrox.

It was then that something unexpected happened.

Lynx, his heart pounding in his chest, stepped forward, his arms raised instinctively as he felt the energy building inside him. The flames of his powers surged within him, a fierce, burning heat that radiated from his core. With a cry, he unleashed the fire, his arms sweeping through the air as bursts of flame shot out toward the Abasimtrox.

The flames hit with brutal force, engulfing the nearest Abasimtrox in fire. The dark figures shrieked as they were pushed back, the fire wrapping around them and forcing them to retreat. Lynx's control over the flames was unlike anything any of them had seen before—his powers surged with an intensity that not only protected them but pushed the dark beings away.

The battlefield shifted instantly.

"Lynx!" Ridge shouted in awe, his eyes wide as he watched his nephew unleash the fire with perfect control, holding off the Abasimtrox in a way that had never been possible before. "That's it! Keep them back!"

Waverly, who had regained her balance, stood beside Ridge, her eyes locked on Lynx as the fire continued to surge from his hands. Her brother's newfound ability was pushing the darkness away, keeping them safe long enough to make a breakthrough.

With the Abasimtrox temporarily repelled, the Tanzloran and Arcmyrin warriors rallied, cutting down the remaining dark beings with deadly precision. The Abasimtrox, their dark forms flickering like dying embers, started to retreat. But just as the battle seemed to be swinging in their favor, the remaining Abasimtrox regrouped and began to charge once more, their red eyes burning with rage.

The Tanzloran warriors, now standing side by side with the Arcmyrin warriors, exchanged glances, and the leader of the Tanzlorans nodded to the Arcmyrin general.

"You must get them through the portal," the Tanzloran leader said, his voice calm despite the chaos around them. "We will hold them off as best we can. The Abasimtrox are regrouping. We cannot let them follow you."

The Arcmyrin general nodded, his golden eyes narrowing as he surveyed the battlefield. "Go now," the Tanzloran leader said, his voice filled with the weight of responsibility. "We will stay and fight. The elders will close the portals once the Beaumonts are safe on Arcmyrin."

Ridge, Waverly, and Lynx exchanged one last look, their hearts filled with gratitude and resolve. They knew that their mission had just begun, but it wouldn't be the same without the warriors who were standing beside them. With one final, determined look, Ridge nodded.

"We're going," he said.

Waverly took a deep breath, feeling the tension in her chest ease. "We'll make it. We've come this far."

Lynx, his fiery energy still pulsing in his veins, smiled fiercely. "We're ready."

Together, the three of them stepped into the opening of the portal, their bodies passing through the threshold of energy and light, leaving the battle behind them.

As they passed through, the sounds of the battlefield—clashing swords, the cries of the Abasimtrox, the roar of the warriors—faded away. The world around them shifted again, and this time, they felt themselves being pulled toward something new.

22

The last thing Ridge, Waverly, and Lynx felt was the sharp pull of the portal as it tugged them through, their bodies propelled into a swirl of energy, light, and sound. The deafening noise of the battle seemed to fade away into nothingness as they plunged deeper into the swirling vortex. For a moment, it felt as though the very fabric of space and time was stretching them to their limits. Then, with a sudden jolt, the world snapped into focus.

They found themselves sprawled on the cold, uneven ground of a vast, unfamiliar landscape. Ridge's body slammed against the earth first, the shock knocking the breath out of him. He gasped for air, trying to orient himself in the dizzying swirl of light that still clung to his vision. The ground beneath him was solid, but the air had a strange quality—heavy yet invigorating.

Waverly, still disoriented, rolled over with a groan, her hands pressing into the soil beneath her. She felt a strange pressure in her chest as the air seemed to push in on her lungs. Lynx, ever the resilient one, was already pulling himself to his knees, his eyes wide as he tried to make sense of their surroundings.

Before they could fully recover, a figure approached them at a swift pace, her silhouette stark against the brightness of the surrounding land. Elara, her tall form shimmering with otherworldly grace, rushed toward them, her golden hued skin glowing faintly in the shifting light.

"Quickly, get away from the portal!" Elara called out, her voice sharp with urgency. "It's still unstable!"

Ridge pushed himself to his feet, his body trembling from the effects of the transport. His eyes scanned the surroundings, the landscape unfamiliar, yet strangely beautiful. The land stretched out in all directions, bathed in a soft golden light. Towering, crystal-like structures glittered in the distance, while the ground beneath them was a mix of rich, deep earth and smooth, shimmering stones.

Waverly slowly pulled herself to her feet, but her legs wobbled as if the gravitational pull of the planet were too much to adjust to all at once. She staggered, barely catching herself, before Elara was at her side, her hand resting lightly on Waverly's arm, steadying her.

"Steady, Waverly," Elara said quickly, her golden eyes scanning her for any signs of distress. "You need to sit until the herbal mixture begins to work. You're acclimating to the environment; it'll pass."

But Waverly shook her head stubbornly, eyes darting across the strange landscape as she tried to shake off the dizziness. "I need to see Dad," she said, her voice filled with desperation. "Where is he? I have to find him."

Ridge, still kneeling on the ground, looked around, his eyes searching through the haze for any sign of his brother. "Where's Lincoln?" he asked, his voice rising with concern. "Elara, where is he? Is he already here?"

Elara's expression softened, but there was something in her eyes—something that suggested she, too, was feeling the pressure of the situation. "He's still in the portal," she said, glancing back at the swirling opening, where the portal's energy was still faintly visible, flickering erratically. "The journey isn't complete yet. But we must focus on your acclimation. The portal is unstable. We must prepare you."

At that very moment, the ground beneath them seemed to rumble. The air was thick with energy, and a low hum filled their ears. They all turned, startled, as a massive wave of water suddenly appeared at the edge of the portal's frame. It was moving at breakneck speed, towering over them as it surged forward like a tidal wave, crashing across the land.

Elara shouted over the roar of the wave, her voice commanding as she pointed to the nearby Arcmyrin warriors, tall olive-skinned beings with golden eyes that shimmered in the light. They stood strong, their bodies shimmering as though they were made from the very energy of the planet itself.

"Prepare yourselves!" Elara called out to the warriors, who immediately ran toward the rushing tide, ready to face whatever it was that was emerging from the portal. Their powerful forms moved with grace and speed, ready to defend the Beaumonts and any others that might appear.

The wave hit the ground with a mighty crash, yet the Arcmyrin warriors rode the crest of it like surfers on a giant sea, their golden eyes focused as they steered the wave, guiding it away from Ridge, Waverly, and Lynx. The water surged forward, wrapping around them, pulling them into the scene like a storm that had come to a violent halt.

Ridge and Waverly struggled to regain their footing, the power of the wave overwhelming them for a moment. But Lynx, always quick on his feet, was already standing tall, his eyes wide in confusion and amazement. He looked toward the warriors, realizing that they were working together to hold back whatever dark force was coming through.

"Is that... dad?" Waverly asked, her eyes locked on the rushing tide. She thought she saw a shadow moving within it, but it was impossible to tell through the haze of water and mist.

"Elara!" Ridge shouted over the sound of the wave, his voice urgent. "What's happening? Is it over?"

Before Elara could answer, the wave receded, the water ebbing back into the portal. It wasn't until the water began to calm that the full impact of the scene became clear. The air grew still again, heavy with anticipation.

The warriors stood firm, their energy bright and unwavering. Elara, still standing by their side, breathed a quiet sigh of relief. "The Abasimtrox are pushing against the portal," she said, her voice heavy. "They've been trying to break through since the portal opened. This is why we need to act quickly."

But just as she was about to turn back to them, a sudden, sharp crack echoed across the land. The portal—still open—began to glitch, the light flickering erratically. The air seemed to vibrate as if something within the portal itself was fighting to stay intact. Then, with an explosive snap, the portal made a loud, disorienting sound like the breaking of glass. The energy around them surged violently, the light flashing so bright that it nearly blinded them.

The portal flickered one last time before it slowly began to collapse, the energy draining from the frame. Ridge, Waverly, and Lynx watched in horror as the portal shrank, its edges crumbling into a thin, shimmering ribbon before snapping completely shut. In mere seconds, the massive doorway to their world had disappeared, leaving behind nothing but an empty, darkened frame.

"No..." Waverly whispered, her voice shaking with disbelief. "It's gone..."

Ridge felt a pit form in his stomach as he realized the weight of the situation. "It's gone. We've lost it." His voice was low, almost strangled with the weight of the truth.

Elara's face darkened as she turned toward the remaining Arcmyrin warriors. "The portal is closed," she said, her voice heavy with regret. "The Abasimtrox will not be able to enter through this way anymore. But this is a blow we cannot afford, as we also can't utilize the portal system. We must act quickly to restore balance."

Just as the air around them seemed to freeze, Waverly, still kneeling in the dirt, suddenly perked up. She stood slowly, her body trembling with the weight of the journey they had just endured, her eyes scanning the space in front of them. "Wait," she gasped, her eyes widening as she looked toward the horizon, her heart skipping a beat. "Dad?!"

23

From the mist, a figure appeared. Slowly at first, but then more clearly—Lincoln stepped through the haze of light, looking slightly disoriented but very much alive. His face was weathered but determined, his expression softening as he spotted Waverly, Ridge, and Lynx standing nearby.

"Dad!" Waverly shouted, her voice breaking with relief and joy. She took a few steps forward, and before anyone could stop her, she ran to him, throwing her arms around his neck.

Lincoln, his expression filled with a mix of exhaustion and joy, embraced her tightly, holding her close. "Waverly... I'm here. I'm really here. And you're here. And Ridge and Lynx too. I never thought I would see this day come."

Ridge stepped forward, his own eyes filled with emotion as he saw his brother, alive and standing in front of him. "Lincoln..." he whispered, his voice choked with emotion.

Lincoln stepped back, taking in the sight of his family—his children, his brother. "I'm so sorry it took me so long," he said, his voice low but filled with love. "We had to do everything we could on Tanzlora... but it's over now. You made it here. We're together."

Elara, standing at the edge of the scene, gave a quiet sigh of relief. "The mission isn't over," she said, her voice firm. "But we've made it through the hardest part. Arcmyrin is ready to support you, as we promised."

Ridge looked at her, his expression hardening with determination. "Then let's get to work."

The landscape of Arcmyrin was breathtaking in its alien beauty, with towering crystal structures and sweeping landscapes bathed in the soft glow of alien suns. The air was fresh, rich with the vibrant energies of a world that pulsed with life, yet there was an unmistakable tension in the atmosphere. As Elara led Lincoln, Ridge, Waverly, and Lynx through the winding paths toward the heart of Arcmyrin, they couldn't help but notice the contrast between the stunning landscape and the palpable unease among the Arcmyrin warriors.

Lincoln walked alongside his children, his eyes occasionally drifting to the warriors flanking them, their shimmering olive skin and golden eyes reflecting the light of their world. They were a formidable force, and yet, their quiet resolve seemed at odds with the beauty around them. They were marching toward something important—something that was critical for the survival of all three planets.

Elara led the group into a vast courtyard, the ground underfoot polished to a smooth, dark sheen, and as they walked, the air hummed with a low, almost imperceptible vibration. Ridge's senses were on edge. The journey through the portal had been disorienting, and though they had successfully made it through, the gravity of the mission ahead was beginning to settle in.

"We're almost there," Elara's voice broke through the silence. Her pace had slowed slightly, and she turned to look at them, her golden eyes filled with a quiet intensity. "The command center is just ahead."

As they approached the large building before them, the structure seemed to rise from the earth itself, its walls of shimmering stone glistening in the ambient light. The building had an organic feel, with sweeping curves and edges that flowed seamlessly into the landscape. It was as if the structure itself was an extension of the planet's natural energy.

Inside, the air was cool, and the space was vast, filled with high-tech equipment and displays that pulsed with soft light. The walls were lined with massive screens showing various data feeds—geographical maps, energy readings, and an array of symbols that Ridge could not decipher.

The room felt both ancient and futuristic at the same time, a perfect representation of Arcmyrin's long history intertwined with its advanced technology.

At the center of the room was a long table, surrounded by Arcmyrin warriors and several other figures Ridge had yet to meet. They stood as a united front, their eyes focused, waiting for their arrival. Ridge's gaze flickered to his family as they gathered at the table. His heart was still pounding from the journey, but now there was a sense of urgency in the air, something far greater than the fear of the unknown.

Elara stepped forward, her voice calm but commanding. "Everyone, these are the Beaumonts—Ridge, Waverly, Lynx, and Lincoln. They are the key to restoring balance, not just to Arcmyrin, but to all the worlds. We need to ensure their safety and guide them through the next steps."

Ridge nodded in acknowledgment to the warriors who stood at attention, their solemn faces betraying none of the fear they must have been feeling. He could feel the weight of their expectations, and in return, he felt a surge of determination. He and his family were at the center of something much larger than they could have imagined. They were here to restore balance—not just to Arcmyrin, but to their very existence.

"Thank you," Lincoln said quietly, his voice carrying the deep, unspoken understanding of the gravity of their situation. "We're ready to do whatever it takes."

Elara gestured toward the large table, where several maps and images were displayed. "Please, sit. We need to discuss the strategy for restoring balance. The planet's ecosystems are failing, the elemental forces are in disarray, and we are on the brink of collapse. We can't afford any missteps."

Ridge, Waverly, and Lynx sat down at the table, with Lincoln taking a seat beside them. Their eyes were drawn to the screens in front of them, each one showing a different aspect of the planet's turmoil. One screen showed the decaying forests—vast swathes of once-thriving greenery now reduced to barren landscapes. Another showed the collapsing rivers, their once-lush banks now withered and dry. The most chilling image, however, was the one showing the massive energy disturbances near the heart of the planet—an unstable core that, if left unchecked, could cause even more devastation.

"Elara," Ridge said, his voice tight with concern, "what's causing this? What is throwing the balance of the elements off? The images... they don't look like anything I've ever seen."

Elara's golden eyes met his, filled with the weight of the knowledge she had been carrying. "It's the Abasimtrox," she said simply, her voice sharp with anger. "They've been manipulating the elemental forces—draining the life energy from Arcmyrin and destabilizing the core. The elements are no longer in harmony. Earth, fire, water, and air are all out of sync. That's why the planet's systems are collapsing."

Waverly, her brow furrowed, leaned forward. "So, the Abasimtrox have been here all along, slowly corrupting everything?"

"Exactly," Elara replied, her voice tense. "They've been using the planet's own elemental forces to gain power. They've disrupted the balance, and now, with the portal closed, they've turned their focus entirely on Arcmyrin, trying to drain it dry."

Lynx, his voice barely above a whisper, spoke up. "But why now? Why attack when the portal is closed?"

"They're desperate," Elara said grimly. "Their plans to open the portal have been thwarted, but they're not done yet. They still have influence, and they know that if they can throw off the elemental balance completely, it will bring all of us to the brink of collapse. They are trying to break the connection between the worlds."

Lincoln, sitting at the table, his face drawn with worry, nodded slowly. "If they succeed, they'll destroy the very foundation that ties our worlds together. Arcmyrin, Earth, and Tanzlora... all of them are at risk."

Ridge clenched his fists, feeling the weight of what they had to do. "So, how do we stop them?"

Elara turned toward one of the warriors, who immediately stepped forward, placing a large map on the table. It showed Arcmyrin's four elemental regions—earth, fire, water, and air—all of which were in a state of severe imbalance. The core of the planet, the place where all the elements converged, was glowing an ominous red.

"To restore balance, you must visit each of the elemental regions and stabilize them," Elara explained. "Each of you is connected to one of the elemental forces. You, Ridge, will align with Earth. Waverly, you with Air. Lynx, you with Fire. And Lincoln, you with Water."

Ridge looked at his family, a mix of apprehension and determination settling over him. "So, we need to heal the planet—each of us using our connection to the elements to stabilize the core?"

Elara nodded. "Precisely. But it won't be easy. The Abasimtrox are already working against us, and their corruption has spread deep into the heart of each elemental force. You'll need to fight through their influence, restoring the balance by harnessing your gifts. Only then will you be able to stabilize the core and bring Arcmyrin back from the brink."

Lincoln stood, his eyes focused and calm. "We're ready. We've come this far. Let's restore the balance."

Elara gave them a brief nod, her gaze turning toward the warriors. "We are ready to begin the restoration process with the Beaumonts here, and they must reconnect with the elemental spirits to restore balance. But they will need guidance and preparation."

The council leader nodded, gesturing toward a series of alcoves in the back of the room, where glowing vials of liquid and bundles of herbs were arranged neatly. "We have prepared the brews that will help the Beaumonts adjust to the planetary energies and begin the process of awakening the spirits. They must first be acclimated to Arcmyrin's energy and environment. We will administer the mixtures to them, and once their bodies have adapted, we will proceed with the ritual."

Ridge's eyes widened slightly as he looked at the vials, sensing the importance of the moment. He had known they would need to face the elements, but he hadn't expected it to be so direct—so physical. "How long will it take for the mixtures to work?" he asked.

"The brews will help you adjust to the planet's atmosphere, gravity, and energy fields," the council leader explained. "It will take some time for your bodies to synchronize with Arcmyrin's core, but once you are acclimated, the elemental spirits will be able to sense you more clearly. The process is not instantaneous, but it will not take long."

Waverly looked at the glowing vials and then back to Elara. "What happens once we're ready? What do we have to do to awaken the spirits?"

Elara's golden eyes gleamed as she met Waverly's gaze. "The spirits can only be awakened when the four of you—Ridge, Waverly, Lynx, and Lincoln—reconnect with the elements inside you. This will require a deep focus, a merging of your energies with those of the planet. Once you align with the elemental forces, you will be able to communicate with the spirits directly. They will guide you in the restoration process. But be warned: the Abasimtrox will not allow this process to go uncontested. They are determined to disrupt the balance, and they will try to stop you."

"Let them try," Ridge said, his voice low and filled with conviction. "We'll do whatever it takes."

Elara nodded with a mixture of pride and respect. "The journey will not be easy. But you will not be alone. Arcmyrin stands with you."

At her signal, the Arcmyrin warriors stepped forward, each holding a vial filled with a shimmering liquid. The warriors moved with practiced precision, carefully offering the mixtures to Ridge, Waverly, and Lynx, one by one. Elara herself handed the final vial to Lincoln, who took it with a steady hand, his gaze never leaving his children. His body was still adjusting to the strange pull of the planet's gravity and energy, but his determination was unwavering.

As they drank the brews, the effects were almost immediate. Their bodies hummed with energy, the warmth of the liquid spreading through them like a current of life force. Waverly closed her eyes as the sensation overtook her, feeling the energy around her flow into her body, calming the turbulence inside her mind. The pressure in her chest eased, and she found herself more grounded, more present.

"Do you feel that?" Waverly asked, her voice soft as she opened her eyes and looked at the others.

Ridge nodded slowly, his hands gripping the edge of a stone table as the energy coursed through him. "It's... strange," he said. "But I feel more connected, somehow. Like the planet is calling to me."

Lynx, who had been the last to drink, now stood tall, his body still adjusting, but his face filled with a sense of purpose. "I feel it too. It's like... we're part of this place."

Elara smiled, satisfied with their progress. "This is just the beginning. The spirits are awakening. You will need to use that connection to restore balance, but first, we must prepare for the next phase."

As the last of the tension left their bodies, Elara's golden eyes glinted with quiet anticipation. "Arcmyrin awaits your guidance. The elemental spirits are waiting for you to lead them back into balance."

But Ridge, Waverly, and Lynx knew that the hardest part was still to come. They had reconnected with the elements, but their journey to restore balance to Arcmyrin had just begun. The spirits were awake, but the danger still loomed.

24

Gran Celia paced restlessly in the quiet parlor of Sage Manor, the familiar ticking of the old clock on the mantelpiece the only sound breaking the stillness. She had tried to focus on the books scattered across the table, but her mind kept drifting to the same thought—her family had been gone for far too long. The uncertainty of their mission, the unknowns of the portal, and the dangers they faced on Arcmyrin all pressed in on her. The sense of helplessness gnawed at her, and it became unbearable. She couldn't sit idle any longer.

"Francis," she said suddenly, breaking the silence. "I need to go down to the gazebo. Something isn't right. I can feel it in my bones."

Francis, who had been quietly studying some notes at the table, looked up at Gran Celia, her expression a mix of concern and curiosity. She closed the book in front of her, her hands still resting lightly on the cover. "What do you mean, Gran Celia? Something is wrong?"

Gran Celia hesitated, her eyes narrowing slightly as she took a deep breath. "I don't know how to explain it. I just feel like... something's off. I need to see it for myself."

Francis stood, pulling on her jacket. "I'll go with you. I can't imagine you'll want to be down there alone."

Together, they left the parlor, their footsteps echoing in the large, empty hallways of the manor. Gran Celia led the way, the path to the gazebo familiar, yet somehow now filled with an uneasy tension. The manor had always been a place of comfort and refuge, but tonight, it felt cold and distant, as if the house itself was holding its breath.

They reached the gazebo, standing in front of the stone steps that led down into the chamber. The air was still, the usual hum of energy that once resonated in the space beneath them absent. Gran Celia's heart quickened as she reached the bottom of the stairs. She paused, her hand resting on the cool, stone railing.

"Do you feel that?" Gran Celia whispered, her voice barely audible.

Francis nodded, looking around in confusion. "It's... quiet. Too quiet."

Gran Celia's heart sank as she stepped forward into the chamber. The crystal gate, once so vibrant and alive with energy, now appeared dark. The crystal structures around it, usually glowing with an ethereal light, were dim, some shattered, their jagged edges like broken teeth in the silence.

Gran Celia's eyes widened, and she moved closer to the orb, her breath catching in her throat. It was no longer the radiant, pulsing sphere they had seen before. Now it was clouded and dark, as though the very essence of the portal had been drained away. The humming energy that used to fill the chamber was gone, replaced by an oppressive silence that seemed to press in from all sides.

"What... what is this?" Gran Celia muttered, more to herself than to Francis, as she reached out to touch the orb. Her fingers barely brushed the surface before she pulled back, as though the very air around it had turned cold and hostile.

"This isn't right, Francis," Gran Celia said, her voice shaking with a sudden rush of panic. "This is impossible. The portal, the energy... it's gone."

Francis moved closer, her expression turning to one of disbelief as she surveyed the scene. "The orb... it's like it's been... severed from whatever was keeping it alive. But there's no sign of damage, no disturbance. It's as if the energy was simply drained."

Gran Celia turned to look toward the other side of the chamber, toward the large room with the table and chairs where Ridge, Waverly, and Lynx had been prepared for their journey. She walked briskly toward it, her heartbeat quickening in her chest. When she reached the table, her stomach twisted into knots. The curved screens that had once displayed the status of the portal and the energy systems were now nothing more than dark, blank surfaces.

"This... this doesn't make sense," she said, her voice tight with the weight of the realization. "Everything is... dark. Empty."

She turned away, trying to steady her breathing, and hurried toward the seed room. She couldn't explain it, but she had to check—had to see with her own eyes that everything was still as it had been. The air felt heavier as she approached the familiar door, and her hand trembled as she turned the knob.

Inside, everything appeared just as it had been before. The shelves still held the vials of herbs and mixtures, the glass bottles shimmering in the dim light. The workbench was neatly arranged, and the bundles of plants were untouched. Yet, there was a deep sense of unease in the air. The feeling of stagnation was palpable, a sense of dread that settled heavily in Gran Celia's chest.

"Francis," she whispered, her voice barely audible. "Look at this. It's all here. But it doesn't feel right. It's... it's like everything is just... waiting. But there's no life, no energy."

Francis stepped into the room, her expression troubled as she took in the stillness. "It's exactly as it was left. But the energy... I don't feel it either. It's like everything's been cut off."

Gran Celia's mind raced, the pieces of the puzzle not fitting together. Everything about this felt wrong. Her pulse was quickening, and a feeling of doom began to settle over her. There was no way of contacting the others. No way of knowing what was happening on Arcmyrin.

"What if something terrible happened?" she whispered, the words leaving her mouth before she could stop them. "What if they..."

"No," Francis interrupted, placing a hand on her shoulder. "We don't know that. They're resilient, they're strong. Whatever's happened, we'll figure it out."

Gran Celia shook her head slowly, unable to shake the feeling of impending disaster. She turned away from the seed room, her steps heavy as she made her way back up the stairs. Her mind was clouded with fear and uncertainty, the heavy silence pressing in around her as they ascended into the gazebo.

As they reached the top of the stairs, Gran Celia stopped in her tracks. She couldn't put it into words, but something inside her had shifted. The world outside had felt disconnected from the reality she had known for so long. She wasn't sure what had happened in the chamber below, but the sense of loss, of something irrevocably broken, felt undeniable.

She slowly made her way to one of the wicker chairs and collapsed into it, her hands trembling in her lap. She stared at the open doorway, once spilling light into the gazebo, now nothing more than a dark, empty passageway.

The light was gone. The portal was gone. The connection they had relied on—the energy, the hope—was shattered. The door to the unknown, to the future, was closed. And in its place was nothing but a void.

Her chest tightened as the full weight of the situation hit her. They had prepared for everything, but nothing had prepared her for this. The space where the portal once stood now felt like the entrance to a tomb. Cold, empty, silent.

And it was only then that the gravity of the moment settled fully in her bones.

Gran Celia sat there, staring into the darkness, her thoughts consumed with worry for her family, for the fate of the planets, and for the unknown dangers that still lurked just beyond the veil.

For the first time, she felt the true weight of what they were up against—and it terrified her.

25

The Arcmyrin landscape stretched out before Lincoln, Ridge, Waverly, and Lynx, a strange and alien world, yet now feeling strangely familiar. They were seated beneath the canopy of a massive crystalline tree, its shimmering branches swaying in a breeze that carried a palpable energy. A group of Arcmyrin warriors stood nearby, their golden eyes scanning the surroundings with calm vigilance. They were part of the group tasked with helping the Beaumonts understand their connection to the elemental spirits that held the planet—and the portal system—together.

Lincoln had been guiding his children through their individual understanding of the elemental powers they carried within them, a legacy of the Beaumont bloodline that stretched back generations. They had each been gifted a unique affinity for one of the four elements—Fire, Water, Earth, and Air. Now, in the stillness of this moment, he could sense that his children were beginning to understand, but there was much more to the connection they needed to grasp.

"Lynx," Lincoln began, his voice steady, but laced with a fatherly tenderness. "You've always had an instinct to protect, haven't you?"

Lynx, sitting cross-legged across from his father, nodded slowly, his brow furrowed in thought. "Yeah, I guess I have. But I still don't get it, Dad. How did I do what I did in the portal? When I... when I used fire. I didn't know I could do that. I just did it."

Lincoln gave a small, knowing smile. "Sometimes, the gifts within us aren't awakened until they are needed. Your fire gift was dormant, Lynx, until that moment when you felt the instinct to protect your family. You felt fear, yes. But you also felt a deep, natural need to protect life. In that split second, the gift that has always been inside you was released."

Waverly, listening intently, leaned forward. "So, fear... protection. That's how our gifts are activated?"

"Exactly," Lincoln replied, his eyes meeting his children's with a mixture of pride and understanding. "Fear and love are two sides of the same coin. You feared for your family's safety, and because of that, your gift to protect life—your fire—was called upon. In that moment, you weren't just using fire to attack. You were using it to preserve life."

Ridge, who had been listening quietly, nodded thoughtfully. "That makes sense. We didn't get the training we expected. It wasn't about learning the power—it was about feeling it. Understanding our connection to the planet, the elements."

Lincoln glanced over at Ridge, his expression softening. "Exactly. You've all felt the pull of the elements since the moment you arrived on Arcmyrin, even if you didn't understand it. Your gifts were always there, but it took a life-or-death situation to release them."

Lynx sat back, clearly processing this new revelation. "So, when I was fighting those Abasimtrox in the portal—when I threw the fire at them—I wasn't just defending myself. I was defending us. All of us."

"That's right," Lincoln affirmed, his voice steady but proud. "That's the essence of what we are, Lynx. We protect what matters most to us. The elements were gifts given to our ancestors by Origin, and we are the ones who must use them to restore balance to this planet and to the portal."

Ridge leaned forward, curiosity evident in his voice. "What about you, Lincoln? You used water in the portal—what was that about?"

Lincoln's expression grew more serious, a flicker of somber remembrance crossing his features. "Water is my gift. And in that moment, I used it to defeat the Abasimtrox and wash them away from the gates. The only way to defeat them within the portal system was to drive them back—to clear the way for the warriors to escape to their respective planets and prevent the Abasimtrox from getting to the gates before the elders shut the system down. Water is cleansing—it washes away what is tainted."

Waverly's brow furrowed as she processed the significance of his words. "So, the elemental spirits... they're connected to the portal. The elements themselves are the key to keeping the balance intact?"

Lincoln nodded, his expression filled with both weight and hope. "Yes. The portal system, the balance of life, the ecosystems—all of it is intertwined with the four elemental forces. Arcmyrin can't survive without them, and neither can the portal. We are the guardians of that balance. But without the full connection to the elemental spirits, the link will weaken. That's what the Abasimtrox seek to exploit—to destroy the link and escape."

Waverly took a deep breath, her mind whirling with the magnitude of their task. "So, we're supposed to reconnect with the spirits? How do we even begin to do that?"

Before Lincoln could respond, the low hum of energy outside the canopy signaled the arrival of another presence. Elara appeared at the edge of their group, her golden eyes shining brightly as she moved toward them. She approached with a quiet grace, her presence commanding and serene.

"Am I interrupting?" Elara asked, her voice gentle but filled with purpose.

Lincoln turned toward her with a smile. "Not at all. I was just explaining to the family what we've learned about our gifts. The connection to the elements is deeper than I think they realized."

Elara's gaze softened as she looked at Ridge, Waverly, and Lynx. "The elemental spirits have already begun to stir, but you are not yet ready to reconnect with them fully. That will require more than just understanding your gifts—it requires surrendering yourself to the planet's core energy. You will need to be in harmony with the very forces that sustain Arcmyrin, or the spirits will not respond."

Ridge looked at Elara with determination. "How do we reach that harmony? What's the first step?"

Elara's gaze shifted to Lincoln, who nodded slightly before speaking. "The first step is always to recognize the truth of the elements within us. You, Ridge, Waverly, Lynx—you each carry a piece of that power. The elemental spirits will not respond unless you can understand that power fully, feel it in your body, mind, and soul. You must let go of doubt and trust that the balance is within you."

Lynx was quiet for a moment before speaking up. "I still don't understand why we're the ones who have to do this. Why us? Why not the Arcmyrins or the Tanzlorans?"

Lincoln turned his gaze to Lynx, his expression gentle but filled with the wisdom of generations. "The Beaumont bloodline is tied to the elements. We were chosen by Origin long before any of this began. Our ancestors were the first to receive the gifts of the elements—Earth, Water, Fire, and Air. But the key to keeping the balance is not in the power of the elements themselves, but in the harmony we maintain with them. That is why we must reconnect with the spirits. Our connection is the anchor that keeps the portal stable."

Elara nodded in agreement, stepping forward to stand next to the group. "You will face great challenges ahead. The Abasimtrox will try everything to keep the elements from coming back together. But the spirits are waiting for you to step into your role. The only way to restore balance to Arcmyrin and to the portal is to awaken them."

At that moment, Waverly spoke, her voice filled with urgency. "But what about Sage Manor? What about Gran Celia and Earth? Are we sure the Abasimtrox haven't found another way through the portal? What if they're already there?"

Elara's golden eyes softened with a reassuring calm. "Earth is safe, Waverly. The Abasimtrox cannot reach it through the portal anymore. We had to destroy the portal system in order to block them from accessing all the worlds. It is the only way to keep the worlds secure. But the contact and communication with Earth are broken. I can no longer appear holographically outside of Arcmyrin."

Waverly felt her heart drop, but Elara's next words offered a sliver of hope. "When the elemental spirits are brought together, the portals may be reopened—but you must first restore balance."

Waverly's eyes widened, the weight of Elara's words sinking in. "So... the only way for us to return to Earth is by uniting the elements and restoring balance?"

"Yes," Elara said quietly. "The only way to bring the portals back online and restore communication with Earth is to reconnect with the spirits and restore the harmony between the worlds. Once that is done, the elemental forces will be in balance, and the portal system will be restored—controlled by those who understand the power and responsibility it carries."

Ridge stood up, a look of resolve crossing his face. "We can't waste time then. Let's do this. We have a lot of work ahead of us, but we'll do whatever it takes to make sure Earth and Arcmyrin are safe."

Elara's eyes gleamed with a mixture of respect and hope. "I have faith in you, Ridge. In all of you. The spirits will guide you, but it is up to you to bring them together."

Lincoln placed a hand on Ridge's shoulder, his voice steady with the knowledge that this journey was just beginning. "The path won't be easy, but we will walk it together."

26

The sun hung low on the horizon, casting long shadows across the shimmering landscape of Arcmyrin. The air was thick with energy, the very atmosphere alive with the pulse of the planet. The Beaumont family—Lincoln, Ridge, Waverly, and Lynx—stood at the edge of a vast valley, surrounded by Arcmyrin warriors who had been assigned to protect them during their journey. Elara had briefed them all about the dangers they might face as they traveled to connect with the elemental spirits. The warriors, tall and imposing with their golden eyes glowing brightly, stood ready, their presence reassuring but the tension in the air palpable.

The journey had already been difficult. The land they traversed was beautiful but wild, with jagged cliffs and dense forests that seemed to stretch endlessly. The Beaumonts had learned to move cautiously, aware that their task would require more than just strength—it would require patience, focus, and the ability to connect with the very fabric of the planet.

"We're heading toward the waterfall," Lincoln said, his voice steady but filled with a sense of purpose. "Mistara, the Water Spirit, resides there. I've felt the pull of the waters before, but it's different now. It's not just about controlling the water. It's about listening to it."

Ridge, his gaze shifting from the landscape to his brother, nodded in agreement. "We've come this far. We need to connect with the spirits and restore balance to Arcmyrin. Let's not waste any more time."

Waverly adjusted the strap of her pack, her mind heavy with the weight of the task ahead. "I've never felt anything like this. The air, the land… everything feels alive in a way I can't explain."

"It's the spirit of Arcmyrin," Lincoln said, his tone low, as though speaking to the very planet. "It's in everything—the trees, the rocks, the rivers, the air. All of it is connected. But it's also unstable. We have to reconnect with the spirits to restore that balance. It starts with Mistara."

Lynx, who had been quiet for most of the journey, finally spoke up. "What happens if we fail? What if the spirits don't listen to us?"

Lincoln's eyes softened. "We won't fail, Lynx. The spirits are waiting for us, even if we can't see them yet. They've been dormant for too long. It's our job to bring them back to life."

As they made their way through the dense woods toward the distant sound of rushing water, the air seemed to grow heavier. The Arcmyrin warriors moved in formation around them, their eyes scanning the surroundings with a keen awareness of the dangers that might lurk in the shadows.

The journey took hours, the landscape shifting from forest to rocky outcrop, until they finally came to the edge of a wide, raging waterfall. The water cascaded down from high cliffs, its power and beauty overwhelming. The roar of the falls drowned out all other sounds as the Beaumonts and their protectors paused at the base of the waterfall, looking up at the dizzying heights above.

"There it is," Lincoln said, his voice filled with awe. "Mistara is in the waters. We need to reach the heart of the falls."

Waverly stepped forward, her eyes fixed on the roiling water. "How do we connect with her? Do we just... step in?"

Lincoln shook his head, his expression serious. "It's not that simple. You must listen to the water. Feel the energy within it. The spirit will respond to you when you are attuned to the flow."

Ridge, ever the skeptic, took a deep breath. "I'm ready. Let's do this."

The Arcmyrin warriors, positioned at various points around the waterfall's base, stood watch, their golden eyes trained on the surroundings. Elara had warned them that the Abasimtrox would stop at nothing to prevent the Beaumonts from reconnecting with the elemental spirits.

They knew the path would not be easy, and as the Beaumonts prepared to approach the waterfall, a chill ran down their spines.

The wind suddenly picked up, howling through the trees and whipping the water into a frenzy. The temperature dropped, and the air became thick with tension. A dark shadow seemed to slip through the edges of the swirling mist, unseen but felt. It was an unnatural presence—one that seemed to twist the very fabric of reality.

Waverly, her senses heightened, looked around. "Did you feel that?" she asked, her voice tense. "Something's... not right."

Lincoln turned toward her, his face hardening. "The Abasimtrox are here. They're trying to stop us. Stay focused. The spirits are within reach."

But as the Beaumonts approached the base of the waterfall, the winds began to intensify, pulling at their bodies, tearing at their clothes. The wind howled like a living thing, and suddenly, the warriors standing guard were being tossed back by the force of the storm. The once-calm waters of the waterfall began to churn violently, as if something was rising beneath the surface.

The sky above darkened as the wind surged into a swirling vortex. A tornadic blast of air whipped around them, sending debris flying and pulling at their feet. It wasn't just the wind—it was something else, something darker. The air felt alive, charged with malevolent energy. It was as if the Abasimtrox were using the very elements against them, trying to prevent them from reaching Mistara.

"Get down!" one of the Arcmyrin warriors shouted, his voice barely audible over the roar of the winds. He and the other warriors attempted to form a defensive perimeter, but the wind was too powerful, and they were tossed back like ragdolls, struggling to hold their ground.

"Keep moving!" Lincoln shouted, grabbing Waverly's arm and pulling her toward the waterfall. "We're not leaving until we reach her!"

But the wind wouldn't let them. The force of the gale grew stronger, swirling around them in chaotic funnels. The Beaumonts were being tossed, their feet lifting from the ground as the tornado-like winds bore down on them. The warriors, though powerful, were struggling to hold their positions against the onslaught. Their golden eyes shone bright, but even they were being buffeted by the brutal force of the storm.

Lynx tried to steady himself, his hands outstretched, but the wind ripped at him, pushing him back with force. His eyes were wide, and he couldn't hear his own voice over the shrieking winds. "Dad! Waverly!" he yelled, his words lost in the chaos.

Lincoln reached out for him, pulling him into a protective stance, but the wind caught him as well, throwing him to the ground. The powerful blast of air pushed them all to their knees, unable to move forward, unable to reach the waterfall.

"Stay together!" Lincoln shouted, his voice barely audible over the storm. He was struggling to keep his footing as the wind twisted around them like a living thing. "We can't let them separate us!"

But it was becoming clear that the winds—powered by the dark force of the Abasimtrox—were too much. The Arcmyrin warriors fought valiantly, but they too were being forced back. The Beaumonts were nearly powerless against the storm that raged around them.

The energy was overwhelming. Lincoln's gift of water was useless against this furious wind. Waverly's connection to the air spirit wasn't enough to counter the force. Lynx, too, could not summon his fire, for the wind was stifling everything in its path.

"Hold on!" Ridge shouted, though his voice was barely heard. He gripped Waverly's arm tightly as the wind threatened to pull them apart.

Just as it seemed like the wind would tear them from their feet, a flash of light—like a beacon—suddenly erupted from the base of the waterfall. The water seemed to shimmer with energy, and a pulse of pure, elemental power shot through the air, momentarily cutting through the howling winds.

But before they could take another step toward the water, the winds pushed harder, the tornadoes growing more violent. The energy that had risen from the falls began to flicker, and it seemed as if their connection to Mistara was slipping through their fingers. The elemental spirits were close, but they couldn't reach them.

Then, just as suddenly as it had begun, the tornado-like winds grew even more intense, throwing them all back. The Beaumonts, the Arcmyrin warriors—everyone was being tossed, hurled into the air like playthings in a storm.

And then, just as quickly, everything went silent.

The wind died down, but the damage had already been done. The Beaumonts and their protectors were left struggling to rise, disoriented and battered by the storm. They could hear the roar of the waterfall in the distance, but it was drowned out by the oppressive silence.

They had been pushed to the brink—and now, it seemed like the dark shadow had won.

27

The air around the Beaumont family and the Arcmyrin warriors was thick with the remnants of the battle they had just fought against the tornado-like winds. The ground beneath them was littered with debris—broken branches, leaves, and the scars of the brutal storm that had just torn through the area. The once majestic waterfall, which had seemed like an inviting beacon of life, now looked almost ominous, its waters churning as if responding to the chaos that had erupted around it.

Lincoln, Ridge, Waverly, and Lynx struggled to rise to their feet, their bodies battered by the relentless winds. The Arcmyrin warriors, though still standing, were visibly shaken, their golden eyes searching the landscape for any further signs of danger. The tornadoes had subsided, but the threat of the dark shadow lingered, like a heavy weight pressing down on them all.

"Are you all right?" Lincoln asked, his voice steady but filled with concern as he checked on his children. He reached out to steady Waverly, who had nearly lost her balance after being knocked to the ground.

"I'm fine," Waverly said through clenched teeth, her face pale but determined. "We just need to push through."

Lynx, equally unsteady but with a determined look on his face, nodded. "We're not giving up. Not now."

Ridge stood beside them, wiping dust from his hands and his clothes. "That was too close. But we're still here, and we're still going."

As they all regrouped, the Arcmyrin warriors began to form a protective circle around them once again, their golden eyes scanning the surroundings. They had fought valiantly, but it was clear that the dark force they were facing wasn't just an external enemy—it was something more insidious, something that seemed to wield the elements themselves against them.

Just as the group began to brace for what might come next, a sudden burst of light illuminated the area. A holographic projection of Elara flickered into view, her tall, elegant form shimmering in the air before them. She looked worn, as though the battle had taken a toll on her as well, but her eyes were filled with unwavering resolve.

"Lincoln," Elara's voice rang out, firm and filled with purpose. "You and your family have come far, but you are not finished yet. The dark force that is trying to keep you from reaching Mistara is relentless, but it can be fought. You must focus."

Lincoln stepped forward, his gaze locking on Elara's holographic form. "We're ready. We'll fight back, but I need to know how to use my power against this wind. It's too strong for us to break through."

Elara's golden eyes shimmered as she gave a small, knowing smile. "You are the key to breaking this storm. The water spirit, Mistara, is deeply connected to the very forces of water that sustain Arcmyrin. To restore balance, you must call on her. But first, you must fight back the tornadoes. Your water gift is strong, Lincoln. Use it to counteract the winds."

Lincoln nodded, the weight of his fatherly resolve settling deep in his chest. "How?"

Elara's projection flickered briefly, and a faint hum filled the air, as though the very space around them was being charged with the energy of Arcmyrin. "Focus on the water inside you. You have always known how to control it, but now you must command it. Call the water to counter the wind. Not just the water of the waterfall, but the very essence of it. You can bend it to your will. You've done it before."

Lincoln closed his eyes for a moment, taking a deep breath as he felt the pulse of the water element within him. He focused, narrowing his mind on the sensation of water—cool, flowing, cleansing. He visualized it, the water swirling and coiling inside him, waiting for his command.

"Lincoln," Elara urged, her voice steady but filled with encouragement. "Remember, you are not fighting the wind with force alone. You must match it with your flow. Water is the ultimate counter to chaos—it seeks balance, it seeks calm."

A ripple of understanding washed over Lincoln. Water was fluid, not meant to be controlled with brute force, but with finesse, with a quiet strength that allowed it to shape its surroundings. He had always known that water was about healing, about nourishment, but now he understood it in a new way.

With a steady breath, Lincoln raised his arms, palms open, facing the raging winds. He could feel the surge of water inside him, rising with every beat of his heart. The winds howled around them, but Lincoln stood firm, focusing on the energy swirling within him.

"Mistara, guide me." Lincoln whispered, his voice low and filled with power. "Guide us to calm."

A sudden wave of energy surged from Lincoln's chest, extending outward like a burst of water, crashing against the wind. At first, the force was met with resistance, but then—slowly—the wind began to calm. The air around them grew still, and the tornadoes began to lose their force. The water he summoned swirled in the air, cutting through the wind like a blade, forcing it back. The Arcmyrin warriors gasped in awe as they watched the power of the water spirit begin to take shape.

The swirling winds faltered as the water flowed in, pushing back the chaos. The tornado-like storms diminished, their fury broken by the strength of the water that Lincoln had called forth. The sense of imbalance that had pervaded the area slowly began to recede.

"It's working!" Waverly shouted, her voice filled with relief. "Dad, you're doing it!"

But just as they thought the battle was over, a shadow appeared in the distance—dark, ominous, and moving swiftly toward them. It was the same shadow they had sensed before, the force behind the storm.

It hovered at the edge of the waterfall, a swirling mass of dark energy, reaching toward them like a hand seeking to pull them back into the chaos.

"Not yet," Lincoln muttered, his voice tight with concentration. "We're not finished."

He took another deep breath, his arms raised once more as he reached deeper into the water within him. He felt the connection to the spirit of the falls—the living pulse of the water. As his focus sharpened, the water around them surged with renewed strength, creating a wall of liquid energy that pushed back against the shadow.

With a great, final surge, Lincoln released all of his power. The water shot forward like a tidal wave, a blast of pure energy that met the shadow head-on. For a moment, the two forces clashed—the swirling wind and dark shadow fought against the flow of water, but it was clear which force held the advantage.

The dark shadow writhed, pushing back against the water's force, but it was no match for the power of the spirit of water. With one last, desperate howl, the shadow was swept away, its presence dissipating into the air like smoke.

The winds calmed, the waters settled, and the land fell silent once more. Lincoln stood, chest heaving, as the others gathered around him, their expressions filled with awe and relief.

"You did it," Waverly said, her voice full of wonder. "The wind is gone. The shadow's gone."

Lincoln nodded, his hands trembling as the power inside him faded. "We've won this round. But Mistara is still waiting."

Ridge, wiping his brow and glancing toward the waterfall, stepped forward. "What do we do now?"

Elara's holographic form appeared once again, her voice calm but filled with a quiet reverence. "Now, you must go to her. Mistara will guide you, now that the path has been cleared. But remember, she is not just a spirit of water—she is the essence of purity, healing, and balance. You must connect with her fully to restore the waters of Arcmyrin."

Lincoln looked at his children, his face set with determination. "Let's go. Mistara is waiting."

Together, the Beaumonts and the Arcmyrin warriors made their way toward the waterfall, the roar of the water now a soothing sound rather than a threat. As they approached the base of the falls, Lincoln felt the pull of the spirit—the living force of water that sustained not just Arcmyrin, but all the worlds connected by the portal system.

He stepped forward, his hands reaching out toward the cascading water, feeling the power within it, ready to connect with Mistara and restore the flow of pure, healing waters to the planet.

And as the water surged forward to meet him, the spirit of Mistara was finally awakened, her presence filling the air with a powerful energy that would heal the wounds of Arcmyrin and set the course for the restoration of balance across the worlds.

28

The mood around the base of the waterfall was one of quiet celebration, but also reflection. The Beaumonts stood in awe as the last remnants of Mistara's power settled over them. The waters had cleansed Arcmyrin's rivers and oceans, their purity now flowing freely across the planet, the land beginning to heal from the wounds the Abasimtrox had inflicted.

Lincoln, Ridge, Waverly, and Lynx gathered together, their hearts lighter than they had been in days. The weight of their responsibility was still heavy, but the connection to Mistara had brought them a renewed sense of hope. The victory, however, was bittersweet. There were still three more spirits to find, each of them an essential piece to restore the balance to Arcmyrin—and to the portal system that connected the worlds.

The Arcmyrin warriors, standing at attention but with a sense of quiet pride, had been watching the Beaumonts in reverence. Elara had joined them once again, her presence as serene as it had been before. She had observed the connection to Mistara from a distance, her golden eyes filled with a quiet appreciation for what had just been accomplished.

"Well done," Elara said, her voice soft but filled with the weight of the words. "You have reawakened Mistara, the water spirit. You've restored balance to the waters of Arcmyrin. But as you know, this is only the beginning."

Ridge exhaled slowly, wiping the sweat from his brow, though a slight smile tugged at his lips. "It feels like we've made some real progress, but I know the road ahead is still long."

Waverly, still standing by the water's edge, looked out at the mist rising from the falls. "What's next, then? Where do we go from here?"

The leader of the Arcmyrin warriors, a tall and commanding figure with golden eyes and silver hair, stepped forward. His name was Rykas, and he had been with them since their arrival on Arcmyrin, offering both guidance and protection. "The next step is to seek out the fire spirit, Ignissa," he said, his voice deep and resonant.

"Ignissa?" Ridge asked, raising an eyebrow. "The fire spirit? Where do we find her?"

Rykas's eyes clouded for a moment, his gaze turning toward the distance. "Normally, Ignissa's home is in the Embre Mountains. These mountains are known for their fiery, volcanic peaks that glow with the reflection of Arcmyrin's twin suns. They are a sight to behold—a constant, smoldering light that never fades. But lately..."

Rykas hesitated, as though unsure how to express the depth of the change. Elara stepped forward, her voice filling the space as she addressed the group.

"The Embre Mountains are no longer as they were," Elara said, her tone serious. "What was once a beacon of flame is now a place of darkness. The fiery glow is gone. The mountains are obscured by dense fog, and there has been no sign of Ignissa for some time. It seems that the spirit of fire has gone underground."

Waverly's brows furrowed. "Gone underground? What does that mean?"

Rykas's eyes shifted toward the distant mountains, his expression filled with concern. "It means that Ignissa is hiding, perhaps retreating from the chaos that has gripped Arcmyrin. The fog that now blankets the mountains is not natural—it's the result of the fire spirit's absence. Her power, the very essence of fire, is missing from the planet's balance. Until she is found, the Embre Mountains will remain in this perpetual state of grayness, cut off from their natural heat."

Lincoln's mind was already racing, processing the information. "So, the fire spirit is hiding because the balance is disturbed. We need to find her and bring her back to restore the warmth, the fire to Arcmyrin."

"Precisely," Rykas affirmed. "Ignissa's return is essential for the restoration of Arcmyrin's ecosystems. Without her, the balance of heat and energy across the planet is out of sync. The fog that now covers the Embre Mountains is just a symptom of a much deeper disturbance."

Lynx, still processing the magnitude of their task, nodded gravely. "So, what do we do now? How do we find her?"

Elara stepped forward, her golden eyes shining with quiet determination. "We must travel to the Embre Mountains and seek her out. But be warned, the path will not be easy. The fog is thick, disorienting, and filled with dangers that we cannot yet predict. But we have no choice. Ignissa's power is the next piece of the puzzle that must be restored."

Ridge glanced at his family, then back at Rykas and Elara. "How long will it take to reach the mountains?"

"The journey to the Embre Mountains from here will take several days on foot," Rykas replied. "We must navigate through the forests and across the plains, avoiding any wild beasts that may have been driven into frenzy by the imbalance. The fog will be our greatest challenge. It has distorted the landscape, making it nearly impossible to navigate without help."

Lincoln nodded, his gaze shifting to the others. "We'll go. We can't afford to waste any time. Ignissa may be the key to bringing everything back into balance."

The group began to prepare for the journey ahead, gathering their supplies and making sure they were ready for whatever lay ahead. The Arcmyrin warriors took their places alongside the Beaumonts, ready to provide protection on the road to the Embre Mountains. The tension in the air was palpable. They had only just begun to heal one part of Arcmyrin, but the rest of the planet still needed their help.

As they began their trek, the landscape gradually shifted from the lush greenery surrounding the waterfall to more barren, rocky terrain.

The temperature dropped, and the air grew dense, filled with an eerie stillness. The dense fog began to settle around them, a cold mist that clung to their clothes and chilled the air.

"This fog..." Waverly said, pulling her cloak tighter around herself. "It's almost like the air itself is sick."

Lincoln nodded, his eyes scanning the horizon. "It's a manifestation of Ignissa's absence. The energy that should be radiating from the mountains is missing. Without the fire spirit, Arcmyrin's equilibrium is off-balance. The land is trying to compensate, but it's not enough."

As they ventured deeper into the mist, the sounds of nature around them seemed muted—distant cries of unseen creatures, the rustle of the wind through the trees, but all of it felt far away. It was as though the land itself was holding its breath.

Lynx, walking beside his father, looked up at him with a mixture of curiosity and concern. "Dad... do you think we'll find Ignissa? I mean, how do we even begin to wake her up?"

Lincoln smiled softly at his son, his voice calm but filled with certainty. "We won't find her by just hoping, Lynx. We have to call to her. Reach into the heart of the Embre Mountains and listen for her response. The spirits respond to our connection—not just our power, but our understanding of their place in the world. Ignissa's fire is not just about destruction. It's about creation, warmth, and life. We need to find the core of that warmth again."

The fog grew thicker as they pressed on, obscuring their view and making it harder to see what lay ahead. The air had grown colder, and every breath felt heavier. They moved cautiously, each step deliberate, knowing that they were entering a dangerous unknown. The Embre Mountains loomed ahead, their peaks hidden in the mist, the very air seeming to throb with an unspoken tension.

"We are close," Rykas said, his voice carrying through the fog. "We must press forward. The spirit of fire awaits."

But as they pushed forward, a distant rumble shook the ground beneath their feet. The fog swirled around them in a violent gust, and the temperature dropped even further, as if the land itself had shifted in response to their presence.

It was then that they realized: the search for Ignissa would not be easy, and the spirit's return would be harder fought than any of them had anticipated.

The fog seemed to thicken, pulling them deeper into the heart of the mountains. And in the distance, a strange and ominous sound echoed through the mist—like the crackling of flames, distant but unmistakable.

They were getting closer. But as they neared the source of the fire spirit's hiding place, they could feel the land itself pushing back.

29

The air in Sage Manor felt heavy, a weight that Gran Celia couldn't shake. Days of worrying about her family's safety—especially her grandchildren's mission—had taken their toll. The silence that hung around the manor was oppressive, and her thoughts swirled with concern. Her connection with the portal had been severed. She couldn't reach them on Arcmyrin. It was like they had slipped away into another world, leaving her stuck in the uncertainty of the unknown.

Gran Celia sat by the window in the parlor, her gaze fixed on the misty blue mountains of Pisgah National Forest just beyond the manor grounds. She had always found peace in the beauty of the forest, but lately, it seemed distant—like she was unable to connect with it the way she used to. It was almost as if the forest shared in her worries.

"Celia?" Francis's voice broke through the quiet, and Gran Celia turned to see her friend standing in the doorway, concern etched on her face.

"Yes?" Gran Celia replied, her voice strained with the weight of everything that had been occupying her mind.

Francis stepped into the room, her expression thoughtful. "You've been inside too much lately. I know you're worried about everything, but you need to get out. It's not good for your health to keep brooding in here."

Gran Celia sighed, leaning back in her chair. "I know, Francis. It's just... it's so hard. I don't know what's happening with them, and I feel like I've lost touch with everything."

Francis nodded, sitting down beside her. "I completely understand, but you've got to do something for yourself. Your mind can't be running in circles like this all the time. You need a change of scenery. Some fresh air. A little break."

Gran Celia's gaze softened, a small smile tugging at her lips. "I suppose you're right. It's just... everything feels so heavy right now. But I don't know if I have the energy for anything much."

"Well," Francis said with a slight grin, "what if we start small? I was thinking—a picnic. It's right behind the manor, in the Pisgah National Forest. The Pink Beds. It's a beautiful spot, and I know it used to do wonders for you when you were feeling down."

Gran Celia raised an eyebrow. "A picnic? In the forest?"

"Yes. You used to take Lincoln and Ridge there when they were boys, didn't you? They loved it there—running around, exploring, playing in the woods." Francis's voice was gentle, but filled with conviction. "I think it would do you some good to be out there again. A little bit of peace, away from the house and the constant worry."

Gran Celia hesitated for a moment, her heart swelling with nostalgia at the mention of her sons. She could see the image in her mind so clearly—Lincoln and Ridge, young and full of energy, running through the trees, their laughter filling the air. How much simpler those days had seemed, how much lighter life had felt.

"You know..." Gran Celia began slowly, her voice tinged with a bittersweet smile. "That might just be what I need. I haven't been to the Pink Beds in ages. It's been too long since I've let myself enjoy the forest the way I used to."

"Then it's settled," Francis said, standing up and crossing to the cupboard. "I'll gather up a picnic basket, and we can head out there. A few hours of peace—no thinking about portals or worlds beyond our own. Just the forest, a lunch, and good company."

Gran Celia stood with Francis, feeling a small spark of something she hadn't felt in days—hope, maybe, or simply the relief that came with taking a break from the constant worry.

Together, they packed up a basket with sandwiches, fruit, and lemonade, a simple meal but one that carried the promise of a peaceful day. As they made their way out the door and toward the Pink Beds, Gran Celia took a deep breath of the fresh mountain air, feeling the cool breeze brush against her skin. It was like a balm to her soul, the weight of her anxieties lifting just slightly.

The Pink Beds area of Pisgah National Forest was just behind Sage Manor, and Gran Celia had always loved it here. The terrain was gentle, with soft meadows and wildflower-filled glades, surrounded by towering trees and the faint murmur of streams. As they approached the picnic area, Gran Celia felt her shoulders relax. The sound of birds singing, the rustling of leaves in the trees—it all felt so familiar, so grounding.

"Do you remember how the boys used to run wild out here?" Gran Celia asked, her voice soft with nostalgia as they set up the picnic at one of the wooden tables.

Francis smiled, glancing around the area. "How could I forget? They'd be up and down those hills, dragging their mother along to look at this rock or that tree, always excited about the next adventure. You used to sit right there on that bench, just watching them, your face lit up with pride."

Gran Celia's heart swelled with the memory. "They were always so full of life, so eager to explore. I don't think they ever understood how much I cherished those moments. How precious they were."

Francis nodded. "I think they knew more than you give them credit for."

Gran Celia took a seat at the table, looking out across the meadow, watching the families that had gathered around picnic tables in the area. Children played in the distance, running and laughing, while their parents sat nearby, sharing a meal, talking, and enjoying the day. It was peaceful here, as if the rest of the world could wait.

"I used to bring Lincoln and Ridge here all the time," Gran Celia murmured, her gaze distant. "When they were younger. I wanted them to learn about nature, about the cradle of forestry here, about the importance of the land. I wanted them to appreciate the world beyond the walls of Sage Manor, to understand the legacy of this land…"

She paused, a soft smile spreading across her face. "I think it worked. They both grew up to respect it, to understand that the world outside their front door is just as important as the one inside."

Francis, sitting across from her, watched her closely. "And now you're passing that same legacy to your grandchildren. That's something to be proud of."

Gran Celia nodded, though her smile faded a bit as a thought passed through her mind. She hadn't heard from Waverly, Lynx, or Ridge in what felt like an eternity. The silence had grown unbearable, even with all the beauty around her. The world felt too big and distant without them near.

She let out a long breath, her hand resting on the edge of the table. "I just want them to come home safely. All of them."

Francis reached across the table, placing a comforting hand on Gran Celia's. "They're strong, Celia. They're doing the work they were meant to do. But they will come back. You'll see."

Gran Celia looked out at the families around them, the children running and laughing in the sunlit glade, the parents sharing quiet moments of peace. It was as though the world outside had paused for just a brief moment, giving her time to catch her breath, to remember what it was like to live in a moment of peace.

With a final, quiet smile, Gran Celia nodded, allowing herself to relax into the day. She needed this—more than she realized. And for the first time in a long while, she felt the weight of her worries lighten, just a little.

The forest, the laughter, the memory of her sons playing in these very woods—it all brought her back to the core of who she was, reminding her that, even in the darkest of times, there could be light.

30

The Embre Mountains were shrouded in an oppressive fog, the dense, swirling mist that had engulfed the once fiery peaks. The fog felt like an enemy in itself—thick, suffocating, disorienting. It was a manifestation of the imbalance, a sign of the fire spirit's absence from the planet. Despite their best efforts, the Beaumont family had found it difficult to make any progress through the haze, the oppressive air preventing them from reaching the source of Ignissa's power.

As they climbed higher into the mountains, the fog seemed to press in on them, wrapping around their bodies like a living thing, blinding their vision and dulling their senses. The cold bite of the mist settled into their bones, and they could feel the weight of their task settling more heavily upon them. They had already faced the storm created by the dark shadow in the valley, and the fog was just another reminder of the chaos they were fighting against.

Lincoln, Ridge, and Waverly were on edge, moving cautiously through the thick air. Lynx, however, seemed unusually calm as he walked in the front, the energy of his flame gift still a recent memory in his mind. Elara, who had appeared to them once again, walked beside them, her golden eyes scanning the fog for any signs of danger.

"This fog won't stop us," Elara said, her voice filled with quiet confidence. "Lynx, you've already unlocked part of your gift. The fire inside you. Now, you must dig deeper. You must use your connection to fight back the fog. You have to summon the force you used in the portal. That was the fire of protection."

Lynx looked at Elara, his face serious, though tinged with uncertainty. "I'll try, but... it wasn't like I was thinking about it when I used the fire before. It just happened. I don't know if I can do it again."

"You can," Elara encouraged, her golden eyes steady on him. "It is within you. The protection of your family, your desire to keep the ones you love safe—that is the key to unlocking your power."

Lynx exhaled deeply, his hands flexing by his sides as he steadied himself. He had already experienced a glimpse of the power he held within, but it was a different thing altogether to call upon it intentionally. He could still feel the rush of heat in his chest, the pulse of flame that had surged through him when he had used it in the portal. His fingers tingled with the memory, but the fog pressed in, thick and unyielding.

"I'll try," he said, the uncertainty in his voice evident.

The group came to a stop at the edge of a narrow ridge, the fog thickening as they paused. Lynx closed his eyes for a moment, focusing inward. He took in a slow breath, remembering the fear and desperation he had felt in the portal when he had used his flame to protect his family. That fear, that deep need to protect those he loved, was what had ignited the fire. He could feel it again, swirling within him, but it was harder to reach through the fog this time.

"I can't see through it," he muttered, frustration beginning to creep into his voice. "It's so thick. I don't know how to break through."

"Don't focus on the fog," Elara advised, her voice calm. "Focus on the fire. The flame within you. Let it burn brighter than the dense mist."

Lynx clenched his fists, his mind focused on the warmth within his chest, the strength of the fire that had protected them before. He felt the heat rising, like a pulse deep inside of him, and he focused everything on bringing that heat to the surface.

For a moment, nothing happened. The fog remained unchanged, swirling around him like a wall of gray. He felt the flame within him flicker, unsure of how to reach it, unsure of how to make it burn hot enough to push the fog back.

But then, suddenly, the heat exploded within him.

A bright flash of light ignited from Lynx's hands, the fire spilling out in tendrils of flame that cut through the fog. The air around him shimmered with heat, the mist pushing back as the fire began to grow, burning brighter and hotter. Lynx's eyes widened in shock as the flames flared to life, casting an orange glow through the fog and illuminating the surrounding mountains.

But the fog wasn't retreating fast enough. The swirling mass seemed to grow thicker, pushing against the flames with an almost deliberate force. Lynx strained, his body trembling with the effort to keep the fire going, but the fog refused to yield.

Waverly, watching her brother struggle, felt her heart race. The feeling of helplessness was overwhelming. "Lynx!" she shouted, her voice edged with panic. She took a step toward him, but the mist was so thick she could barely see him through the haze.

Suddenly, a surge of fear and anger shot through Waverly. She couldn't lose Lynx. She wouldn't let the fog swallow him. The anger at the dark shadows that had been tormenting them, the fear of losing her brother, fueled something deep within her.

"I won't let you take him!" she shouted, her voice ringing with the power of her own determination.

Before she even realized what she was doing, Waverly raised her arms, focusing all her energy on the fog that surrounded them. The wind began to pick up around her, swirling violently, responding to the force of her anger. She felt the air around her, tugging at the mist as it thickened in front of her. With a shout, she thrust her hands forward.

The air responded.

With a great, forceful gust, Waverly commanded the fog to lift. It wasn't just the power of the wind—it was her connection to the air spirit, the natural flow of energy that she had learned to control. The fog swirled and lifted, its thick mass breaking apart as the wind rose to her command. The fog didn't fight back this time—it parted, lifting away from Lynx and from the others. The path cleared, the visibility improving as the mist was swept aside.

As the fog cleared, Lynx's fire blazed brighter, the flames pushing back against the remaining haze. The air around them grew warmer, the oppressive chill of the fog dissipating as Waverly's power drove it back.

Lynx, now able to see clearly, turned to his sister, his face filled with gratitude. "Waverly... you did it."

Waverly, still trembling from the effort, nodded, though she could barely catch her breath. "I couldn't let it take you. I couldn't lose you."

Elara's holographic figure appeared beside them, her voice filled with awe. "You've done it. You've called upon the power of the air and fire spirits. The fog is gone."

Ridge, who had been watching from the edge of the group, stepped forward with a relieved smile. "That was incredible, Waverly. You both were incredible."

But it was the sight ahead that made them all freeze in awe.

The fog, now completely lifted, revealed a hidden cave entrance at the base of the mountains. The walls of the cave seemed to glow with an unnatural light, a soft, golden radiance that spilled from within, casting long shadows across the ground. The entrance was framed with rocks that shimmered with the warmth of fire, as though the very stone itself was alive with energy.

"It's her," Elara whispered, her golden eyes wide with recognition. "Ignissa is inside. The fire spirit has been waiting for you."

Lynx, his heart pounding, took a deep breath. He could feel the heat of the cave calling to him, the warmth of the fire spirit reaching out to him. He took a step forward, his resolve firm.

"We're not just here to find her," Lynx said, his voice steady with newfound strength. "We're here to bring her back. To restore the balance."

As they walked toward the cave, the light within it grew brighter, the heat radiating from the entrance, and the Beaumonts knew that they were one step closer to restoring Arcmyrin's balance. They were not just travelers in this world—they were its guardians. And the fire spirit, Ignissa, would be the next force they would unite with.

31

Deep beneath the surface of Arcmyrin, in the labyrinthine tunnels that wove through the planet's core, a dark and brooding presence stirred. The caverns were far from natural—distorted by centuries of manipulation, their walls slick with an oily black sheen that seemed to absorb light instead of reflecting it. The atmosphere was thick with an unnatural energy, a malevolent force that pulsed through the very veins of the planet. Here, in the deepest recesses of Arcmyrin, the shadows that had been battling the Beaumont family for control of the planet now seethed in silence, gathering strength for another strike.

At the center of this darkened lair, on a platform carved from the very rock of the planet, stood Patereon. He was unlike the shadow creatures that served him, a dark figure twisted by hatred and envy. His form was human—tall, gaunt, with skin that hung loosely from his bones, his face lined with age and fury. His eyes, black as midnight, glowed with an inner fire, but it was not the fire of life—it was the fire of vengeance, a hunger for power that no amount of time or failure could extinguish.

The shadow creatures, their forms formless and dark, huddled in the cavernous space around him, shuddering as he spoke. The leader's voice was a low rasp, tinged with an almost unbearable anger.

"Fools!" Patereon's voice cracked like a whip through the damp, heavy air. His words were laced with venom, each one dripping with contempt. "How could you let them win? How could you let a few youngsters defeat you? I should have known better than to trust you with the fate of this planet. You were so sure of victory, yet now you've lost it all. Arcmyrin is slipping through our fingers, and you let it happen!"

The dark shadows in the room writhed, their forms shifting in response to his fury. They were no more than extensions of his will, creatures of darkness and malice, bound to do his bidding. And yet, in their failure, even they trembled before the wrath of their master.

"You let them—the Beaumonts—escape the trap," Patereon hissed, spitting the name as though it were poison on his tongue. "Ridge, Lincoln, Waverly, and Lynx. I had Arcmyrin almost within my grasp. I almost wiped them out—almost! And now, they are stronger than ever. Their elemental spirits have awoken, their power has multiplied, and they will come for us. They will come for me."

A cold laugh escaped his lips, filled with bitterness and disdain. "I should have finished them when I had the chance. But no matter. They will fall. Because unlike them, I have powers that they cannot even begin to comprehend. They are not the only ones with gifts, are they?"

He turned sharply, his piercing gaze cutting through the room as he scanned his shadowy followers. "You think I have no power left, don't you? You think you've seen the extent of my strength. But you've only seen the beginning."

The shadows swirled around him, though none of them dared to speak. They had learned long ago that silence was their only defense when Patereon's rage was unleashed.

Patereon continued, his voice lower now, yet filled with a chilling promise. "The Beaumonts have their gifts. The elements. Water, fire, air, earth—each one of them touched by the forces of Arcmyrin itself. But they are only part of the picture. They cannot comprehend the true depths of power. Not the way I do."

His gnarled hands clenched into fists as he took a step toward the shadows, his voice rising again with newfound intensity. "I am not simply a man, not merely one of them. I have harnessed the powers of this world, and I have forced its supernatural powers into submission. Arcmyrin's gifts are not limited to those born of its elements. I control the core. I control the shadows that fester beneath the surface of this world, and with them, I will destroy the Beaumonts and everything they stand for."

The air seemed to thrum with a dark energy as Patereon's words hit the shadows like an electric charge. The temperature in the room dropped, and the once-silent forms around him began to hum with anticipation, their dark eyes gleaming in the faint light of the cavern.

"Patereon, master," one of the shadow beings finally spoke, its voice a rasping whisper, "we... we will find another way. The Beaumonts—"

Patereon's head snapped around, his eyes blazing. "Another way? You think I don't know that? You think I'm sitting idly by, letting them run free? We're not talking about another way—we're talking about annihilation. Arcmyrin is mine, and I will have it."

He raised his hands, palms open, and the shadows around him quivered in response. Dark tendrils of energy shot out from his fingertips, slithering like serpents, spreading throughout the cavern. The walls pulsed with a dark glow as Patereon called upon the very core of the planet itself. His power was immense, fueled by centuries of hidden rage and a desperate need for control.

"I've waited for this day too long," Patereon muttered to himself, his voice now a low growl. "The Beaumonts believe they have control of the elements, that they will bring balance to this broken world. They're wrong. Balance is an illusion. Power is the only truth."

He paused, his eyes narrowing as he thought of his next move. His grip tightened on the air around him, a palpable force of will that made the shadows curl in on themselves.

"I will use them. The Beaumonts think they are the saviors of this world. They believe they are chosen to bring Arcmyrin back into harmony. But they don't understand that the world was never meant to be in harmony. The elements were never meant to work together. I will tear them apart, one by one."

He began to pace, the energy in the room shifting with his every step. "I will break the spirits. I will shatter their connection. I will make them beg for their destruction."

The shadow creatures, though still cowering, felt the raw power in Patereon's words, and in his mind, they could already hear the destruction his plan would bring. The Beaumonts, despite their gifts, would not be able to stop him. He had been patient, and now, it was his time.

"Prepare yourselves," Patereon's voice rang through the cavern like a bell. "We will strike soon, and we will strike hard. They will not expect what is coming. Arcmyrin will be mine, and the Beaumonts will be nothing more than a memory."

A deep, rumbling laugh reverberated through the cavern. It was dark, foreboding—a laugh filled with hatred and the promise of destruction. Patereon had always believed that power belonged to those who were willing to take it, and he would not let the Beaumonts stand in his way.

"I've waited long enough. And now, the real war begins."

With that, Patereon's dark supernatural powers began to pulse through the very core of Arcmyrin, calling to the shadows that still lingered beneath the surface, preparing for the final battle that would determine the fate of the planet—and the Beaumonts.

32

The entrance to the cave was small, almost concealed beneath a tangled mass of vines and rock, but once the fog had cleared, the way forward had become clear. The air was thick with heat, but not the usual oppressive warmth of the fog; this was different. This heat was alive, vibrant, pulsing with energy, as though the very walls of the cave were breathing. Lynx could feel it in his chest, the heat that called to him, beckoning him inside.

His feet crunched softly against the gravel as he entered the cave, the glow from within casting long shadows across the jagged stone walls. The cave's interior was massive, the walls smooth and etched with ancient markings, symbols that pulsed with faint light. The ground was uneven, rocky, and though the air was heavy with heat, it was not suffocating. Instead, it felt like the very essence of fire itself was waiting, dormant but alive, ready to awaken.

Lynx's heart pounded in his chest, and for a moment, doubt crept in. He had fought against the storm on Embre Mountain, struggled to control the fire within him, but this—this felt different. The weight of the task ahead, the responsibility to awaken Ignissa, to restore the balance to Arcmyrin and to the portal system, pressed heavily on his shoulders.

But then he remembered his family—their faces, their voices, the fear he had felt when the Abasimtrox had attacked them in the portal. He remembered how the fire inside him had surged to protect them, how his instincts had guided him to use the power he didn't fully understand. He wasn't just fighting for himself anymore; he was fighting for everyone.

With a deep breath, Lynx stepped further into the cave, his senses on full alert. The heat around him grew stronger, more intense, as if the cave itself was a furnace, and then, in the distance, he saw it—a glow, faint at first, then growing brighter, as if a fire was slowly kindling in the heart of the cave.

He quickened his pace, and as he rounded a bend in the stone, he saw her.

At the center of the cavern, a massive figure rose from the ground, the air around her shimmering with heat. She was made of flame—her body flickering and twisting, radiating a warmth that seemed to bend the very air. Her form was ethereal, made of fire, but somehow stable, her energy pure and focused. Her eyes, burning with golden light, turned to meet his.

"Ignissa," Lynx whispered, awe filling his voice as he stepped closer, unable to look away from the fire spirit who had once been lost to the world.

The fire spirit's gaze softened as she observed him. "Lynx Beaumont," she spoke his name, her voice like crackling flames, soothing yet powerful. "You have come. I have felt your presence."

Lynx stood still for a moment, unsure of what to say, but the words seemed to come on their own. "I've been trying to understand my gift. The fire inside me—it came out when I needed it most. But I didn't know it was you I was connected to. I didn't know this was the reason."

Ignissa's flame-like form shifted, a tendril of fire curling around her, almost like a comforting embrace. "You have always known, Lynx. Your gift was awakened by necessity, by your love for your family, by your desire to protect. That is the heart of fire—passion, purpose, destruction and rebirth. But it is not just the destruction of the enemy, the removal of the shadow. It is the creation of light, warmth, and life."

Lynx took a step forward, his eyes narrowing as the flames around Ignissa seemed to intensify. "But I didn't feel like I was in control. It was all so... sudden."

"That is the nature of fire," Ignissa said, her voice almost tender. "It is wild, unpredictable, and yet always purposeful. Your fear and your love unlocked it, and now that you understand its depth, its true nature, you can wield it with intention."

Lynx's eyes widened as he absorbed her words. He had always known there was something primal about fire, something beyond its mere heat and light. He had felt it when the flames had erupted in the portal, when he had feared for his life and the lives of his family. But there was something more now—something deeper that he could barely comprehend.

"I don't know if I'm ready for this," he said, his voice barely above a whisper. "I don't know if I can control all of it."

Ignissa tilted her head, her form flickering as if she were smiling, the fire around her brightening. "You are more ready than you realize, Lynx. You do not need to control it with your mind. You must feel it with your heart. The fire inside you will guide you. And now, I will guide you."

Lynx felt a rush of warmth, the heat around him intensifying, but it was not overwhelming. It felt right. It felt like a part of him, and with it came an incredible sense of clarity. The fire within him was not just a destructive force; it was an integral part of the world's balance, a force that could protect and create.

"Now, Lynx," Ignissa said, her voice growing steady and strong, "I need you to release me. The planet—and the worlds—are depending on you. My flames must return to the skies. Arcmyrin needs me, and the portal system needs me. It is time for me to burn again, to bring light to the darkness."

Lynx nodded, his heart racing with a mix of awe and purpose. "I'm ready," he said, and the words felt right. "I'm ready to release you."

He stretched out his hands, feeling the heat rise from his core, from the fire that had once terrified him. This time, there was no fear. He was no longer trying to control the fire; he was working with it, letting it flow through him, channeling its power.

As he called upon the fire, the flames in the cave began to grow, rising up from Ignissa's form, filling the cavern with a brilliant, blinding light.

The fire surged through the air, dancing in patterns that Lynx could only begin to understand. It was like the flame was no longer something outside of him; it was an extension of himself.

With a final, triumphant roar, Ignissa's form burst into a thousand sparks, flying into the air like an explosion of fire, lighting the entire cave with an intense, warm glow. The flames stretched high into the ceiling, illuminating the darkened cave, filling every corner with radiant heat and light.

Lynx, his arms outstretched, felt the fire flow through him, and for the first time, he truly understood it. It was not chaos. It was not destruction. It was balance—the balance of life and death, of creation and destruction, of light and dark. And as the fire spread out from the cave, he knew that Arcmyrin was about to change.

Ignissa's voice rang out, calm and powerful, filling the cavern. "Lynx, you have set me free. Now, I will restore the balance. Arcmyrin will burn with my light once again. The worlds will know the power of fire—and with it, the power of rebirth."

Lynx stood there, his body trembling from the intensity of the experience, but his heart filled with pride. The fire had been awakened, but so had he. He was no longer just a young boy unsure of his power. He was a force—their force—ready to restore balance, not just to Arcmyrin, but to the portal system that connected all the worlds.

The flame of Ignissa, the fire spirit, burned brightly once more, lighting the path ahead. The balance was slowly, but surely, returning.

As Lynx turned to leave the cave, the fire still flickering in the distance, he knew that the battle was far from over. But now, with the power of the fire spirit at his command, he was ready for whatever lay ahead.

Arcmyrin would burn brightly again. And the Beaumonts would be the ones to ensure that the light of the spirits would never fade again.

33

The sky above the Embre Mountains had shifted from the intense heat of the day to the cooling embrace of twilight. The fading suns cast long shadows across the rugged terrain, painting the land in hues of gold and purple. After their successful connection with Ignissa, the fire spirit, the Beaumonts had felt an overwhelming sense of accomplishment. But there was little time to revel in their victory—the journey was far from over.

The warriors had led the Beaumonts to a small camping area nestled in a sheltered valley, a quiet spot far from the mountains' dangers. Here, the trees grew tall and dense, providing a canopy of shade beneath which they could rest. The ground was softer, the air cooler, and the sound of a nearby stream provided a soothing background to the otherwise still night. It was a rare moment of peace, and for the first time in what felt like forever, the Beaumonts could breathe easy.

The Arcmyrin warriors had set up a fire pit in the center of the campsite, and with their help, the Beaumonts quickly settled into the area. The warriors also provided more herbal mixtures, brewed from plants native to Arcmyrin, which were designed to help sustain them during the next leg of their journey. These would help the family stay energized and acclimate to the world's unique atmosphere, but they were also given a meal of human food to enjoy—a small comfort, a reminder of home.

Sitting around the fire, the family settled into a rare moment of quiet reflection. They shared their thoughts about everything they had experienced so far, the weight of the journey still fresh in their minds, but the flicker of hope growing stronger with each passing moment.

"I can't believe we've already connected with two of the spirits," Ridge said, his voice filled with wonder as he stared into the fire. "Mistara, Ignissa... It feels like just yesterday we were stumbling through that chamber beneath the gazebo."

Waverly nodded, her eyes still wide from the events of the past few days. "And now... the planet's healing. We've actually released them from whatever dark shadow had kept them captive. It's hard to believe."

Lynx shifted beside her, the warmth from the fire casting flickering shadows across his face. "I still can't believe I did it—we did it. I was so scared, but then, in the moment when I needed to protect you, the fire just came to me. It was like... like something clicked."

"Ignissa," Lincoln said, his voice tinged with a sense of quiet pride. "The fire spirit is not just about destruction—it's about life. Creation. You helped unlock that."

"Yeah, I felt it too," Waverly said, glancing at her brother. "The power of it. It felt so... freeing. The world needs that balance, Lynx. The water spirit and the fire spirit—they're the beginning of something much bigger."

Ridge sighed and leaned back, crossing his arms behind his head as he lay on the grass. "We've done well so far. But I can't shake the feeling that there's more to come. We've released two spirits, but the Abasimtrox are still out there. And they won't stop."

"We'll be ready for them," Lincoln said, a steady resolve in his voice. "We've come too far to let them take this from us."

The crackling of the fire was the only sound for a moment before the warriors, having finished their own meal, began to settle into their places around the campsite. The night had fallen quiet, and even the air seemed to settle into a deep calm. It was a welcome change from the tension of the day.

At that moment, Elara's holographic form appeared before them, her shimmering presence flickering in the air as if she were made of light itself. Her golden eyes met theirs with a look of both pride and recognition.

"You have done well, all of you," Elara said, her voice carrying with it the weight of the acknowledgement. "I can see it now, the planet healing—its rivers running clean again, its warmth returning to the mountains. The balance is shifting."

"We couldn't have done it without your help," Ridge said, nodding in appreciation toward Elara.

"You have done the hard work," Elara replied. "But more remains. You have awakened two spirits, and with that, you've unlocked the first step to restoring balance. The Arcmyrin Council can now see the progress—our world is healing, and the link to the portal system is strengthening."

"But there's still more to do," Waverly said quietly. She had always been the most focused on their mission, and the exhaustion from their journey had not dulled her sense of responsibility. "What's next?"

"There are still two more elemental spirits to awaken—Earth and Air," Elara said, her voice calm but filled with the weight of what lay ahead. "The work you've done so far has paved the way, but you must rest tonight. Tomorrow will bring new challenges. The journey will not be easy, and the Abasimtrox will not relent."

The fire crackled, sending sparks into the air as the group fell into a thoughtful silence. They had come so far, but they knew the next step would be just as difficult. The weight of what lay ahead hung heavy in the air.

"Get rest," Elara urged. "You've earned it. Tomorrow, the journey continues. But for now, take the night to recover. We'll be ready for whatever comes next."

As her form began to flicker and fade, the group settled back into their blankets, grateful for the rare moment of peace. The warriors had gathered their own fire nearby, and the quiet hum of the Arcmyrin camp filled the night. The sounds of the forest were peaceful, and the moonlight bathed everything in a soft, silver glow. It felt like a moment suspended in time—a fleeting respite before the next storm.

The next morning came quickly. The sun had risen early, casting its pale light over the mountains. Waverly, however, had already woken up, feeling the need to clear her mind before the day began. She rose quietly from the blanket, careful not to wake Lynx, who was still curled up beside her, fast asleep.

The air was cool and fresh, the fog that had covered the mountains the previous day now dissipated into a soft mist that hovered near the ground. Waverly inhaled deeply, feeling the weight of everything they had accomplished, but also the enormity of the task ahead.

She decided to take a walk. The forest was beautiful this early, bathed in the soft light of dawn, and the stillness seemed to offer her some solace. She walked slowly, allowing herself to take in the sights—the towering trees, the delicate ferns, and the faint sound of a nearby stream. It was a moment of peace, a moment for her to feel grounded again.

Her footsteps grew more purposeful as she ventured further into the woods, the peaceful solitude offering a brief escape from the pressures of their mission. But as she stepped carefully through a patch of thick grass, her foot sank into something soft.

At first, she thought it was just wet ground, but then it pulled—her foot sinking further with a sudden, eerie tug. She gasped, trying to pull her leg back, but it was too late. Her other foot quickly followed suit, and before she could react, the earth beneath her was swallowing her whole.

She screamed, panic rising in her chest as the ground beneath her became a sticky, wet trap. The more she struggled, the faster the quicksand seemed to pull her in. Her hands flailed out for something—anything—to grab onto, but there was nothing nearby.

"Help!" Waverly screamed, her voice rising in a desperate cry. "Help! I'm stuck!"

The mist seemed to blur her vision, and the forest around her became a blur of shapes. Her heart pounded as she tried to move, but the more she struggled, the deeper she sank into the quicksand.

"Someone! Please!" she cried out, the ground threatening to consume her. The fear was real now—this was no longer a simple walk. This was dangerous.

Her breath came in sharp gasps, her heart racing with terror as the weight of the earth pressed in on her. She needed help. Desperately.

34

Ridge's dream was an explosion of sound, the reverberating bass of a rock-and-roll concert vibrating through his chest. He could feel the energy of the crowd pulsing around him, a sea of people swaying to the beat of the music. It was everything he had ever loved—the noise, the thrill, the rush of being part of something so visceral.

The lights were flashing in strobe patterns, and the sound was deafening as the band played their anthem, the music carrying through the air like a force of nature. Ridge could feel the music seeping into his bones, alive in every part of him.

And then, over it all, there was a scream—a loud, high-pitched cry that made Ridge's head snap around in annoyance. It was too shrill, too insistent. The scream cut through the crowd like a knife, drowning out the sweet melody of the song he was so lost in.

He turned to find the source. A woman, standing at the front, her hands raised in the air, screaming so loudly that her voice seemed to pierce the very music itself. Ridge winced, his mind struggling to block out the noise.

"Come on," he muttered, half-irritated, half-amused. He tried to focus on the music again, but the scream only got louder, more jarring, drowning out everything else.

Suddenly, the sound was unbearable, more overwhelming than the music, more insistent. Ridge's frustration flared. The song, the crowd, the energy—it was all starting to slip away, to fade into the background, replaced by that maddening, never-ending scream.

And then, with a jolt that felt like a shock to his system, Ridge bolted upright from his cot.

His breath was ragged, and for a moment, he didn't know where he was. The noise had stopped. The concert had dissolved into the quiet of the dawn. Ridge's eyes darted around in panic, and the fog of sleep cleared enough for him to realize where he was—back in the camp, not in some crowded concert hall. His heart raced as the remnants of the dream faded into the cool early morning air.

Something was wrong.

He quickly scanned the campsite. The fire was dimming, and Lynx, Lincoln, and the warriors were still asleep. But then it hit him—the space beside him was empty.

Waverly.

"Waverly!" Ridge's voice cracked through the stillness, panic gripping him as his mind raced. She was gone. Where had she gone?

His instincts kicked in before his thoughts could catch up. He didn't even think about waking anyone else. Ridge sprang to his feet, tearing through the campsite and toward the shadows at the edge of the valley. The faint sound of screams pierced the air—Waverly's screams.

His heart stopped.

Waverly's voice.

He could hear the fear in her voice, her voice growing fainter with each scream.

"Waverly!" Ridge shouted again, running toward the sound. His legs pumped furiously as his heart thudded in his chest. He knew he couldn't waste time. She was in danger, and the screams told him it was getting worse. The panic in his veins grew.

Ridge reached the edge of the valley, and there—through the trees and morning fog—he saw it.

Waverly was sinking. Her feet and legs were buried up to her knees, the ground beneath her more like quicksand, swallowing her whole. She was struggling, her arms flailing, but she was sinking fast. Her face was barely above the surface, her eyes wide with terror.

Her screams were frantic now, barely a whisper as the earth beneath her seemed to drag her further down.

"No!" Ridge's chest tightened. He rushed forward, his eyes never leaving her.

The warriors stirred behind him, Lincoln and Lynx rushing to his side as they all neared the edge of the sinkhole. "Waverly!" Lincoln shouted, his voice hoarse with urgency.

Ridge reached the edge of the quicksand-like trap just as Waverly's body sank deeper. She was screaming in terror, her voice weak, the panic in her chest growing.

"Waverly, stay calm!" Ridge shouted, his voice cracking with raw fear. "We're coming for you! Stay calm, okay?"

His hands reached out, but he wasn't sure how to help her. The earth was swallowing her, the sand shifting like water, pulling her deeper with every second. Ridge's mind raced, and in that moment, something—something inside him clicked.

His eyes narrowed. He felt the stirring within him—it was raw, untamed.

"Solidify!" Ridge shouted, his hand shooting forward toward the shifting ground beneath her.

The air around him seemed to shimmer as his power swirled outward, wrapping around the quicksand-like trap. For a heartbeat, nothing happened, but then the ground beneath Waverly began to harden, solidifying around her legs, locking her in place. It wasn't enough to pull her free—but it stopped her from sinking further.

She gasped, her body trembling from the strain. "Ridge!" she cried out, her voice desperate.

But Ridge knew something was wrong. As soon as he spoke, Lincoln's voice rang out behind him.

"Ridge, stop! You're trapping her!"

Ridge's heart skipped a beat as he realized what he had done. The earth had solidified—but in doing so, he had inadvertently trapped Waverly even more, her body held fast by the thick, hardened earth.

"No!" Ridge shouted, his hands shaking as he pulled at the earth with all his strength. "I didn't mean to—I—"

"Back off!" Lincoln ordered, his voice urgent. The Arcmyrin warrior leader, Rykas, was already barking commands to his people, who raced to find tools to help. But it was Lynx who reached Ridge first, his face full of panic.

"Don't just stand there, we need to dig her out!" Lynx cried, his hands already scrambling through the hardened ground, desperately trying to free Waverly.

"I'll help!" Ridge shouted, falling to his knees beside his nephew. They both dug into the ground with frantic urgency, their hands scraping through the hard earth, trying to create enough space to free Waverly.

"We need something better," Rykas called out to his warriors, his voice sharp. "We must find a shovel or a spade! Quickly!"

The warriors scattered, leaving Ridge and Lynx to dig with their bare hands, their desperation growing as the seconds ticked by.

Minutes passed—long, agonizing minutes—and they were making little headway. Ridge's arms were burning, his hands scraped raw from the rough earth, but he kept going. Waverly's cries were softer now, her voice weakening.

Ridge's heart pounded. He couldn't lose her. Not like this. Not after everything they had fought for. He had to get her out.

Finally, after what felt like hours, Ridge stood up, his chest heaving with effort. He turned to the others. "Everyone, get back! I have to do this my way."

"What are you doing?" Lincoln shouted, his eyes filled with fear.

"Just trust me," Ridge said, his voice strained. He turned to Waverly, kneeling behind her, and placed his hands on the earth on either side of her shoulders. "Waverly, close your eyes. Trust me."

She nodded, her face pale and exhausted, but she closed her eyes as Ridge directed.

With all his strength, Ridge slammed his fists into the earth on either side of her, sending shockwaves through the ground. The earth cracked open beneath him, splitting like the shell of an egg. He forced his fists through the hard ground, breaking up the dirt as he went.

Finally, with a great heave, Ridge reached Waverly's sides and pulled her free, his arms locking around her as he dragged her up and out of the earth.

She gasped, coughing for air, and Ridge collapsed back, taking her with him. The ground was still shaking beneath them, the echoes of the force Ridge had used still rippling through the air.

The warriors around them cheered, their voices filled with relief, but their triumph was short-lived.

Suddenly, the earth beneath them groaned. The ground trembled, the very mountains shuddering beneath their feet.

Ridge's heart leapt into his throat.

Something was coming.

35

The ground trembled beneath their feet. At first, it was a subtle vibration, almost imperceptible, but it quickly grew stronger, a low rumbling that set the air humming with ominous energy. The peaceful silence of the camp was shattered by the unmistakable sound of shifting earth—a dark, unsettling sound as though the very core of Arcmyrin was waking up, stretching, and reaching toward them.

"Do you feel that?" Waverly's voice broke the stillness, her eyes darting around as she took in the sudden shift in the atmosphere. The air was thick with tension, the ground around them quivering with an unnatural force.

Ridge, still holding onto Waverly after the desperate rescue, stiffened. "Something's wrong. Get ready."

The warriors, ever vigilant, immediately dropped into battle stances, their eyes scanning the horizon. They weren't sure what was coming, but they were prepared for anything. Lincoln's gaze sharpened as he tried to make sense of the growing disturbance.

And then, through the morning fog and shadows, they saw it.

At first, it was just a ripple in the earth, dark shadows stretching upward from the ground like tendrils of smoke. But as the shadows took form, they began to crawl toward the group, coiling and twisting like living things. They moved with purpose, slowly and deliberately, as if drawn to the family like magnets, their dark presence permeating the air around them.

"I don't like this," Lynx said, his voice a low growl, his body instinctively tense. He didn't need to ask. He knew these shadows—he could feel them in his bones. They were a harbinger of something far worse.

"They're coming for us," Ridge muttered, "All of them."

The shadows seemed to pulse with an unholy energy, their movements jerky and unnatural. And in the midst of this mass of darkness, there was a figure—a human shape. As it drew closer, the figure became clearer, emerging from the swirling shadows like a dark lord rising from the depths of the earth.

Lincoln's heart skipped a beat as he saw the figure's face.

"No..." Lincoln whispered under his breath, his stomach twisting in a mixture of disbelief and fury.

Ridge looked at him, confused. "What is it, Lincoln?"

Lincoln took a step forward, his eyes locked on the figure. His voice was barely a whisper, but it carried a weight that made the air feel even thicker. "It's Gideon."

Ridge's expression shifted from confusion to shock. "Our uncle...?"

Lincoln's face was a mask of anger, the recognition clear in his eyes. His hands clenched into fists. "Not anymore. He's no longer our uncle."

The figure—Gideon, or whatever he had become—stepped fully into the clearing, his presence radiating with a dark energy that seemed to infect the very ground beneath his feet. His skin was pale, his once-kind features twisted by years of betrayal, and his eyes glowed with an unnatural light, flickering with malice.

He smiled as he looked at Lincoln, Ridge, and the rest of the group, the shadows around him moving like extensions of his will. The dark mist that followed him felt like it was closing in on the group, suffocating the very air around them.

"Lincoln," Gideon's voice was cold, taunting. "It's been a long time, hasn't it? I see you've found your way here, just as I knew you would."

Waverly, still trying to make sense of the situation, looked between Lincoln and Gideon. "What's going on?" Her voice was shaky, still unsure of how to process what was happening. "Who is he?"

Ridge's gaze was fixed on the man who had once been a part of their family, the man who had once been a trusted ally. Now, he was something else—something dangerous. "This isn't Gideon anymore," Ridge said, his voice tinged with disgust. "This is something much worse."

The air crackled with the rising tension, the warriors on high alert. But it was Elara's voice that pierced the silence next, her holographic form materializing in front of them. The golden glow of her eyes shone with righteous fury.

"Gideon," she spat, her voice a mixture of disgust and disbelief. "Or should I say Patereon now?"

Gideon—Patereon—smirked, his eyes flashing with dark amusement. "Ah, Elara. Always so quick to judge. You should learn to call me by my true name. Patereon—the one who will rise to claim Arcmyrin and bring it into the new order. The true order."

The air around the group seemed to grow heavier, the temperature rising as if Arcmyrin itself were reacting to Patereon's words. The shadows surged forward, their mass shifting like a storm about to descend upon them.

"You've failed, Elara," Patereon continued, his voice full of contempt. "I will rule this planet. Arcmyrin was meant to be mine. You should have never allowed the Beaumonts to interfere. But no matter, the world will be mine soon enough. Once I conquer this planet, I will move on to Tanzlora. And then Earth... Earth will be last. I'll wipe out the legacy of the Beaumont family—every last trace of your so-called 'special' gifts. The universe doesn't need your kind of order."

Lincoln took a step forward, his anger palpable. "You've betrayed everyone, Gideon. You've brought ruin to our worlds. There's no redemption for you."

Patereon's laughter filled the air, bitter and full of malice. "Redemption? Do you think I need it? No, Lincoln. What I've done has been a necessary evolution. The old order is weak. It's time for something stronger, something real. The Beaumonts have no place in the new world I will create."

Elara's form flickered, her voice cutting through the tension. "You were chosen by Origin to hold the gift of Air, Gideon. You were meant to be a protector of Arcmyrin, a force for good. And yet, you chose the path of darkness. Now, you will face the consequences of that choice. Your day of reckoning will come, and when you stand before Origin, there will be no forgiveness for the evil you've wrought."

Patereon scoffed, his eyes narrowing. "I will not be judged by the likes of you. I will be the one to decide the fate of Arcmyrin—and all the worlds connected to it."

Before anyone could react, Patereon's hand shot out toward them, his fingers pointed in their direction. The ground beneath them began to shake violently as dark energy rippled through the air. The shadows surged forward, swirling like a storm, and before anyone could react, Patereon turned to face them one last time.

His eyes locked on Waverly, and his lips curled into a cruel smile.

"You and I, Waverly," Patereon said slowly, his voice dark and venomous. "We share the same gift. The gift of Air. But you will never be able to reach Ambreela, the spirit of Air. You will never connect with her the way I have. I alone hold the true connection to her. You will never be able to call her power—she belongs to me."

He took a long, drawn-out breath, as if savoring the moment. "I may have failed today, but I will not fail again. There is only room in this universe for one person to hold the connection to Ambreela. And that person... is me."

With those final words, Patereon raised his hand, and the shadows surged around him, engulfing him in darkness. In an instant, he and his followers disappeared back into the earth, leaving only a whisper of his presence behind.

The ground trembled once more, as if Arcmyrin itself was recoiling from Patereon's threat. The warriors stood frozen, the air still thick with the weight of what had just occurred.

The Beaumonts stood together, their bodies tense, their minds racing with the enormity of the words they had just heard. The threat was not over—it was just beginning.

36

The lingering feeling of unease hung heavy in the air long after Patereon and his dark shadows disappeared into the earth. The ground, still trembling from his ominous retreat, had settled into an eerie silence that made it feel as though the world was holding its breath. The Beaumonts, still standing in their battle stances, exchanged tense glances. The Arcmyrin warriors, having seen many battles in their time, were visibly unsettled by the appearance of Patereon—and the threat he had just issued.

Lincoln stood tall, his fists clenched at his sides, his face filled with a quiet fury. Ridge and Waverly were still trying to process everything they had just witnessed, the gravity of Patereon's words sinking in. Lynx, ever the skeptic, crossed his arms over his chest, though his eyes held an unreadable expression.

"What now?" Ridge finally asked, breaking the silence. His voice was thick with disbelief. "That was a warning. We're not safe here."

"We never were," Lincoln said, his voice calm but edged with anger. "Patereon's words were a declaration of war. He wants Arcmyrin, Tanzlora, and Earth—all of them. And he's not going to stop until he gets them."

Waverly's eyes were wide with concern. "He's lying, right? He can't possibly have Ambreela's connection—she's... she's a part of me too."

But there was doubt in her voice, the fear creeping in despite her resolve. She had seen the way Patereon had spoken, the absolute certainty in his voice that only one person could hold the connection to the spirit of Air. She had always known that her gift was something special, something vital, but Patereon's claim gnawed at her. Could she really reach Ambreela?

"We have to go after him," Lincoln said, breaking her thoughts. "We can't let him gather his strength, and we certainly can't let him spread his poison through Arcmyrin and beyond."

Rykas, the Arcmyrin warrior leader, stepped forward. His gaze was hard, his golden eyes sharp with focus. "The warriors are ready to defend you," he said, his voice unwavering. "We've trained for such a time as this. But you're right—Patereon will not stop. If he is truly the one who controls the connection to Ambreela, then we need to stop him before he manipulates that power for evil."

"Then we have to find him," Ridge said, his voice filled with determination. "We can't just sit around waiting for him to strike again. I don't care how strong he is—we'll fight him together."

Waverly nodded, her mind still reeling from Patereon's words. She could feel the weight of her gift now more than ever, the pressure to prove herself, to connect with Ambreela and fulfill the legacy of the Beaumonts. It was an impossible task, but she had never backed down from a challenge before.

"We will find him," she said, her voice steady. "But we can't do it alone. We need to reach the next spirit—Earth. We need more guidance, and we need to restore balance. We can't waste time."

Lynx stepped up beside her, his expression serious, though his hands remained tucked in his pockets. "I'm with you, Waverly. We've come this far, and I won't let Patereon win. But we need a plan. Charging into his lair isn't going to do anything but get us killed."

"We know where we need to go," Lincoln said, turning his gaze toward the distant horizon. "The next spirit—Terraveta—should be in the Greenway Plains. We'll need to get there fast, before Patereon can figure out a way to release her for his own gain."

"We'll need more than just speed," Rykas added. "We will need to pass through the Windspire Cliffs which are dangerous. They're high and unpredictable. If we are to succeed, we will need both strength and strategy."

"And stealth," Ridge muttered, eyes scanning the landscape, his mind already turning to the next challenge. "Patereon knows we're after him. We need to be smart."

With a final look at each other, the group knew the time for reflection had passed. It was time for action. The warriors prepared their gear, and the Beaumonts readied themselves for what lay ahead. The weight of the morning was already pressing on their shoulders. They had a long way to go.

As the warriors and the Beaumonts set out from the camp, the winds around the mountains began to pick up, swirling like a warning. The air felt charged, crackling with the energy of the land itself. Waverly felt the pull of the winds, as though Ambreela was calling to her, urging her to come closer, to seek her power.

The journey through the Windspire Cliffs was long, the terrain rough and uneven. The forest gradually gave way to rocky outcroppings and sweeping grasslands. The warriors led the way, their sharp eyes scanning the terrain for any signs of danger. Lincoln and Ridge kept a close eye on the surrounding cliffs, aware that Patereon's presence could be anywhere.

As they traveled deeper into the heart of Arcmyrin, Waverly began to focus inward. She knew she needed to connect with Ambreela, to call upon the spirit of Air and awaken her true power. She had felt the stirrings of it inside her, the wind that tugged at her hair, the pressure in her chest as though the very air around her was alive. But Patereon's words still haunted her.

She glanced at her family, her heart heavy with the burden of the task ahead. She had to prove herself. She had to show them that she could reach Ambreela.

Nightfall came quickly, and with it, a rising wind. The warriors set up camp near a small stream, the sound of the rushing water soothing in the otherwise still air. The wind around them howled through the trees, the trees themselves swaying and creaking under the pressure of the gusts. It felt as if the wind was alive, an unpredictable force waiting to be tamed.

Waverly sat by the fire, her hands clasped together as she stared into the flames. She could feel the pull of Ambreela's power deep within her, but it was hard to focus. Her mind kept drifting back to Patereon's words. Was he right? Did she really have the connection to Ambreela that he had claimed? Was she really strong enough to awaken the spirit of Air and restore balance?

She felt a hand on her shoulder and turned to find Lincoln standing beside her, his expression soft but filled with concern.

"You're thinking too much," he said, his voice calm. "You've already proven yourself. You've helped me connect with Mistara, and Lynx to Ignissa. You're ready for this. You just have to believe in yourself."

Waverly looked at him, the weight of his words sinking in. "I don't know if I can, dad. I don't know if I can reach Ambreela."

"You already have, when you lifted the fog to save your brother," he said, his voice full of conviction. "We all have our doubts, Waverly. But you're stronger than you think. And we're all in this together. You won't face this alone."

Waverly's eyes softened as she nodded, the weight of her fears lifting slightly. Her family's support was all she needed. She didn't have to prove herself alone. Together, they were unstoppable.

As the night deepened and the fire flickered in the quiet air, Waverly closed her eyes, letting the wind surround her. She allowed herself to relax, to feel the spirit of Air tugging at her, pulling her closer to the heart of Arcmyrin. She had to trust herself.

And then, as if summoned by her thoughts, the wind shifted. It swirled around her, gentle at first, and then stronger, as if calling to her, beckoning her to follow.

A soft whisper in the wind, almost like a voice, seemed to say, Come, Waverly.

Her eyes snapped open. The wind was rising, swirling with the promise of something greater. Ambreela's presence was there, just out of reach.

She stood, her heart racing, her breath steady as she began to follow the wind, ready to connect with the spirit of Air and reclaim her power. The others followed behind her, their expressions filled with determination. But ahead of them, the Windspire Cliffs loomed—a dark, towering mountain range, the winds howling between them.

37

The journey to the Windspire Cliffs had been long, the treacherous terrain slowing their progress as the wind picked up and the air grew colder. Despite their growing urgency, the Beaumont family had been making their way through the rocky paths that wound deeper into Arcmyrin's wild heart. The warriors, ever watchful, led them through the dense, unyielding forests, the path to the Windspire now uncertain.

But just as they began to feel the weight of their fatigue, Rykas, the Arcmyrin warrior leader, stopped abruptly at the base of a massive stone formation—a cliffside nearly hidden from view by thick trees. His keen eyes swept over the area, the air around him buzzing with energy.

"We're close," he muttered, his voice low. He turned to the group, his golden eyes gleaming with a sense of reverence. "The spirit of Earth lies here, in the heart of Arcmyrin. Terraveta."

Terraveta.

Waverly felt the name resonate through her very bones, a soft vibration that seemed to come from deep within the earth itself. She had heard of the spirits—Mistara, Ignissa, and now, the name of Earth herself. But she had never imagined that she would stand on the very ground where they resided, where the world's balance was restored.

"Is she... inside?" Ridge asked, his voice steady but filled with a quiet awe.

Rykas nodded. "The spirit of Earth is not like the others. Terraveta is not bound by location in the same way as the other spirits. She is of the land itself, as old as Arcmyrin, and her presence permeates the very earth beneath our feet. To awaken her, we must offer ourselves to the land and open ourselves to the deep currents of power that lie hidden within."

The group exchanged glances. Waverly took a deep breath, grounding herself in the moment. She had already watched her family connect with the spirits of water and fire. But this—this was different. The spirit of Earth was the cornerstone, the foundation that connected all of Arcmyrin. Without Terraveta, the land itself would wither.

They made their way to the stone formation, the air thick with anticipation. The trees here were ancient, their roots spreading deep into the ground, wrapping around boulders and cliffs. The land seemed to pulse with life, a steady rhythm that echoed through their feet and into their hearts.

"I don't understand," Ridge said, his eyes narrowed as he surveyed the rocky outcrop. "How do I reach her? How do I call out to the spirit of Earth?"

"It's not a question of reaching her," Rykas explained. "The spirit of Earth is present in all things—the trees, the stones, the very soil beneath us. It is about opening your senses to her presence, connecting with the land itself."

As the group stood before the cliffside, the wind shifted around them, carrying the unmistakable scent of wet earth and rich soil. Ridge closed his eyes, reaching inward, letting the vibrations from the ground rise through his body. The earth seemed to hum beneath him, a steady pulse, as if it were alive, breathing. His senses heightened, and he could feel the weight of centuries in the very soil beneath his feet.

Suddenly, the ground trembled beneath them. Not in fear, but as though something ancient was awakening.

From the depths of the stone formation, a soft glow began to emerge—a warm, golden light that seemed to come from deep within the earth. The rocks around them shifted, parting slowly as though the earth itself was making way for something. The light grew brighter, and from the fissures in the rocks, a figure began to materialize.

She was massive—towering over them like the very cliffs themselves. Terraveta's form was made of earth and stone, her body woven with roots and vines, flowing like rivers of rock and soil. Her skin was a warm brown, like the earth after a rain, and her eyes glowed with the light of the stars. She was both ancient and timeless, her presence as enduring as the planet itself.

"Terraveta," Ridge whispered, awe filling his voice.

The earth spirit turned her glowing gaze to the group, and though she spoke with the voice of the land, it was a voice that resonated with the deep, soft rumble of the planet's core.

"Beaumonts," she said, her voice gentle yet powerful, "you have come seeking balance. You have awakened the waters and the fires. But it is the earth that will bind it all together."

Ridge stepped forward, feeling the earth's pull more than ever. "We seek your help," he said, his voice steady but tinged with urgency. "We need to find Ambreela, the spirit of Air. She is the last element we need to restore balance to Arcmyrin. Will you help us?"

Terraveta's eyes seemed to shimmer with ancient wisdom, the weight of her gaze enveloping them all. She paused for a moment, as if considering their request, before speaking again.

"The air and the earth are deeply connected," she said softly, the rumble of her voice like the sound of distant thunder. "But the path to Ambreela is not one that can be easily traversed. The shadows that rise from the depths of the core of Arcmyrin are working to tear the balance apart. They seek to control the elements, to pervert the gifts of Origin. And they will stop at nothing to take what they believe is theirs."

Lincoln's expression darkened at the mention of the shadows. "Patereon," he muttered, his voice tight with anger.

Terraveta's gaze shifted to him, and her voice softened. "Yes. Patereon, the one who was once called Gideon. He betrayed his gift, and now, the shadows that fester within him seek to consume all. He is not just a danger to Arcmyrin—he is a threat to the very balance of all the worlds."

Waverly felt a chill run down her spine. She had known that the dark forces they were facing were dangerous, but hearing the weight of Terraveta's words made it clear just how dire their situation was.

"We need Ambreela," Ridge said, stepping forward. "We need to connect with the spirit of Air before Patereon can manipulate that power for himself. Please, Terraveta, show us the way."

The earth spirit's gaze softened. "To find Ambreela, you must first understand the heart of the planet itself. The core of Arcmyrin is where the elements converge, where the deepest forces of the world are held in balance. If you wish to reach Ambreela, you must pass through the core. But be warned—the path is perilous. The shadows that have risen from the depths will stop at nothing to prevent you from reaching your goal."

The air seemed to thicken around them, the ground pulsing with an energy that was both inviting and ominous.

"We are ready," Lincoln said, his voice unwavering. "We've come this far, and we won't stop until we've restored balance."

Terraveta's eyes softened, and she nodded slowly. "Then you must travel to the heart of Arcmyrin, where the core lies. The shadows will try to mislead you, to turn you away from your path. But you must stay true to your purpose. Trust in the gifts you hold."

Ridge felt a surge of energy within him at Terraveta's words. The air around him seemed to hum with possibility. He closed his eyes, allowing himself to sink deeper into the connection he was beginning to form with the earth. He could feel the pulse of the land, the deep rhythm of the world itself.

"We will go to the core," Ridge said, his voice filled with conviction. "And we will face whatever comes."

Terraveta's form seemed to flicker with light as if in approval, her golden eyes shimmering brightly.

"Then go with my blessing," she said, her voice rumbling like the sound of the earth shifting. "The journey will not be easy, but you will not face it alone. The earth will guide you."

With a final nod, the earth spirit began to fade back into the rocks, her form dissolving into the stone as if she were one with the land itself. The glow from her eyes slowly dimmed, but her presence lingered in the air, filling the group with a quiet sense of peace and strength.

As Terraveta disappeared, the warriors began to prepare for the next part of their journey. Ridge, feeling the weight of his connection to the earth spirit, turned to his family. His heart was still racing, but he knew they were closer than ever to their goal. The next step was to find the core of Arcmyrin, to face the shadows, and to seek out Ambreela.

"We have to move quickly," Rykas said, his voice resolute. "The longer we wait, the more Patereon will consolidate his power."

The group nodded, determination in their hearts. They had faced down fire, water, and earth—and now, they would face the very core of Arcmyrin itself.

The final piece of the puzzle was within reach. They would restore balance to the elements—and, with it, to the worlds they sought to protect.

38

Back at Sage Manor, the air was still and warm, the sun casting its afternoon light over the manicured gardens. The gazebo, an iconic feature of the estate, stood proudly in the center of the garden, surrounded by ivy-covered trellises and fragrant blooms that had long been nurtured by the land. The quiet hum of nature seemed to settle over everything, a soft background of birdsong and the distant rustle of leaves in the breeze.

Gran Celia sat in her favorite chair in the gazebo, the cool porcelain of her teacup held gently in her hands. Across from her, Francis Roller settled into her seat, her own teacup resting on the small wooden table between them. The two women had spent many afternoons here, drinking tea and discussing everything from family history to the matters of the world beyond their quiet home. Today, the conversation drifted toward a subject that had weighed heavily on Gran Celia's heart: the legacy of the Beaumont family and the remarkable connection they had with the land.

"I've been thinking a lot lately, Francis," Gran Celia began, her voice soft but filled with a quiet reverence. "About how far back this connection to the land goes. About how we—our family—have always been tied to the Earth."

Francis looked up, her curiosity piqued. "What do you mean?"

Gran Celia sighed, her gaze drifting out toward the sprawling gardens that surrounded them. The legacy of the Beaumont family was etched into every stone, every plant, and every part of the land. It was as if their story and the land's story were one and the same, intertwined through centuries of history. "It all started with Galen," she said, her voice growing softer. "Galen Alexander Ridgely Beaumont. The patriarch of this family."

Francis leaned forward, intrigued. "Tell me more. I know bits and pieces about him through the archives in the library, but I've never heard the full story."

Gran Celia's eyes softened as she began to recount the tale, the memories flooding back as if they had never left. "Galen was a man ahead of his time, a visionary, really. He wasn't just a farmer or a landowner. He was a lover of the Earth in a way I don't think anyone fully understood, even back then. He was a pioneer of sorts, but not just in the traditional sense. He had a gift—something that set him apart from everyone else."

Gran Celia paused, her fingers tracing the rim of her teacup, lost in thought. "He had an innate connection to the land—he could hear it, feel it in ways that no one else could. There are stories passed down through the family of how he would walk the land for hours, sometimes days, just listening. And when he planted, Francis—when he planted, it was like the Earth itself responded. The trees, the crops, the flowers—they grew quicker and stronger than anything anyone had seen before. It was as if the land wanted to grow for him, to flourish beneath his touch."

Francis sat in rapt attention, her eyes wide with wonder. "So, he wasn't just planting things like anyone else would?"

"No," Gran Celia said, her voice tinged with awe. "He was more than a gardener or a farmer. Galen was a steward of the land. He found a way to restore balance to the soil, to make it richer, more fertile. He came to this area for the cradle of forestry—the secret to the deep, ancient connection that exists between the Earth and all its living things. He was among those who pioneered techniques of reforestation, methods that allowed the land to heal itself, to regrow what had been taken, to restore what had been lost."

Gran Celia paused, her eyes distant as she thought back to the old stories. "You see, Galen had something no one else had. He was so in tune with the Earth. There's even a legend that he could speak to the trees, listen to them in a way no one else could. It's said that he could make the trees grow taller and stronger, faster than any other farmer or planter, simply by speaking to them."

Francis was quiet for a moment, taking in the enormity of the tale. "That's incredible. So, this connection—this ability to understand the land—it wasn't just something he had learned, it was a gift?"

Gran Celia nodded. "Yes. It was a gift from Origin. And over the years, that gift was passed down through the generations. Each Beaumont heir, each member of the family, learned from Galen's wisdom. We became stewards of the land, protectors of the Earth's balance, and we've carried that responsibility with us ever since. But even though we've done our part, I fear the Earth's connection is weakening. The world is changing, and so much of what Galen set in motion is being disrupted by forces we cannot control."

The weight of Gran Celia's words hung heavy in the air, and Francis understood the depth of her concern. The Beaumont family had always been close to the Earth, its roots growing deep in the soil of history. But now, with the disruption of the planet Arcmyrin's balance—especially with the threat of the Abasimtrox—it seemed as though that legacy was being threatened.

"It sounds like Galen was more than just a patriarch of the family. He was a guardian," Francis said softly, her voice reflecting the weight of Gran Celia's tale.

"A guardian, yes," Gran Celia agreed. "But more than that—he was a bridge. A bridge between the human world and the natural world. And through him, the Beaumonts became part of the Earth's greater legacy. And now, Lincoln, Waverly, Lynx, and Ridge—they carry that legacy forward, but the world is changing, and the balance is tipping."

As they sat there, lost in the conversation, the garden around them continued to hum with the quiet sounds of nature. A soft breeze stirred the leaves of the trees, and the scent of roses and jasmine filled the air. But for Gran Celia, there was more than just the physical world around her. The deep connection to the Earth, the legacy of Galen, seemed to seep through her veins. She could feel it, as though the land itself was speaking to her, reminding her of the importance of their family's mission.

The silence stretched between them, comfortable but heavy with unspoken thoughts, until Francis broke it gently. "Celia, can you tell me more about the portal?"

The portal had always been a part of their family's history, a mysterious relic hidden beneath the manor's grounds, and it had taken on an even more crucial role now that Gran Celia's children and grandchildren were caught up in the cosmic forces threatening the world.

"I don't know," Gran Celia admitted. "I don't fully understand the connection. But it seems... linked somehow, doesn't it? The portal, the elemental spirits, the land... I think they're all connected in ways we still don't fully comprehend."

A soft breeze blew through the gazebo, stirring the ivy around the pillars. Gran Celia glanced out over the manicured gardens again, her heart heavy with the weight of everything that had happened. She knew the family had come far, but the path ahead was still uncertain. The Beaumonts had a legacy to uphold, but with every passing day, the stakes seemed to grow higher.

"I fear," Gran Celia said softly, "that the balance we've fought for is fragile. That it's slipping through our fingers."

Francis didn't respond immediately. Instead, she let the quiet stretch between them, allowing Gran Celia's words to sink in. She knew that the weight of this legacy was not something that could easily be carried, but it had been passed down through generations for a reason. And now, as the world teetered on the brink of imbalance, the Beaumont family would once again have to rise to the challenge.

As the two women sat in comfortable silence, the warmth of the afternoon sun began to fade, casting long shadows across the garden. Gran Celia's eyes wandered back toward the stone doorway that led to the chamber beneath the gazebo—the very chamber where the portal lay hidden in darkness now, its energies gone.

"Francis," Gran Celia said, her voice trembling slightly. "Look."

Francis followed her gaze and frowned. There, emerging from the stone doorway that led to the chamber, a faint, flickering glow seemed to pulse from within. It was dim at first, just a soft illumination that seemed to pulse in time with the rhythm of the earth itself, as if the land were responding to something deep within.

"Do you see that?" Gran Celia asked, her voice tinged with disbelief.

Francis squinted, her brow furrowing. "Yes... It's faint, but it's there. Almost like a light. But how?"

Gran Celia rose slowly, her gaze fixed on the glowing light. "The portal or the orb... Something is happening."

They both stood, their chairs creaking as they pushed them back. Francis's heart began to race, her curiosity piqued, and her hand instinctively reached out toward Gran Celia's arm, steadying herself as they both approached the chamber door.

Gran Celia's pulse quickened, her instincts telling her that something was changing. Something deep within the chamber was awakening.

"I need to see this for myself," she murmured. "Either the portal or the orb is reacting... but to what?"

The glow from the doorway intensified slightly as they approached, casting a soft halo of light across the stone steps. The air seemed to hum with a quiet energy, and for the first time in a long while, Gran Celia felt something she hadn't in days—hope.

The door to the chamber beckoned.

39

The atmosphere inside the tent was thick with tension. Around a makeshift table they constructed out of large round stones, stood the Arcmyrin warriors and Elara, her holographic form shimmering with golden light in the center. They had gathered here to plan their next move—an essential and dangerous step on their journey to confront Patereon and release Ambreela, the spirit of Air.

The Arcmyrians had gathered together many times in the past to determine strategy for winning battles they faced, but the plans they were making today would be unlike any other.

Elara's form flickered slightly, her golden eyes intense as she addressed the warriors and the Beaumont family. "We are approaching a dangerous time, my friends. Patereon is not just a threat to Arcmyrin, but to all the worlds connected through the portal system. We must act swiftly to reach the core and release Ambreela before Patereon can corrupt her spirit and use her power for his own ends."

The Arcmyrian warriors nodded, their faces grim. They were warriors, used to facing battles of all kinds, but this was something different. Patereon—formerly known as Gideon—was no ordinary enemy. He had turned against his own kind, embracing darkness and wielding the power of the shadows. Now, with the gift of Air—once his own, and now shared with Waverly—he was poised to gain control of the element and reshape Arcmyrin to his twisted vision.

"Once we reach the core of Arcmyrin," Rykas, the Arcmyrian warrior leader, spoke up, his voice filled with resolve, "we will have to face not only Patereon, but the very heart of the planet itself. The balance of the elements is fragile, and if Patereon has truly corrupted the connection to Ambreela, we will need to act quickly to restore it."

Elara's gaze shifted to Waverly, her voice softer now. "Waverly, you are the key to releasing Ambreela. You share the gift of Air with Patereon, and you are the only one capable of reaching her. But the question remains: Can you do it?"

Waverly's heart skipped a beat at the weight of Elara's words. She had been preparing herself for this mission, but now, faced with the reality of what they were asking her to do, a cold knot of fear twisted in her stomach. "I can try," Waverly said, her voice trembling slightly. "I've watched the others connect with the elemental spirits—Mistara, Ignissa—but this... this is different."

Ridge, who had been standing silently beside Waverly, stepped forward. "You will do it," he said firmly, his eyes locked on his niece. "We've come this far, and we've seen what you can do. You're not alone in this."

Lincoln nodded in agreement, his voice steady. "We're with you, Waverly. No matter what."

Elara's form shimmered, and she placed a hand over her heart in a gesture of both comfort and warning. "Waverly, this is not just a matter of reaching Ambreela. The connection you share with Patereon is a double-edged sword. You must release Ambreela from his grasp—but it is unclear whether that will be enough. To truly free her, you may have to face Patereon directly."

At this, the room grew quiet. The weight of her words hung heavily over the group. Patereon's betrayal was well-known, but the thought of confronting him—facing the very man who had once been part of their family, who had once been a trusted ally—was almost unthinkable.

Waverly glanced at her family. Her heart was racing, her mind swirling with questions. Could she really face him? Could she truly defeat someone who had once been part of her family's legacy, even if he had turned to darkness?

Elara seemed to sense Waverly's uncertainty. "Waverly, I know this is difficult. But you must understand that if Patereon is not stopped, he will destroy everything. The connection you share with Ambreela is what gives you the power to restore balance. But it also means you must be the one to free her—by whatever means necessary."

The words felt like a cold wave washing over Waverly. She had never killed anything before—not intentionally. The most she had ever done was step on bugs in the woods accidentally crushing them beneath her heel. But this? This was different. This was a life she would be ending—a life that, until recently, had been part of her family. The gravity of the decision was too much to bear.

"I—I don't know if I can," Waverly whispered, her voice cracking with uncertainty. "I've never done anything like this before. Even with everything Patereon has done, I've never... I don't know if I can bring myself to kill him."

The room fell silent again, the weight of her words hanging in the air like a thick fog. Lincoln, who had been silently watching his daughter, stepped forward and placed a reassuring hand on her shoulder.

"You don't have to do this alone," Lincoln said softly. "We're all here. We've been through hell and back. You're strong enough for this. But if it comes to it—if you have to make that choice—remember that you're not just fighting for yourself. You're fighting for everyone. For Arcmyrin. For the whole universe."

Ridge stood beside Lincoln, his posture solid with determination. "You don't have to be afraid, Waverly. We'll all be with you. And when the time comes, if it comes to that, you'll make the choice that needs to be made. No one is asking you to do this alone."

Waverly swallowed hard, trying to steady her breath. The weight of their words was heavy, but it was the truth. This wasn't just about one life—it was about the fate of the entire worlds.

Elara, who had been watching Waverly closely, nodded. "You are not alone, Waverly. You will have all of us. But know this—if you cannot release Ambreela without facing Patereon, you must do what is necessary. You are the key to the balance of the elements. And sometimes, to restore balance, you must make hard choices."

The room fell silent again as everyone seemed to take in Elara's words. Waverly's mind was spinning, trying to grasp the enormity of what they were asking of her. The thought of it made her stomach churn.

Rykas, sensing the weight of the moment, stepped forward. "We will go with you, Waverly. We will protect you, every step of the way. But if it comes to the point where you must face him—where you must stop him for good—know that it is not you who will be making the decision alone. The whole of Arcmyrin stands with you."

Waverly nodded slowly, her heart pounding in her chest. The warriors' presence gave her strength, but the fear still lingered. She had never taken a life before, and now she was being asked to make a decision that could change the course of everything.

"We'll support you," Ridge said again, his voice filled with determination. "But you are the one who will decide how this ends. We're with you, no matter what."

Waverly closed her eyes, feeling the weight of their trust and their support. She was overwhelmed with the responsibility, but she knew they were right. This wasn't just about her—it was about the balance of the elements, about protecting her family, and about ensuring the safety of the worlds that depended on Arcmyrin.

After a long, tense silence, Elara spoke again, her voice filled with both compassion and resolve.

"We will move forward with the plan," Elara said.

40

Gran Celia descended the stone staircase, her heart pounding with anticipation. The stairwell was narrow and cold, the walls of the ancient manor cool to the touch. At the bottom of the staircase, they entered the large chamber.

Gran Celia's gaze immediately fell on the large orb in the center of the room. It was glowing faintly, casting a soft, iridescent light that seemed to pulse in time with her own heartbeat.

As Gran Celia approached, she noticed the small flame inside the orb, flickering gently. It hovered above a small puddle of iridescent water that shimmered with an ethereal glow, casting reflections across the chamber. The flame was no ordinary light; it seemed to shift, to grow, and to flicker in a way that was both magical and familiar.

Gran Celia gasped softly as she gazed at the phenomenon. "It's... it's a sign," she whispered in awe. "Francis, something is happening on Arcmyrin."

Francis, who had been following closely behind, stopped just a few paces away, her breath catching in her throat. She stared at the orb, her mind racing as a familiar sensation washed over her. There was something about the orb, something about the light within it, that felt strangely familiar. She took a step closer, narrowing her eyes as she tried to make sense of it.

Then it hit her—a memory, so vivid it was almost as if she could reach out and touch it.

"Celia..." Francis said, her voice trembling with disbelief. "I've seen this before. I've seen this exact thing. It's in a painting. In the parlor."

Gran Celia turned toward her, her excitement still buzzing in her chest. "What do you mean? What painting?"

Francis's gaze was fixed on the orb, her eyes wide with recognition. "The painting. The one over the mantel in the parlor." She stepped closer to the orb, her voice trailing off. "This looks exactly like what's in that painting."

Gran Celia's brow furrowed as she turned her attention back to the orb. She had never seen the connection before, but now that Francis had pointed it out, she could feel the truth in her words. The water, the flame—everything about this moment seemed to echo the painting Victoria had created decades ago. It was a family heirloom and had been hanging over the mantel in the parlor from the day Galen placed it there.

She had always admired the artwork, but never before had she considered its significance. The painting had always been a source of beauty and mystery, hanging proudly in the parlor. It depicted a serene and iridescent pond, set against a backdrop of deep blue ridge mountains. The sky was alive with hues of purples and pinks, the clouds wispy and windswept across the sky.

But the most striking feature of the painting had always been the sun. Instead of the typical golden orb that most landscape paintings portrayed, Victoria's painting had shown a large, flickering flame in place of the sun, casting its light and warmth over the entire scene. It had always seemed out of place, but now, standing before the orb, Gran Celia realized it had been a symbol—a sign.

Francis looked at Gran Celia, her face filled with urgency. "Celia, we have to look at the painting now. There's a connection—this orb, this flame—it's the same as what's in the painting. We need to see it for ourselves. We need to understand what it means."

Gran Celia shook her head, her excitement bubbling over. "I can't leave it. This is a sign, Francis, I agree. The portal—it's awakening. It's opening up. My family... they're coming back. This is what we've been waiting for."

"But Celia," Francis pressed, "this could be the key to unlocking the mystery of the portal. If there's a connection between the painting and this orb, then we might be able to understand what it's trying to tell us. We need to find the answers. The family could be closer than we think."

Gran Celia hesitated, her gaze flicking between the orb and Francis. She had spent days waiting for a sign like this, hoping that the portal would reactivate. And now, it seemed that it would, that the light and flame inside the orb were indications of that and she did not want to miss this moment.

But at the same time, Francis was right. There was a deeper meaning to this, something hidden within the family's history that she couldn't ignore.

With a final glance at the orb, Gran Celia sighed and nodded. "You're right, Francis. We need to see the painting. If there's a connection, we must understand it. Let's go."

Francis led the way, her pace quickening as they ascended the stone staircase, her mind racing with possibilities. Gran Celia followed close behind, her heart still fluttering with the excitement of what lay ahead.

As they reached the parlor, Francis crossed the room to the mantel, where the large painting of the iridescent pond had hung for decades. The light from the fire flickered off the glass, casting shadows across the vibrant colors of the scene. The painting had always been a source of wonder, but now, standing before it, it felt like a map—a guide to something much larger than either of them had ever imagined.

Gran Celia stood beside Francis, staring at the painting, her breath catching as she saw the similarities between it and the orb in the chamber. The sky, the colors, the flame in place of the sun—everything about the scene matched the orb.

"This is it," Gran Celia whispered, her fingers trembling as she traced the outline of the flame in the painting. "This is what's been calling us all these years. This is the portal, the heart of it all."

Francis nodded slowly, her eyes filled with a mix of awe and realization. "The flame in the painting... it's not just a symbol of light. It's a beacon. It's a signal. And it's tied to the portal. The flame is the key."

Gran Celia felt a deep sense of connection, as though the mystery of the portal had finally begun to unravel. The painting had always seemed like a work of art, a beautiful landscape, but now, it was clear that it held the answers they had been searching for all along. The flame in the sky was not just a light—it was a force, a beacon that had been guiding them toward the truth.

But there was something more—something even more profound than the connection between the orb and the painting. Gran Celia could feel it deep in her bones, a sense of something ancient awakening, a force that was larger than any one family, any one person. This was not just about the Beaumonts—it was about the balance of the worlds.

"This flame," Gran Celia murmured, "it's not just a light. It's a force, a power that will guide us back to the truth."

Francis looked at Gran Celia, her expression filled with both wonder and concern. "Celia, what do you think it means? The orb, the flame... everything we've seen?"

Gran Celia's eyes flickered with understanding, but there was a sadness in her gaze too. "It means the portal is opening again. It means that my family is coming back through. And it means that the Earth, the balance—it's shifting. Something has begun, and we can't stop it. But I don't think we're meant to."

As they stood there, staring at the painting, Gran Celia's heart filled with a mixture of hope and trepidation. The family's legacy was being reborn, the portal was awakening, and their journey was only just beginning.

"I think," Gran Celia said softly, her voice full of resolve, "it's time for us to step forward and follow the light."

41

The suns had set, casting a dim orange glow over the rugged landscape of Arcmyrin as the group made camp on the edge of a cliff, the wind whipping through the trees and rustling the leaves. Waverly sat on a large rock near the fire, her arms wrapped around her knees, staring out at the horizon. The night was quiet, but the weight of her thoughts was loud and relentless. Every time she closed her eyes, she saw Patereon's face—twisted by darkness, filled with malice and a power she could barely comprehend.

But worse still, she could hear his words echoing in her mind: "You will never be able to reach Ambreela, the spirit of Air. I have the connection. It is mine."

A shiver ran through her body, and she pressed her hand to her chest as though to calm the storm brewing inside her. She had never wanted to kill anyone—not even Patereon, despite the atrocities he had committed. She had never taken a life—how could she now? But Elara's words haunted her. If it came to it, she might have to kill Patereon in order to free Ambreela.

Waverly closed her eyes tightly, trying to block out the images of the battle to come, but the weight of her mission, the fear of what it might require of her, was overwhelming. She wasn't sure she was strong enough for what was ahead.

Beside her, Lynx was sitting cross-legged on the ground, his youthful face lit by the firelight. He was too young to fully grasp the gravity of the situation, but that didn't make him any less present. He had always been a source of comfort to her, even if sometimes his words were... well, a bit off.

"Hey," Lynx said, his voice full of innocence and, as always, unintentional bluntness. "You know, I think it'll be okay. I mean, Gideon's old, right? He's, like, super old. Like, ancient. He's not going to be around much longer anyway."

Waverly's head snapped toward her brother, confusion and disbelief flashing in her eyes. "What are you talking about, Lynx?"

Lynx shrugged nonchalantly, the fire reflecting in his eyes. "Well, I mean... he's been doing evil stuff for a while. He's super old, and evil people don't live as long as good people. So, you're kind of doing him a favor, right? Freeing him from being evil. Plus, if you kill him, you're saving the worlds, so..." He trailed off, clearly thinking of the logic behind his words. "It's a win-win."

Waverly's mouth fell open, her heart sinking at the casual way Lynx spoke of life and death. She wanted to lash out, to scream that he didn't understand, that no one did, but instead, she just sat there, stunned and speechless. Lynx was too young, too innocent to understand the depth of what she was facing, and that was part of the problem.

In an uncharacteristic move, Waverly stood abruptly, turning her back to him. She couldn't process what he had said. She didn't want to think about it. The thought of taking Patereon's life—of ending anyone's life—made her stomach twist. And yet, the crushing weight of the mission she had to complete settled on her shoulders more heavily with every passing second.

She didn't respond to Lynx, didn't turn around to explain herself. She simply walked away, heading toward the far side of the camp, where the trees grew denser. She needed space, needed time to think alone. The sound of her footsteps was drowned out by the wind, but her thoughts were louder than ever.

Lynx didn't understand. No one did. The fear, the doubt, the anxiety gnawed at her, and the quiet loneliness of the situation seemed to grow, expanding like a black hole in her chest. Elara had said she would not be alone. That was true, in a sense. She had her family, the Arcmyrian warriors, but at the core of it, this was her mission. She was the one who shared the connection with Patereon, the one who could free Ambreela. But no one could understand how she was feeling. Not truly.

The night was cold, and as she walked deeper into the trees, she felt the chill of the wind biting at her skin. She hugged her arms tighter around herself, wishing that the world could stop for just a moment. A small part of her wished for the peaceful days back at Sage Manor when things were simpler, before they knew about the portal, before they knew about the dangers that lay ahead.

But those days were gone. The war they were fighting now was bigger than any of them could imagine.

She found a large rock near the base of a tree and sat down, wrapping her knees to her chest. She gazed at the stars above, the expanse of the universe stretching out before her. The quietness of the night only made her feel more isolated. It was as if she were on the edge of the world, standing alone in the vastness of it all, unsure of what to do next.

Why had it all come to this? Why had she been chosen for this mission? She was just a girl from Galen Valley, a girl who had lived a relatively quiet life. And now, here she was, standing on a strange world, tasked with saving it from destruction—and possibly having to kill the very person who had once been part of her family.

She closed her eyes, trying to shut out the storm of thoughts. "I can't do this," she whispered to herself. "I can't kill anyone. Not even Patereon."

The sound of the wind seemed to respond, its soft whispers brushing against her skin, but she couldn't shake the weight of her fear. She had never taken a life before—not in any deliberate way. She couldn't just end someone's life, even if they were evil, even if they deserved it. She didn't know how to reconcile that.

The wind stirred again, a strange feeling stirring in the air around her. The breeze felt... different. Warmer, perhaps, as if it carried something more than just the coolness of the night. Her mind flickered back to the words of Elara. "You are the key. You have the power to release Ambreela."

Her heart raced at the thought of Ambreela. The spirit of Air, the one who had been trapped for so long by the dark shadows. She had to free her. But how? What would it cost her?

Suddenly, as if the world had shifted in response to her plea, Waverly felt a soft pressure against her chest. It wasn't physical, but it was unmistakable—a presence, a feeling that she wasn't as alone as she had thought. The air around her shimmered, and then, with a sudden burst of warmth, she felt a presence in her mind.

She gasped, her eyes flying open, and before her stood a vision—a figure clothed in shimmering white light, her form ethereal and radiant, her features soft and gentle. Waverly's breath caught in her throat as she recognized the spirit before her.

"Ambreela," Waverly whispered, standing quickly.

The spirit of Air smiled warmly, her eyes filled with an ancient wisdom. "Waverly, you have come."

Waverly's heart thudded in her chest. "I... I don't know what to do," she said, her voice trembling. "I can't do this. I can't kill Patereon, even if he's become evil. I don't know if I'm strong enough. I've never killed anyone before."

Ambreela's form shimmered gently, her presence calming. "You are stronger than you realize, Waverly. Your gift is vast, and it is meant to set things right. The path before you is not an easy one, but it is necessary. You are the one who can release me, and in doing so, restore balance."

Waverly shook her head, her chest tight with emotion. "But... but what if it requires killing him? What if I have to take his life to free you? I can't do that. I can't live with that."

Ambreela's voice was soft but filled with an unwavering understanding. "You do not have to kill to release me, Waverly. Your fear holds you back. But you must face your inner darkness to free me. Patereon's time has come, yes, but his life is not for you to take. It is his own choices that have led him to this point."

The vision of Ambreela began to fade, but her presence lingered in Waverly's heart. "Do not let fear guide you, Waverly," she said softly. "You are not alone. And you will be ready when the time comes."

With that, the vision of Ambreela faded, leaving Waverly alone in the quiet stillness of the forest. Her heart was pounding, but something had changed inside her. The fear that had gripped her seemed to lessen, replaced by a deeper sense of clarity.

She could do this. She didn't have to kill Patereon. She would find another way—there had to be another way.

Waverly stood up, a new determination in her step. She would free Ambreela. She would restore balance to Arcmyrin. And she would do it on her terms.

As she turned back toward the camp, she felt the weight of the world pressing on her, but she felt a new strength rising within her, the clarity Ambreela had given her beginning to settle into her bones. The fear still lingered, but now it was tempered by the understanding that the path ahead was hers to shape, not bound by the harsh necessity she had once feared. She would face the darkness, but she would do so on her own terms.

As she returned to the camp, the others had gathered around the fire, speaking in low tones. Ridge was standing near the edge of the camp, his back to her, and Lincoln was checking their supplies. Lynx, ever the curious one, noticed her first.

"Hey, Waverly! Where'd you run off to?" Lynx called, his youthful curiosity shining through as he stood up from his spot by the fire.

Waverly smiled faintly, not ready to share the depth of what she had just experienced. "Just needed some air," she replied, her voice steady but filled with a quiet resolve that surprised even her. She felt more sure now, more at peace with the challenge that lay ahead.

She moved toward the fire, where her family had made camp. Ridge turned around at the sound of her voice, his expression softening when he saw the determined look on her face.

"There you are," he said, his voice a mix of relief and concern. "You've been gone for a while. You okay?"

Waverly nodded slowly, her eyes meeting his. "I'm okay. I'm ready." The words felt like a weight lifting off her chest. She was ready.

Lincoln, noticing the change in her demeanor, stepped closer. "Are you sure?" he asked, his voice laced with both love and caution. She was his daughter and he was being protective of her, seeing the burden on her shoulders made him hesitant to let her carry it alone. "This won't be easy."

"I know," Waverly said quietly. "But I'm not alone. I'm not alone in this. And I'll find a way to make it right." She met his gaze, her resolve hardening. "I'll release Ambreela. I'll restore the balance."

Ridge's eyes softened, and he placed a hand on her shoulder. "Whatever happens, Waverly, we're with you. We'll stand by you every step of the way."

Lynx nodded eagerly, as if the whole conversation made perfect sense to him. "Yeah! We've got your back. No matter what. And anyway, if you can get Ambreela to help, I bet she'll make sure everything goes right."

Waverly's heart lifted at their words, though the uncertainty still lingered deep inside her. She knew she couldn't predict what would happen when they reached the core of Arcmyrin. She didn't know if she'd be able to connect with Ambreela in time, or if Patereon's power would be too strong. But she knew one thing for certain—she would face it. She would meet the challenge and do whatever it took to restore balance to the worlds.

As the night stretched on, the fire crackled and popped, sending sparks up into the cool night air. The warriors had settled in for the night, their quiet murmurs fading as they drifted off to sleep. But Waverly remained awake, her thoughts racing as she sat on the edge of the camp, lost in the stars above.

The weight of the decision she would soon have to make still pressed on her, but now she could feel Ambreela's presence with her, like a gentle whisper in the wind. She closed her eyes, remembering the spirit's words: You are not alone.

"Tomorrow," Waverly whispered to herself, "we face what comes. Together."

42

The early morning light broke through the thick canopy of trees, casting long shadows over the rugged terrain of Arcmyrin. The air was crisp and cool, the sound of distant winds whispering through the trees. Waverly awoke with a start, the familiar weight of the mission pressing heavily on her chest. The night had brought no peace—only dreams that had deepened her resolve. Now, it was time to face the task at hand.

The fire had burned low, and the warriors were already preparing their packs. Lincoln, Ridge, and Lynx were all up, ready to face the journey that would take them to the core of Arcmyrin. Waverly felt a flutter of nervous anticipation in her stomach. They had spent so long preparing for this moment, but nothing could truly prepare them for what lay ahead.

She stood, brushing the dirt from her clothes and taking a deep breath, trying to steady her nerves. She couldn't afford to hesitate—not now. The fate of Arcmyrin, and the worlds beyond it, rested on her shoulders.

The group gathered their things, and after a quick, quiet breakfast, they set off toward the heart of Arcmyrin. The path was treacherous, filled with jagged rocks, thorny underbrush, and steep inclines. The warriors led the way, clearing the path with their practiced precision, but the terrain was harsh. Every step felt like they were descending deeper into the unknown. The trees grew more sparse as they climbed higher, the air thick with the scent of damp earth and something more... acrid.

Waverly could feel the change in the atmosphere as they moved forward. The air seemed to grow heavier, the wind carrying with it a faint, sour stench. It was as if the very land was sick—decaying, withering beneath their feet.

"I don't like this," Lynx said, his voice filled with unease. He wiped his brow and squinted at the path ahead. "It smells... wrong."

Ridge turned to look at him, a sharpness in his eyes. "Stay focused, Lynx. We're almost there."

But Waverly could sense the tension in the air—the uncertainty of what lay ahead. She had felt it in her dreams, the growing darkness that loomed on the horizon, and she knew they were approaching the final trial.

As they pushed forward, the land began to shift. The once-lush green forests gave way to ashen plains, the trees twisted and withered, their leaves crumbling as if they had been scorched by fire. The air grew thicker, the scent of rot growing stronger with each step. Waverly's heart beat faster, her mind racing with the growing dread that something was terribly wrong.

"I've never seen anything like this," Lincoln muttered, his voice strained. "This... this is the heart of Arcmyrin? It's... dying."

The warriors paused, their eyes scanning the barren landscape. Rykas, their leader, frowned as he surveyed the area. "It's not supposed to be like this," he said, his voice low and tense. "We're close. Very close."

Then, as if to confirm his words, the ground beneath them began to rumble, and a thick plume of smoke rose in the distance, curling up into the sky. The stench became unbearable—an acrid, sulfuric smell that made Waverly's stomach turn. It was as if the very core of the planet was being corrupted, leaking its poison into the world above.

The warriors exchanged wary glances. Rykas led them forward, his steps cautious, as the group neared the source of the smoke. When they finally reached the outer rims of the core, Waverly froze.

In front of them lay a lake—no, not a lake. It was more like a vast, black pool of goo, thick and glistening like tar. It stretched out before them, the surface bubbling and shifting as if it were alive. The smoke rose from it in thick plumes, swirling upward and darkening the sky above. The stench was overwhelming now, filling their nostrils with the scent of decay and rot.

"Is this... the core?" Waverly asked, her voice barely above a whisper. The sight before her was like something from a nightmare. She had expected something dark, something corrupted by Patereon's influence, but not this. The lake was foul, its surface slick and almost pulsing with an unnatural rhythm.

"This is where it begins," Rykas said grimly, his gaze fixed on the black pool. "The heart of Arcmyrin—this is what's left of it. The poison, the corruption—it all begins here."

Waverly swallowed hard, her throat tight. The sight was too much to bear. She could feel the weight of the task ahead of her—the mission to free Ambreela, to restore balance, but right now, all she could think of was how to get past the toxic lake in front of them.

"Can we cross it?" Ridge asked, stepping forward. He was as determined as ever, but the sight of the black goo made him pause.

"I don't know," Rykas replied, shaking his head. "I've never seen anything like this before. There's a great darkness here. It's a trap, for sure."

"Trap?" Waverly asked, her voice rising in alarm. "You mean this... this thing could be a trap?"

Rykas nodded. "We're close to the core of Arcmyrin, and the dark forces are watching us. The Abasimtrox and Patereon—they've set up defenses here to keep us from reaching the heart. This lake—this corruption—it's part of their trap."

The realization hit Waverly like a physical blow. They had been walking into a trap all along. The path to Ambreela was not only perilous but designed to stop them. The core of Arcmyrin was not a place of power or restoration—it was a place of decay and control. The very essence of the planet had been corrupted.

"Then we have no choice," Lincoln said, his voice full of quiet resolve. "We push forward."

"Not yet," Rykas warned. "We need to be careful. This lake... it may look like tar, but it's not just a simple obstacle. The goo is thick, and there's no telling what's beneath the surface."

"We can't go back," Waverly said, her voice filled with urgency. "If this is part of the trap, we have to get through it. Ambreela is on the other side."

Ridge looked over at her, his expression softening. "Waverly's right. We can't afford to wait. We need to cross, and we need to cross now."

The warriors readied their weapons, the group falling into a defensive stance. Rykas stepped forward, his eyes scanning the black lake before them. He motioned for the group to stay back.

"This may be our only chance," he said, his voice filled with authority. "But we must be quick. If the Abasimtrox are nearby, we can't waste any more time."

Waverly nodded, her determination hardening. She glanced at Lynx, who stood beside her, his youthful face filled with an unspoken question. She didn't know how they would make it across, but she knew one thing for sure—this was the only way forward. They had to get to the core. They had to free Ambreela.

"I'll go first," Rykas said, his voice calm. "Stay behind me. Stay close."

As Rykas carefully approached the edge of the black goo, his feet sinking slightly into the muck, the others followed closely. The surface of the goo rippled, but there was no sign of what lay beneath. It was as though the lake itself was alive—waiting, watching, breathing.

The warriors kept their weapons ready, eyes scanning the horizon for any sign of movement. The black lake stretched out before them like a dark abyss, threatening to swallow them whole. The air was thick with a sense of unease, as if the very land was trying to push them back.

"Do you feel that?" Lynx whispered, his voice filled with a sense of dread. "It feels like something's watching us."

"I feel it too," Waverly admitted, her voice quiet but filled with an edge of fear. She couldn't shake the feeling that they were being watched—that something was lurking beneath the surface of the lake, waiting to strike.

Rykas stepped carefully, his boots sinking slightly into the tar-like substance as he moved forward. The rest of the group followed, but the pace was slow, deliberate. Every step felt like a trap, every footfall uncertain.

Waverly's heart raced. Whatever lay ahead, whatever the Abasimtrox had planned, they had to be ready. The moment they crossed this black lake, they would be closer than ever to the core—and to confronting Patereon, to freeing Ambreela.

But with each step, the fear of what was to come grew heavier, as the darkness beneath them seemed to pulse with a life of its own.

43

The late afternoon sun poured through the tall windows of Sage Manor's parlor, casting long shadows over the polished hardwood floors. The air inside the room was still and quiet, the only sound the soft creak of the old house settling, and the rustling of Gran Celia's shawl. The room, with its deep, warm tones, was one of the few places that still felt untouched by the weight of the world outside. It was a space of comfort, of history, and now—of discovery.

Francis Roller stood near the fireplace, her gaze fixed on the large painting. Gran Celia stood quietly beside her, her eyes focused on the canvas as well. The two women had stood there for some time, both lost in thought, pondering the significance of the painting.

Francis had been studying it in increasing detail, her mind piecing together the images, the symbols, and the subtle clues woven into the brushstrokes. It was a beautiful landscape, certainly. But there was more to it—so much more. The painting was not just a depiction of a serene pond with rolling hills and towering mountains. It was a guide. A symbol of something far more powerful and far-reaching than anyone could have realized.

Gran Celia's voice broke the silence, her words calm but filled with a quiet intensity. "We've been staring at this painting for a while, Francis. Do you see something more now? Something I don't?"

Francis turned to face Gran Celia, her eyes bright with excitement, the realization hitting her like a spark of electricity. "Yes, Celia, I think I do. This painting... I've seen it in a new light. I believe it's depicting the elemental spirits—water, earth, air, and fire—in perfect balance and harmony."

Gran Celia blinked in surprise, leaning in closer as she processed the words. "The elemental spirits? How do you mean?"

Francis took a deep breath and stepped up closer to the painting, standing before it with a sense of awe. "Look at the water, Celia," she said, pointing to the serene pond at the center of the canvas. "It's calm, peaceful, but there's an energy in it—something flowing beneath the surface. Water is the spirit of Mistara. It's fluid, adaptable, and yet it has the power to shape entire landscapes. Notice how the water here, despite being still, is depicted with light ripples, hinting at its hidden power, its quiet force."

Gran Celia's eyes followed Francis's finger as she traced the water's surface, and she nodded slowly. "I see. But what about the land? The mountains? They seem so solid, almost unyielding."

Francis's gaze shifted to the distant blue mountains in the background, their jagged peaks rising high above the pond. "That's the earth, Celia. Terraveta. The mountains are stable, strong—protective. But look at how the land meets the sky. The curves of the hills suggest growth, life, and movement. Earth, though solid, is always connected to life and change. The land, like the spirit of earth itself, nurtures and supports. It holds everything in place."

Gran Celia's eyes softened, as if the connection she was making with the painting was something tangible. "And the clouds, Francis? What do they represent?"

Francis smiled slightly, her gaze softening as she looked at the swirling, windswept clouds that filled the upper part of the canvas. The sky was painted in hues of pinks, purples, and soft blues, with clouds drifting in every direction as though being tugged by an unseen force. "That's the spirit of air—Ambreela. The clouds are fluid, constantly shifting and moving. Just as the air carries sound, whispers, and change, the clouds here are an expression of that power. They're sweeping across the sky, traveling, never settling in one place for too long. Air is the force of movement and change—unseen, but always present."

Gran Celia leaned forward, her eyes focusing on the intricate details of the swirling clouds, now understanding the connection Francis was making. "I see it. The air connects everything, moves everything. It is the lifeblood of the world, and it's always in motion."

Francis nodded, her hand hovering over the painting as she continued her analysis. "And then there's the flame."

Gran Celia's eyes followed Francis's hand to the blazing, flickering light in the sky, where the sun should have been. Instead of the expected golden orb, the painting depicted a large, flickering flame, shining brightly and lending warmth to the entire scene. The flame, though odd in its placement, was radiant, its light seeming to spread across the entire landscape.

"Fire," Francis said, her voice filled with reverence. "Ignissa. The flame is fierce, dangerous, but also a force of transformation. It has the power to create and destroy. It fuels life, provides warmth, and yet, it can consume everything in its path. The flame here is symbolic of that dual nature—its ability to nurture and destroy. And notice how it stands out in the painting, how it is the only source of light. It is both the most powerful force in this scene and the most destructive."

Gran Celia absorbed every word, her mind racing as she began to understand what Francis was seeing. The painting, once merely a beautiful landscape, now seemed like a key—a map to understanding the elemental spirits, their balance, and their connection to the portal.

"You believe," Gran Celia began slowly, "that this painting is showing us the balance of the elements—their harmony. And that this balance is what we need to restore?"

Francis nodded, her eyes sparkling with insight. "Exactly. Each element—water, earth, air, and fire—is represented here. They are intertwined, connected, and working together to create balance. If any one of them is disrupted, if one falls out of harmony, then the world suffers. The elemental spirits must remain in balance to sustain the energy of the portal, to keep the worlds connected."

Gran Celia stood up, her heart quickening as the weight of the discovery sank in. "So, the flame—the fire—is key. The spirit of fire must be released. That's the last step we need to complete."

"Yes," Francis confirmed. "And once the spirits are released, once balance is restored, the portal will be stabilized. But without the right harmony, the portal will falter, and the darkness will take hold."

Gran Celia took a deep breath, turning to face the painting again. The once-ordinary scene had taken on an entirely new significance. This wasn't just a work of art—it was a map, a guide to restoring balance, a guide to saving Arcmyrin, and perhaps all the worlds that depended on it.

Her gaze lingered on the flame, the symbol of fire, and she felt a deep connection to the history of the Beaumont family. For generations, they had been protectors of the land, stewards of the Earth's energy. Galen, Jameson, Ridge, and Lincoln—each had carried a piece of this legacy, each had contributed to the balance. And now, Waverly and Lynx would have to carry that legacy forward.

Gran Celia's voice was low and steady as she spoke. "We've always known there was something special about this family. Galen—he knew it too. The portal, the spirits, the balance of the elements—it was all part of the plan. This painting is showing us what is needed. They must free the spirits and restore the balance."

Francis looked at her with a quiet understanding. "The portal will open again, Celia. The flames are flickering, the water is present in the orb. The spirits are telling us."

Gran Celia took a step back, her fingers brushing against the cool surface of the painting as though trying to glean more wisdom from it. "We are so close now. So close to bringing them back. To restoring the balance."

She paused for a moment, taking in the whole of the scene before her. The water, the earth, the air, the fire—each element was a piece of the puzzle. For the first time in days, Gran Celia felt hope blooming in her chest.

44

Waverly's heart pounded in her chest as they approached the rim of the core. She could feel the weight of their mission pressing down on her, each step heavier than the last. The darkness that loomed before them threatened to overwhelm her, to stop them from reaching their destination.

But as they stepped closer, Waverly felt a sudden shift in the air—a sensation that stirred the wind around them. A quiet, familiar whisper began to hum beneath her skin. The air itself seemed to crackle with energy, as though the world was responding to her presence.

"It's them," Waverly whispered to her family, her eyes widening in realization.

Lincoln, Ridge, and Lynx turned toward her, sensing the change in the air. The warriors, too, slowed their steps, looking around warily. But it was clear that Waverly wasn't speaking about anything they could see.

She closed her eyes for a moment, focusing on the pull she felt deep within her—the sensation of the spirits, their presence strong and unwavering, calling to her from beyond the veil.

A gust of wind swirled around them, and the earth beneath their feet rumbled softly as if in recognition. Then, out of the swirling mist, three figures appeared before them, their forms shimmering like ethereal beings woven from the very elements themselves.

Mistara, the spirit of water, appeared first. Her form was fluid, graceful, with long strands of water cascading around her like flowing ribbons. Her eyes were a soft blue, shimmering with the light of the oceans, and her presence was like a refreshing breeze after a storm.

Next, Ignissa materialized from the crackling air around them. She was a towering figure of flame, her body wreathed in flickering fire that danced and swirled with every movement. Her golden eyes burned brightly, reflecting both the strength and ferocity of the fire within her.

Finally, Terraveta, the spirit of earth, stepped forward. Her form was solid and ancient, woven from the rocks and soil of Arcmyrin itself. Her skin was like rich brown stone, and her eyes glowed with the deep wisdom of the land. She emanated a quiet strength, the kind that had endured for millennia.

Together, the three elemental spirits formed a circle around the Beaumonts and the warriors, their presence powerful and undeniable.

"We are with you," Mistara's voice echoed softly, her tone gentle yet filled with a deep, calming power. "We are here to aid you in your final journey. The path to the core is treacherous, but you will not face it alone."

Waverly felt a rush of relief wash over her as she looked at the three spirits. "I've never felt anything like this," she said, her voice trembling with a mix of awe and gratitude. "I didn't think you'd be able to help us directly. We've come so far, but I don't know how we can defeat Patereon. His power is too great."

Ignissa, her fiery form glowing brighter with each passing moment, stepped forward. "Patereon's power is derived from his darkness, from his refusal to embrace the balance of the elements. He is the embodiment of imbalance, and to defeat him, you must restore that balance."

Terraveta, her voice like the rumble of distant thunder, nodded in agreement. "The core of Arcmyrin has been corrupted, poisoned by Patereon's greed. But the elements are the key. The power of water, fire, earth, and air must converge. Together, you can neutralize the darkness he wields."

Waverly looked at them, her mind racing. "But how? We've already released the spirits of water, fire, and earth. How do we reach the core now and face Patereon?"

Mistara's eyes softened, her watery form rippling with the movement of the wind around them. "You are connected to the elements, Waverly. You hold the power of air, and with it, the key to breaking the bond Patereon has with the core. But you cannot do this alone. You must call upon the other spirits—fire, water, and earth—together in perfect harmony."

Ignissa's flame flickered fiercely, her voice passionate. "Patereon has kept the balance from you, but it is within your power to restore it. All you need is the courage to bring the elements together, to stand united with your family, and to trust in the strength of the spirits."

Terraveta's steady gaze met Waverly's, her voice calm but filled with immense weight. "The core is where the elements converge. It is where you will find the heart of Arcmyrin, and where the final battle must take place. But be warned—Patereon will not go down easily. He will use every ounce of his power to keep you from reaching the core."

Rykas, the Arcmyrin warrior leader, stepped forward, his sword in hand, ready for the battle that lay ahead. "Then we face him together. We will help you reach the core. We will fight alongside you."

Waverly felt her heart swell with the support of her family and the warriors. But still, doubts lingered in her mind. "I'm afraid," she admitted, her voice barely above a whisper. "What if I can't do this? What if I can't control the power, or reach Ambreela in time? What if..."

Mistara stepped closer, her watery form enveloping Waverly in a comforting, soothing mist. "Fear is the greatest enemy of all, Waverly. But it does not control you. You are stronger than you think, and you carry the power of the air within you. Trust in yourself, and trust in the bond you share with the spirits. Together, you will restore the balance."

The words washed over Waverly like a cool, cleansing rain. She could feel the warmth of the fire from Ignissa, the grounding presence of Terraveta's earth, and the calming embrace of Mistara's waters. The four elements were within her, and they were within the land itself. With them, she could face the darkness that had taken hold of Arcmyrin.

She turned to her family, the warriors, and the spirits who stood around her. "I'm ready," she said, her voice filled with newfound determination. "Let's do this. We have to stop Patereon and restore the balance."

Ignissa's flame burned brighter, and Terraveta's stone-like form seemed to grow even more solid. "Then let us guide you," said Ignissa. "We will show you the way."

Terraveta stepped forward, her voice steady. "We have given you the power, Waverly. The path to the core is not far now. But you must hold fast to your connection to the elements. Trust in them as they trust in you."

Together, the spirits and the warriors led the way, with Waverly at the forefront, her heart beating in time with the rhythms of the earth. The journey to the core was fraught with dangers, but now she knew that she carried the strength of the elements, the courage of her family, and the guidance of the spirits.

As they moved closer to the core, the air grew thick with tension. But Waverly felt a flicker of hope.

45

As Waverly, Ridge, Lynx, Lincoln, and the Arcmyrian warriors stood at the edge of the core, the heart of Arcmyrin loomed before them. It was a twisted and desolate landscape of blackened earth and swirling darkness. The very ground seemed to writhe beneath their feet, as if it were alive, pulsing with malevolent energy. The core was no longer the vibrant, life-sustaining force it once was—it had been corrupted by Patereon's influence, transformed into a place of decay and destruction.

Waverly took a deep breath, her heart pounding in her chest. The weight of the mission pressed down on her, but the presence of the three elemental spirits—the spirits of water, fire, and earth—was a comforting force. Mistara, Ignissa, and Terraveta stood alongside her, their elemental energies radiating outward like a shield against the darkness. The air shimmered with their power, and though fear gnawed at her, Waverly felt a quiet strength building within her. She was not alone. The spirits and her family were with her.

"This is it," Waverly said, her voice steady despite the turmoil within. "We have to free Ambreela and restore balance. We can't let Patereon corrupt this place any longer."

Rykas, the Arcmyrian warrior leader, nodded grimly. "We will hold off the dark shadows as best we can, but it's up to you to reach Ambreela and restore the core. We will fight with you, Waverly. But you must act quickly."

Patereon's influence was already apparent. The air was thick with smoke, and dark, swirling shadows moved ominously across the landscape. The once-beautiful core of Arcmyrin was now a twisted, sickening reflection of its former self. The lake of black goo that had once served as a beautiful prismatic barrier now seemed to pulse with malevolent energy, as if the land itself was suffering.

Waverly clenched her fists, feeling the wind stir around her. The spirits had told her that she would need to call upon the elements in perfect harmony to break Patereon's hold. But what if it wasn't enough? What if she failed?

"Waverly," Mistara's voice echoed in her mind, calming her nerves. "The balance is within you. Trust in the elements. Trust in yourself."

Waverly nodded, her resolve hardening. She could do this. She had to.

Suddenly, a powerful, guttural laugh echoed through the air. The dark shadows parted, revealing the figure of Patereon standing at the center of the corrupted core. His once-human form was now twisted, corrupted by the darkness he had embraced. His skin was ashen, his eyes glowing red, and a swirling vortex of shadows hovered around him like a storm. He grinned wickedly as he surveyed the group, his eyes locking onto Waverly.

"So, the little girl with the power of the wind has come to challenge me," Patereon sneered, his voice dripping with malice. "You have no idea what you're up against. This world, this planet, is mine. And soon, the entire universe will be under my control. The balance is already broken, and you are too weak to stop me."

Waverly stepped forward, the wind around her picking up in response to her determination. "You're wrong, Patereon," she said, her voice clear and strong. "We're not weak. We're not alone. And we're going to stop you."

Patereon's smile faltered for a moment, and the shadows around him rippled with unease. "You think you can stop me? You think the elemental spirits will help you? You're just a child playing at power."

"That's where you're wrong," Ridge interjected, stepping beside Waverly, his eyes filled with unwavering confidence. "She's not alone. We're all in this together. And you're going to lose."

The warriors stood ready, their weapons drawn, as the three elemental spirits prepared for battle. Mistara, her form shimmering with the light of the oceans, raised her arms, and a wave of water surged forward, crashing against the dark shadows. Ignissa, her flames rising high into the air, launched a barrage of fire at Patereon's dark minions, each blast lighting up the sky with intense heat. Terraveta, the earth spirit, stomped her foot, causing the ground to shake and split, sending jagged rocks flying toward the shadows.

Patereon snarled as the spirits' attacks pushed back his minions, but he was not defeated so easily. He raised his arms, summoning a vortex of dark energy that swirled around him, forming into sharp tendrils that lashed out at the group. The shadows struck with devastating force, but Waverly stood her ground, feeling the wind surge around her, ready to respond.

"Now, Waverly!" Elara's voice rang out through the air, her holographic form appearing beside them, giving them the last push they needed. "Unite the elements! Bring the spirits together!"

Waverly closed her eyes, focusing on the connection she had with the elements. She reached out with her mind, feeling the wind swirling around her, the heat of the flames, the strength of the earth beneath her feet, and the flow of water in the distance. All of them were connected—water, fire, earth, and air. And it was time to bring them together.

"Together," Waverly whispered, her voice carrying over the battlefield, "Elements, Unite!"

The wind roared as she raised her arms, calling upon the spirits to unite. The flames from Ignissa grew higher, swirling around the wind as it picked up speed. The earth beneath them trembled, and water from Mistara's form began to rise, swirling with the air. For a moment, everything seemed to freeze in place, as if the world itself was holding its breath.

Then, with a tremendous roar, the four elements surged together, forming a whirlwind of light, fire, water, and earth that collided with

Patereon's darkness. The light was blinding, the energy overwhelming. The dark shadows that had once surrounded Patereon faltered, retreating as the combined force of the elements pushed them back.

"No!" Patereon shouted, his voice laced with fear and anger. "You cannot defeat me! I am the darkness!"

But as the elemental storm collided with him, the darkness began to crumble, the shadows retreating, unable to withstand the purity and strength of the elements in harmony. Waverly could feel the power of the spirits, the unity between them all, as the final surge of energy swept through the battlefield.

Patereon screamed in agony as the elements tore through his dark form, shattering the twisted energy he had created. The darkness that had once consumed him began to dissipate, leaving only the remnants of the corrupted man he had once been.

With a final, defiant roar, Patereon was gone—his power shattered, the shadows fading into nothingness.

Waverly stood, panting, her body exhausted but her heart filled with a deep, unwavering sense of relief. Her hands were sore, her legs shaky, but the battle was over. The darkness had receded, and with it, the suffocating weight of fear that had pressed so heavily on her chest. She could feel the pulse of the land beneath her feet, no longer twisted and corrupted by the darkness. The air around her had cleared, the fire's heat no longer a threat but a warm, comforting embrace. And the water—once polluted and bound by Patereon's malice—now shimmered with clarity, flowing freely once more.

In the distance, she saw her.

Ambreela.

The spirit of Air appeared as a glowing figure in the distance, her ethereal form swirling with the gentlest of winds, her presence a calming, almost celestial presence that seemed to lift the very atmosphere around them. As she moved closer, the sky above Waverly seemed to clear, the winds picking up gently, and the air grew lighter, freer. Waverly's heart leapt in her chest as she took a step forward, drawn to Ambreela, the final spirit they had fought so hard to release.

The spirit of Air floated toward her, her translucent form sparkling like sunlight on water, her presence both graceful and powerful. When Ambreela reached Waverly, she extended her arms, the winds around her growing stronger as they began to swirl and dance. Waverly took another step, and before she knew it, she was engulfed by the wind, a soft but exhilarating breeze wrapping around her as Ambreela's energy intertwined with her own.

For a brief moment, Waverly felt as though the world itself was breathing through her. The wind rushed through her hair, and the sense of freedom, of lightness, washed over her. She could feel the essence of Ambreela within her, the power of air and the spirit's wisdom coursing through her veins. It was as if the very air she breathed had come alive, and it filled her with the strength and clarity to carry on the legacy of her family—and of the elements.

Ambreela's voice, soft but strong, filled Waverly's mind. "You have done it, Waverly. The balance is restored. I am free. You are free. The elements are united, and Arcmyrin will heal. We are one."

Waverly's heart swelled with emotion as she raised her arms, feeling the spirits of water, fire, earth, and air come together within her. The connection between them was undeniable, and she could feel their power surging within her.

Around them, the other elemental spirits appeared, their forms glowing with their respective energies—Mistara, the spirit of Water, shimmering like liquid glass; Ignissa, the spirit of Fire, her flames burning brightly and fiercely; and Terraveta, the spirit of Earth, standing strong and steady like the rocks and soil of Arcmyrin itself.

They had all been freed, all connected to the world and the Beaumont family once more. The balance that had been disrupted was now restored, and the energy in the air felt alive with possibility.

Waverly turned to see her family and the Arcmyrin warriors standing together, their faces bright with joy and relief. Ridge, Lynx, and Lincoln were all grinning widely, their eyes filled with pride. The warriors were silent, but their expressions spoke volumes, a shared sense of triumph in their gaze.

Ridge, unable to contain his excitement, stepped forward with a wide grin. "Victory," he exclaimed, his voice thick with emotion. "You did it, Waverly. You freed Ambreela."

Lynx, always quick to celebrate, clapped his sister on the back, his grin infectious. "That was amazing! I knew you could do it! We all did!"

Lincoln stepped forward, his hand resting on Waverly's shoulder. "You've restored the balance, Waverly. This—this is what we were fighting for."

The three elemental spirits moved closer to the group, their energies filling the air with warmth, water, air, and earth. Ignissa's flames burned brighter, casting a soft light over the gathered group. Mistara's waters shimmered like a thousand droplets of light, reflecting the joy of the moment. Terraveta's grounding presence seemed to settle the earth beneath them, and the land itself seemed to breathe in relief.

Ambreela's voice echoed again in Waverly's mind, soft and full of gratitude. "You have done more than restore balance, Waverly. You have united us all. You have freed us from the darkness. The worlds are safe because of you, and because of your family."

Waverly smiled up at the spirit of Air, her heart full. "We did it together. All of us," she said, her voice quiet but filled with pride. "The world is whole again. Arcmyrin is healing. And the balance has been restored."

The warriors and her family cheered, the sound echoing through the landscape, their voices carrying the joy and relief they all felt. The land around them seemed to respond, the once-dead soil now rich with vitality, the air fresh and clear, the waters sparkling with life. The elements were no longer in conflict—they were whole, restored, and united in a way that Waverly never could have imagined before this journey began.

As the spirits gathered together, they began to speak in unison, their voices like a harmonious melody. "Arcmyrin will heal. The portal will remain closed, but it will always be ready when the balance is needed again. The elements are no longer separated. They are united, and the worlds will know peace."

Waverly could feel the energy of the spirits—of water, fire, earth, and air—surging within her, their power now a part of her, their connection to her stronger than ever. It was as though she could feel the pulse of the earth itself, the warmth of the fire, the gentle flow of water, and the breath of the air all living within her. She wasn't just Waverly anymore—she was a part of something much greater, something far more powerful than she had ever understood before.

The spirits had trusted her, and she had trusted in them.

46

Gran Celia stood in the chamber, her breath steady but her heart racing with anticipation. Beside her, Francis was carefully studying the orb, her eyes narrowed in concentration as she gazed at the swirling patterns within.

The orb had always been a mysterious object, its true purpose unclear. But now, as the Beaumonts had unleashed the elemental spirits one by one, the orb seemed to be reacting, its once still surface now alive with subtle movements.

The flame that had once been faint and flickering now blazed brightly within the orb, swirling and crackling like a living fire. The water had grown clearer, its surface shimmering with the cool, gentle movement of an ocean breeze. And now, for the first time, Celia could make out the faint outline of mountains, jagged and majestic, like the ones painted in Victoria's masterpiece.

The sight of the mountains made her heart swell with hope. The painting had been the first clue, the first sign that everything was connected, and now, with the orb reflecting that very same imagery, the pieces of the puzzle were slowly starting to fit together.

Francis turned to Celia, her face lit with excitement. "Celia, do you see it?" she asked, her voice filled with awe. "The mountains—they're here. The element of Earth, represented in the orb. It's a sign. Each element that has been released is now filling the orb, becoming part of it again."

Gran Celia stepped closer to the orb, her eyes tracing the contours of the mountains. She could feel the energy within them—solid, grounded, ancient. Earth was the spirit that had always connected with her family, the one that had given them the strength to endure through the ages. Now, that spirit was returning to its rightful place.

"I see it," Celia said softly, her voice full of wonder. "The earth, the mountains... it's like the world itself is waking up."

Francis nodded, her gaze fixed on the orb as if searching for more signs. "It is. And look—there, do you see it? The water. It's flowing now, more clearly than before. This is the sign of Mistara's return. The flame is there too, Ignissa's fire still burning bright. It's as if each release of the spirits is being marked here. The orb is showing us that they are all returning to their rightful place."

Gran Celia smiled, her heart lifting at the sight. "And what about Air?" she asked, her voice barely above a whisper. "Do you think we'll see it too?"

Francis's eyes glimmered with a knowing sparkle. "I believe we will," she said with certainty. "We've seen the signs of water, earth, and fire. It only makes sense that Air will appear next."

Celia's mind raced as she imagined it—what the orb would look like when Air appeared. Would it be like the wispy clouds from the painting? Would it swirl gently, ethereal and light, just like Ambreela's presence in the world? She could almost feel the air itself stirring with anticipation, as though the orb was waiting for the final piece to complete the puzzle.

"I think you're right, Francis," Gran Celia said, a sense of peace settling over her. "The elements are coming together. The balance is being restored."

They both stood there for a moment, silently watching the orb as the faint shapes of the mountains, the flickering flame, and the shimmering water seemed to pulse and move in sync. It was a strange and beautiful sight—a sign of unity, of restoration, and of the spirits coming back together.

"I can't believe it," Celia said softly, her eyes still fixed on the orb. "It's happening, Francis. Arcmyrin is healing."

Francis nodded, her expression full of excitement. "It is, Celia. And this orb—it's showing us that the spirits are returning to their rightful places. The worlds will be in balance once more."

Gran Celia took a deep breath, feeling the weight of the moment settle into her chest. She had known that the restoration of balance was important, but seeing it in this form, in the orb before her, was something entirely different. This was a connection to the past, to her family's legacy, and to the future that they were now shaping together.

"We've come so far," Gran Celia said, her voice filled with awe. "But there's still more to do."

Francis nodded, her gaze never leaving the orb. "Yes, but the first step is almost complete. The elements are in place."

Gran Celia turned toward the staircase, a thought forming in her mind. "I think we should wait in the gazebo. It feels like the right place to be."

Francis smiled, her eyes alight with the same excitement. "That sounds perfect."

Together, they climbed the stone staircase, their steps light as they made their way back up. Gran Celia couldn't help but feel a deep sense of connection to everything around her—the house, the land, her family. All of it was bound together by the elements, by the spirits, and by the legacy that had been passed down through generations.

As the group stood together, Waverly felt the world around her come alive with energy. The winds danced through the air, the flames of Ignissa crackled softly, and the waters of Mistara shimmered like precious jewels. The earth beneath their feet seemed to hum with life, and even the sky above appeared brighter, lighter—full of hope.

"It's over," Waverly whispered, a quiet smile on her lips. "We've saved Arcmyrin."

Her family and the Arcmyrian warriors gathered around her, their expressions filled with awe and gratitude. Lincoln, Ridge, and Lynx stood with her, their arms wrapped around each other, sharing this moment of victory. The elemental spirits surrounded them, their forms radiant with energy and life, and for the first time in a long while, the worlds felt right.

Together, they had overcome the darkness. Together, they had restored balance.

And for the first time in what felt like forever, the worlds were at peace.

As the winds swirled gently around them, Waverly closed her eyes, feeling the harmony of the elements coursing through her. She was no longer just a part of her family. She was a part of the world—of all the worlds.

The gazebo sat in the center of the vast garden, the trees and flowers around it beginning to bloom once more, a testament to the healing that was happening both within and around them. Celia and Francis settled into the wicker chairs, looking out over the landscape, the distant mountains barely visible through the mist.

The air was still, but there was an unmistakable feeling that something was about to change.

Gran Celia took a seat, her hands resting in her lap, a soft smile on her face. "I think we'll see Air soon, Francis. It's only a matter of time."

Francis nodded, her gaze still fixed on the horizon. "Yes. And when it comes, the circle will be complete. The balance will be restored."

The minutes stretched by in quiet anticipation, the two women lost in their thoughts. The peace that surrounded them was only disturbed by the faintest shift in the air—a soft, almost imperceptible breeze that whispered through the trees.

Gran Celia's heart skipped a beat as she felt it, the faintest stir of wind—like the first breath of a storm on the horizon.

"I think it's coming," Celia whispered, her voice full of awe.

Francis smiled, her eyes gleaming with excitement. "It is."

They sat there together, the two of them watching as the wind began to pick up. The orb below, now glowing softly with the presence of earth, fire, and water, shimmered with new life. It seemed to pulse with anticipation, as though it, too, was waiting for Air to join it, to complete the circle.

And then, like a gentle whisper, it came.

A soft wisp of clouds appeared in the orb, swirling gently and forming the shape of a breeze. The air shimmered as the clouds danced across the surface, bringing with them the spirit of Air—Ambreela.

Gran Celia rose from the chair and grabbed Francis by the hand leading her back down the stone staircase and to the orb. What greeted them made Gran Celia gasp in wonder.

The orb grew brighter, the air around them seemed to come alive, filling the chamber with a gentle breeze. It was as if the very world had exhaled a sigh of relief.

Ambreela's presence filled the space, gentle and powerful, and Gran Celia could feel the connection in the very air she breathed. The balance was complete.

"Air is here," Celia whispered, her voice full of awe.

Francis smiled, her heart light with the realization. "And with it, the balance of the worlds is restored."

Together, they stood in silence, the breeze caressing their skin, the elements united in peace and harmony. The orb had shown them. The spirits were free, and with them, the Beaumont family had restored balance to Arcmyrin and the worlds.

47

The last of the shadows had dissipated, and the air around them was still. The battlefield, once a tumultuous clash of light and dark, was now eerily calm, the ground beneath their feet solid and steady. The elemental spirits, free at last, had begun their work of healing Arcmyrin, and the Beaumont family, along with their allies, stood at the edge of the core, the weight of their victory settling in.

Waverly, standing tall but weary from the battle, couldn't help but feel a rush of gratitude. The elemental spirits—Mistara, Ignissa, Terraveta, and now Ambreela—had all played their part. But there was one other force that had been with them, one that had guided them through the darkest moments.

As if summoned by Waverly's thoughts, Elara's holographic form appeared before them. The light that radiated from her was soft yet powerful, her presence a constant source of strength and wisdom. She looked at them, a deep pride in her eyes, as her form flickered with the brightness of the stars.

"You've done it," Elara's voice echoed, clear and resonant. "You have freed the spirits, restored the balance, and defeated the darkness. Arcmyrin and the other worlds will heal, thanks to your efforts."

Waverly smiled, a mix of exhaustion and relief filling her heart. "Thank you, Elara," she said, her voice filled with gratitude. "You were with us every step of the way, especially during the battle. I don't know if we could've done it without you pushing me over the finish line."

Elara's gaze softened, and the gentle breeze of the wind seemed to stir around her as she spoke. "You had the strength within you all along, Waverly. But your courage and determination are what truly made the difference. You brought the balance back to the worlds, and you did so with the support of your family, the warriors, and the elemental spirits."

Waverly nodded, feeling the weight of Elara's words settle in. She had come so far, faced so much. And now, it felt like the world was finally at peace.

But Lynx, always curious, wasn't satisfied with just the victory. His mind was already turning to the next questions, the next steps.

"So, if the portal's closed," Lynx started, his voice laced with both curiosity and concern, "how do we get back home to Earth? To Sage Manor? Gran Celia will be waiting for us."

Elara's eyes flickered as she regarded him, her expression thoughtful. "The portal is indeed closed for now. We had to ensure that it remained sealed in order to prevent any further corruption. The energies have been restored, and the elemental spirits are free. But the portal was never meant to be opened and closed at will. It exists to keep the balance, and that must be respected."

Lynx frowned slightly, his brow furrowing. "But we still need to get back home, right? We can't just leave Sage Manor empty, and Gran Celia's been waiting for us. How do we get back?"

Elara's voice took on a calming tone, and a soft breeze picked up around them, as if reassuring them. "The portal will remain closed for now, but that does not mean you will be stuck here. There are other ways to return home, though they may not be immediate. We will work with the energy of the elements and find a way to create a safe passage."

Lynx nodded, but another thought struck him. His eyes turned toward his father, Lincoln, a question burning in his mind.

"What about Mom?" Lynx asked suddenly, his voice filled with both hope and uncertainty. "How do we get her from Tanzlora to Earth? I want her there with us. She's been away for so long."

Lincoln glanced at Lynx, his expression both pained and thoughtful. He had been so focused on their mission, on freeing the spirits and restoring balance, that the thought of returning home to Earth had seemed distant, almost unreachable. But now, with the dark forces defeated, the time to rebuild had come. The family's reunion had yet to be completed, and Lynx's question echoed in his heart.

"I want her back with us too," Lincoln said softly, his voice thick with emotion. "I've been thinking about it, but I'm not sure what the best course of action is. The portal system is closed, and even if it could be reopened, the risks are too great. But I will do whatever it takes to bring your mother home, Lynx."

Lynx looked at his father with wide eyes, his youthful curiosity mixed with a deep sense of hope. "So, are you coming back with us to Earth, Dad?"

The question hung in the air, a simple one, but it carried the weight of their family's future. Lincoln's gaze softened, and he stepped forward, resting a hand on Lynx's shoulder. He hadn't expected this question, but it was one that had been brewing in his mind as well.

"I don't know," Lincoln admitted, his voice low. "There's still work to be done here, on Arcmyrin. We've restored the balance, but there are many changes to make, many wounds to heal. Arcmyrin needs me, Lynx. I just need to figure out what the next steps are for all of us."

Lynx nodded, processing his father's words with the earnestness only a child could muster. He wanted his family to be whole again, wanted his mother to be with them, and the uncertainty of it all made him feel unsettled. But he understood. For now, they had won the battle, but the journey forward wasn't clear.

"Ok, Dad," Lynx said quietly, his usual enthusiasm tempered by the weight of the conversation. "I just... I don't want things to be all messed up. I want to know that we're all going to be okay. That Mom's coming home."

Waverly placed a reassuring hand on her brother's back, offering him a smile. "We'll figure it out, Lynx. Together, we'll make it work. We've been through worse, haven't we?"

Lynx grinned up at her, the spark of optimism returning to his eyes. "Yeah, I guess we have." Then, his expression shifted slightly, as if another thought had struck him. "So, about that portal... how long do you think it'll take before we can get back home?"

Elara, who had been observing the exchange, stepped forward with a gentle smile. "The portal may remain closed for a while longer, but there is always a way. The bond you share with the elements is stronger than anything. When the time is right, you'll know. The elements will guide you, as they have guided you all along. For now, enjoy the peace, for the balance has been restored."

Waverly nodded, taking a deep breath as the weight of the moment began to settle in. They had won. Arcmyrin was free, and the darkness had been vanquished. But the journey was far from over. There were still loose ends to tie, still healing to be done. And the path forward wasn't clear.

"Thanks, Elara," Waverly said, her voice filled with gratitude. "You've helped us every step of the way. I don't think we could've done it without you."

Elara's holographic form glowed brighter for a moment, her expression full of pride. "You've done it, Waverly. You've saved Arcmyrin, and you've freed the spirits. You've completed the mission. Now, it's time to move forward. The world has been restored, and the journey is yours to continue."

As Elara's form began to fade, the family stood together, the elemental spirits still present in the air around them, their energy a soft hum in the atmosphere. They had achieved the impossible, but there was still work to be done. With Lynx's question lingering in the air, Waverly couldn't help but feel the pull of Earth, of Sage Manor, and of Gran Celia waiting for their return.

48

That night, the Beaumonts were given accommodations within the Arcmyrin community, allowing them to rest after their triumph. Their quarters were simple but comfortable in pods designed to blend into the surrounding ecosystem.

The Arcmyrian living quarters were unlike anything Waverly, Lynx and Ridge had ever seen before. The sleek, rectangular structure stood tall against the vibrant Arcmyrin landscape, its design both futuristic and seamlessly integrated into the environment. As they approached, Waverly noticed the clear, shimmering glass-like panels that encased the lower levels, giving the impression of a biodome floating above the ground.

Rykas and Arcmyrian warriors led the way, explaining the layout of the structure as they walked. "You will see that the structure is composed of three family pods, each stacked vertically in sets of two, forming a compact yet efficient living space for multiple families," Rykas said.

He went on to tell them that at the base of each structure were large, rectangular boxes filled with growing herbs, vegetables, and various plants native to Arcmyrin that thrived in the open air. These underground growing areas were connected to the biodomes above, allowing each family to sustain their own food supply.

As they reached the base of the structure, Ridge took in the intricate growing system, amazed by the innovation. "So, everything you grow down here is used to support the families living above?"

"Exactly," Rykas replied. "It's an entirely self-sustaining system. The plants below thrive in the natural soil and air outside, while the more delicate or exotic plants are grown inside the biodomes. We harvest food from both to ensure we always have enough."

They stepped into a lift located on one of the shorter sides of the rectangular structure, which gently hummed as it carried them upward. As the lift ascended, Ridge and Waverly could see the intricate biodome pods on the lower levels of each family's unit. Clear silica-glass-like enclosures surrounded lush gardens, vibrant with life. Inside the domes, they could see families tending to their plants, preparing meals, and dining together.

Rykas gestured to the biodome below them as they ascended. "Each family has a pod for living and a pod for gardening, cooking, and dining. It's efficient and helps maintain a close connection to the environment we've been working so hard to restore."

Finally, the lift reached the top unit. This level of the family pod was a solid-walled rectangle, housing the living space, while the lower rectangle beneath was the biodome. Rykas led the way as the door slid open, revealing a cozy family gathering area bathed in soft, natural light.

"This is the main family space," he said, gesturing around the room. "We keep it simple—just enough space for rest and comfort."

The family gathering area was warm and inviting, with seating arranged around a central table. A sliding door on one side led to a personal cleaning area, where a sleek shower system and sink were tucked away.

Further back, the sleeping area was divided into two spaces, with minimalistic bedding and storage. Waverly could tell the Arcmyrians had made the most of the compact space, focusing on functionality and simplicity.

"We'll all be staying here together?" Lynx asked, his voice filled with awe as he took it all in.

"Yes," Lincoln replied with a smile. "This is plenty of room for all of us. It may be smaller than you're used to, but we will be comfortable."

"Thank you, Rykas," Lincoln said as he turned to the leader of the Arcmyrian warriors, "we are deeply grateful for your protection and hospitality."

"It is us that are grateful to you," replied Rykas, "for restoring Arcmyrin and the worlds."

After Rykas and the warriors left, the family started to settle in. They made their way back down the lift to the biodome level. The lower pod was a wonder in itself—an open, glass-encased space filled with a lush garden of fruits, vegetables, and herbs. The cooking area was cleverly integrated into the space, with a small dining area nearby, creating an environment where the process of growing, preparing, and eating food was deeply interconnected.

Ridge marveled at the balance of simplicity and technological advancement. "It's incredible how this space functions so efficiently. Everything you need is here—self-sustaining, low-impact living."

Lincoln smiled, watching his family take it all in.

The evening had fallen gently on Arcmyrin, and the living quarters they were staying in, nestled within one of the Arcmyrian city-bases, were cozy and welcoming after the long, grueling journey to restore balance to the planets. After the final battle against Patereon and the dark shadows, it was nice to have a moment of peace, even if the world outside was still settling from the upheaval. The family, their faces weary but content, gathered around a large table in the center of the room, their dinner spread before them.

Lynx, ever the inquisitive one, had eaten little so far. Instead, he sat with his elbows on the table, his brow furrowed in thought, the excitement from the battle still buzzing in his veins, mixed with a million new questions. The peaceful atmosphere of their meal gave him a rare moment to reflect, and with that reflection came an endless stream of curiosity.

"So, Dad," Lynx said, looking across the table at Lincoln, his voice full of curiosity, "is Tanzlora anything like Arcmyrin?"

Lincoln, who had been sipping from his glass of water, paused, then put it down with a soft chuckle. He hadn't expected this question, but it was typical of Lynx to always want to know more about the unknown.

"That's an interesting question, Lynx," Lincoln began, glancing between his children. "Tanzlora is very different from Arcmyrin, but there are similarities. Both planets are ancient, both rich with life, but where Arcmyrin has always been a place of balance between the elements, Tanzlora... it's more about harmony within nature, and the interconnectedness of all life forms."

Ridge, who had been cutting into his meal, paused at his brother's words. "But not eco pods, right?" he teased with a grin, giving Lincoln an exaggerated sidelong glance. "Tanzlora doesn't have all that fancy stuff you're used to, like eco pods and automated everything. I'm betting you'd much prefer Arcmyrin's home base than Tanzlora."

Lincoln nodded, "Tanzlora is different. Instead of eco pods, the cities are built more naturally—blending into the planet's landscape. The people live in harmony with nature, building structures that use the land's resources without disturbing the planet's natural state."

Lynx frowned thoughtfully as he processed this new information. "So, if Tanzlora doesn't have eco pods, how do they keep everything balanced?"

Lincoln replied, "Simple. They just live in tune with the planet, Lynx. They don't need fancy tech to survive. They've mastered living off the land, using the energy from the planet and its ecosystems to maintain balance without relying on artificial systems."

Lynx wasn't convinced. "So... no tech? That sounds like it might be a bit... I don't know... old-fashioned?"

Lincoln chuckled, leaning back in his chair. "Old-fashioned?" he echoed. "Not at all. Tanzlora has a very advanced way of integrating nature with technology, but it's not the same as what is here on Arcmyrin. The planet provides for the people in ways that are far more... instinctive, I suppose. It's about connection with the earth, the plants, the creatures. They have a deep, spiritual bond with their planet."

Waverly tilted her head, her voice curious. "But if there's no tech, how do they communicate with the outside world? How do they talk to Earth or Arcmyrin when they need to?"

"Ah, well, that's where things get interesting," Lincoln said with a smile. "Tanzlora uses organic technology—like plants that act as communicators, and natural forces that send signals. It's a unique kind of innovation. They've figured out how to use the planet's own resources to connect with other places without needing the kind of tech they use on Arcmyrin."

Lynx's eyes sparkled with fascination, clearly impressed. "Wait, so no screens or wires? Just... plants talking to each other? That's wild!"

Lincoln laughed. "Yeah, it's a different world, Lynx. But I think you'd like it. You'd probably end up talking to trees like you're best friends." He teased, nudging his son with his elbow.

Waverly chuckled, but there was a certain wistful look in her eyes. "I'm sure it's beautiful. I want to visit there one day. It sounds... peaceful."

"Believe me," Lincoln said softly, his voice a little distant, "it is. And it's always been my dream to bring you two to Tanzlora. To be able to travel back and forth between all planets. To be intergalactic citizens of the universe."

Lynx, who had been watching his father carefully, blinked and asked, "So... is that your plan, Dad? Is that why you're staying here on Arcmyrin? To help fix things? To be able to travel like that? Or... are you going to come back with us?"

The question hung in the air, and the warmth of the room seemed to quiet for a moment. Lincoln's gaze softened as he looked at his son. He knew this moment had been coming—the question that would decide what was next for him, for the family. It wasn't an easy decision. His heart longed for his family on Earth, for Gran Celia and the home they had left behind. But Arcmyrin was a planet in need of healing, and he couldn't turn his back on it either. Then there was Tanzlora, he had a life there too.

"I've been thinking about it, Lynx," Lincoln said quietly, his eyes meeting his son's. "Arcmyrin has been through a lot. It needs time, and it needs people who can help it recover. But Earth...Tanzlora... your mother... they all need me too. So yes, I will come back. But I'll need to finish some work here first. I've already made plans for the future of Arcmyrin, and I want to see them through. But when the time is right, I'll be with you. We'll all go back home."

Lynx, for the first time, didn't press for more details. Instead, he smiled and nodded, understanding that his father had to do what was right for all worlds.

"Good," Lynx said, his voice full of reassurance. "Because I can't wait to get back to Sage Manor. I have my own room there!"

Ridge grinned, and Waverly, too, smiled softly, though there was a faint trace of sadness in her eyes. "We'll all be together again soon," she said quietly.

They all sat in comfortable silence for a moment, the weight of the conversation settling around them. The food was simple but filling, a welcome change after their long journey. As the family finished their meal, the warmth of their togetherness was a balm to the chaos of the past. Arcmyrin, the battles, the portal, and the dark forces—they were all behind them now.

But ahead of them lay the future—the future of their family.

As Lynx finished the last of his meal, he leaned back in his chair with a satisfied sigh. "This is what I've been waiting for," he said, his eyes sparkling. "A nice, normal dinner. Next time we eat, can we have something with more spice? This was kind of boring."

Ridge chuckled, giving him a playful nudge. "You've got a one-track mind, little dude. You think about food more than anything else."

Lynx just grinned. "It's important. You've gotta stay fueled for whatever comes next."

Waverly smiled, her heart light as she looked around at her family. No matter what the future held, they would be ready. Together.

49

The morning was quiet, the soft chirping of birds the only sound breaking the stillness of the early hours. Gran Celia stood in the gazebo, her hands wringing in nervous motion, her eyes flicking from one corner of the garden to another. The sun had risen higher, casting warm golden rays across the manicured lawns, but the peace of the day did nothing to calm the swirling anxiety that had been building in her chest for the past several days.

It had been over a week since the orb had shown the elemental spirits balanced, and Gran Celia couldn't shake the feeling that something was off. She had tried to keep herself occupied with the day-to-day tasks of the manor, tried to distract herself with work or even conversations with Francis, but her thoughts always returned to the same thing: Why hasn't the family returned?

She stepped forward, pacing the stone floor of the gazebo, her footsteps measured and quick. The rhythmic sound of her movement was soothing for only a moment before the questions began to swirl once again. She stopped, glancing toward the distant chamber below the manor, where the orb had continued to pulse brightly in the absence of her family's return.

"Francis," she called, her voice tight with a mixture of concern and confusion. "I just don't understand. Why hasn't the portal reactivated? Why hasn't there been any sign of them? The orb is still glowing, but the screens... the portal system, everything—it's silent, dark. It's like something's blocking it, but I don't feel any dark forces behind this delay. What do you think?"

Francis, who had been standing nearby watching the morning light spill across the garden, turned toward her with a steady gaze. Gran Celia's pacing and restlessness were becoming more pronounced each day, and though she could understand the worry that had set in, Francis remained calm, a steady presence amid Gran Celia's growing unease.

"I know how you feel," Francis replied gently, moving closer to the edge of the gazebo to stand next to her. "It's hard not knowing what's happening. It's unlike anything we've experienced before. But you're right about one thing: I don't sense any dark forces either."

Gran Celia's brows furrowed slightly. "You're certain?"

Francis nodded, her tone reassuring. "I'm certain. If there were any remnants of dark influence, if there were still dark shadows lurking in the background, I would sense them. The balance has been restored. The spirits are free, and Arcmyrin is beginning to heal. But the fact that the portal remains dark—it's a mystery."

Gran Celia sighed deeply, her shoulders heavy with the weight of the unknown. "I know what you mean. It feels like we've been waiting for ages. The screens in the chamber remain dark, and despite the orb's light, nothing happens. It's as if the portal has become... dormant."

She looked down at her hands, still twisting nervously, and then back up at Francis. "But I know it's not because of dark forces. I feel it deep inside—I don't sense anything threatening. I don't even think the portal is closed. I think it's waiting... waiting for something."

Francis studied her closely, her eyes thoughtful. "You're right. We're in uncharted territory here. But this is a good thing, Celia. The portal isn't closed, not in the way it was before. It's just... dormant. Perhaps it's waiting for something from them. The connection with the elements is unlike anything we've encountered. It could be that they're still completing the final phase of the mission. Maybe there's a natural cycle the portal has to go through before it opens again."

Gran Celia stopped pacing for a moment, her eyes narrowing slightly. "A cycle? What do you mean?"

Francis shrugged. "Perhaps the spirits have to align in a specific way. Maybe the portal system, once activated, is tied to the rhythm of the planets themselves. Arcmyrin is still recovering, still balancing the energies, and the portal could be part of that delicate process. They've restored the balance, but there's a chance that the final steps require time, patience. We may need to wait for the right alignment—of the planets, of the elements."

Gran Celia considered this, but the tension in her chest didn't ease. "But why so long? It's been over a week."

"I understand," Francis said, her voice warm with empathy. "The wait is frustrating, and I can see it's weighing on you. But remember, Celia, this isn't just about bringing the family back. It's about restoring the balance on a cosmic level. The work they've done has been monumental. Arcmyrin itself needed them—and now, the elements are returning to their rightful places. Perhaps the portal can't be opened again until everything has fully stabilized. They've done their part, and now the universe might need a moment to reset."

Gran Celia stood still, her eyes drifting once more toward the distant chamber, where the faint flicker of the orb glowed brightly, almost as if it was waiting for something. The light seemed to call to her, its pulse steady but still filled with a kind of quiet anticipation. There was something calming in the orb's glow, and though she couldn't fully understand it, she knew in her heart that the family would return—when the time was right.

"I hope you're right, Francis," Gran Celia said finally, her voice quieter now, more thoughtful. "I just wish I could know that they're safe. That everything's going as planned."

"They will be, Celia," Francis reassured her. "You've raised them well. They've faced unimaginable obstacles and come through victorious. They've proven themselves—now we just have to trust that the spirits and the universe will do their part."

Gran Celia smiled faintly, grateful for Francis's calming presence. "You're right, as usual. I just can't shake the feeling that we're on the cusp of something—something important. But for now, we wait."

Francis nodded, her gaze following Celia's to the distant, glowing orb. "We wait. But we also remember the victory we've already won. The darkness is gone. The spirits are free. Arcmyrin will heal, and the balance will be restored. They will come home."

Gran Celia turned and gave Francis a small, thankful smile. "I suppose you're right. It's just... difficult to wait, isn't it? After all we've been through, all we've fought for."

Francis's voice softened. "Yes. But sometimes, the greatest strength is in the patience to let things unfold as they need to. The universe is in motion, Celia. Your family will return when it's time. And when they do, they will be stronger for all they've experienced."

Gran Celia nodded, a sense of peace settling over her as the words sank in. She wasn't certain of when they would return, or when the portal would open again, but deep inside, she could feel the connection, the undeniable truth that her family was safe. The balance had been restored, and the world was healing.

As she stood there, Francis beside her, a soft breeze stirred in the gazebo, making the leaves rustle gently in the trees around them. The quiet sound filled the space, and for the first time in days, Gran Celia felt a sense of calm.

They would return. The elements had done their part. And soon, the portal would open again, bringing them back home.

But for now, they waited. And that was enough.

50

The living quarters were quiet as the sun began to set over Arcmyrin, casting a soft glow through the windows. Ridge, Lincoln, Waverly, and Lynx sat around the low table in the center of the room. The aftereffects of their hard-won battle were still fresh in their minds, but for the first time in days, they felt a sense of relief. The weight of their mission, the fear of failure, had been lifted. Arcmyrin was healing. The elemental spirits were freed. Now, all that remained was to return to Earth, to Sage Manor, and reunite with Gran Celia.

But even though the victory was theirs, the waiting felt endless. The portal had remained closed. It was as though something was still in flux, something just out of reach.

Waverly sat next to Lynx, her eyes distant as she thought about home, about their life on Earth. She couldn't wait to see Gran Celia again, to feel the familiar comfort of the manor. Lynx, ever restless, kept glancing toward the door, clearly eager for whatever news would come next. Lincoln and Ridge exchanged quiet words, each lost in their own thoughts as well.

Then, the air in the room seemed to hum, and a soft shimmer appeared by the doorway. The familiar presence of Elara materialized in front of them, her physical form more vibrant than ever before, a comforting glow surrounding her. The energy she emanated was calming but filled with purpose.

"You've been waiting long enough," Elara said with a smile, her voice echoing gently. "It's time."

The family looked up at her, surprise flickering across their faces. The wait had seemed interminable, and to see her now, here—so tangible and present—brought a sense of finality to their uncertainty.

"Time?" Ridge echoed, his voice filled with both anticipation and confusion. "What do you mean? The portal's still closed."

Elara nodded. "The Tanzloran elders have agreed to activate the portal just long enough for you to return home to Earth. But it will only remain open for a short time, just enough to bring all of you back together with Gran Celia. After that, it will close again, and the portal system will be sealed for a while. The balance has been restored, and the elements are in harmony once more. It's safe now. The journey is ready to begin."

Lincoln, who had been silent until now, stood from his seat, his brow furrowing. "The portal will open again? For us to return home?"

"Yes," Elara confirmed. "I will escort you—Ridge, Lincoln, Waverly, and Lynx—from Arcmyrin back to Earth. But there's more. Keelee will be escorting Bethany and the children from Tanzlora. They'll meet you on Earth."

Waverly's heart skipped a beat, and she looked at her father. "Children? What children?"

Elara gave a soft, knowing smile. "Lincoln and Bethany have children—two young ones—from their time on Tanzlora. The elders have agreed for Keelee to bring them through the portal once it's open." She turned to Lincoln, "They don't know? You did not divulge this to your family?"

The room fell silent. Waverly looked at her father, confusion and disbelief written on her face. "Wait. You and mom have... more children? Why didn't you tell us about this?" She couldn't hide the shock in her voice.

Lincoln met her gaze, his expression unreadable for a moment. "It's something I've kept to myself," he said softly, his voice laced with a quiet sadness. "It's complicated, I didn't want to bring up the past. It was never the right time. But now... now it is."

Lynx, who had been listening intently, leaned forward with a grin. "So, we have more family? More siblings? How many more siblings?" he asked, his excitement building as he processed the news.

Ridge let out a short laugh, shaking his head in disbelief. "More kids? So, we're going to have a full house when we get home, huh?"

Waverly's mind was still reeling. "But why didn't you tell us about them? How could you keep something like that from us?"

Elara's voice was calm, her gaze softening as she looked at Waverly. "It wasn't an easy decision for Lincoln and Bethany, and it wasn't something he could share until now. But the time has come for your family to be whole again. The children from Tanzlora are part of that journey. The portal will bring them to you, to your home."

Lincoln, his voice low and steady, spoke again. "It's not something I ever expected, Waverly. I'm sure it's a lot to take in. But now, it's time for us to move forward as a family."

Ridge, ever the optimist, broke the tension with his usual easy grin. "Well, I'm all for meeting new family members. More people to boss around. I'll be the first to show them the ropes." He winked at Lynx, who was bouncing in his seat, clearly excited about the idea of meeting new siblings.

Lynx's excitement was palpable as he leaned forward. "Do they know we're coming? Do they know we're their family? I can't wait to meet them!" His eyes were wide with enthusiasm.

Elara nodded. "They know. The elders on Tanzlora have kept them informed, and they are eager to meet their family. They have been raised in safety on Tanzlora, but now that the portal is opening, it is time for them to join you on Earth."

Waverly's mind raced with thoughts of her mother, of the children she'd left behind, and now—this new information. New siblings. Children she never knew existed. The idea was both exciting and overwhelming. She turned to her father, searching his face for answers.

"How old are they?" Waverly asked, still trying to wrap her mind around it all. "What are they like?"

Lincoln sighed, his eyes softening as he met her gaze. "They're young, five years old. They've been raised on Tanzlora, Earth will be a foreign place to them. But they're part of this family, Waverly. They are Beaumonts. And when the time comes, when we all meet, I ask you to welcome them with open arms."

Waverly stood up slowly, her hands trembling slightly as she took in the weight of the moment. The family was about to be reunited in a way she had never expected. More siblings—children she never knew existed—would soon join them. The unknowns seemed endless, but one thing was certain: they would be a family again, together at last.

Lynx grinned, his excitement bubbling over. "I can't wait to meet them! Wait, how many? I don't think you ever answered that question, dad."

"Two," said Lincoln, "a boy and a girl, twins."

"Cool!" exclaimed Lynx.

"What are their names?" asked Waverly.

"Maya and Maddox." replied Lincoln.

Waverly took a deep breath, her gaze softening as she turned to Elara. "So, when does this happen? How soon can we go home?"

"The portal will open in three days," Elara said, her voice full of certainty. "In that time, you will have everything prepared. Keelee and the elders will send Bethany and the children through, and I will be with all of you every step of the way, escorting you back to Earth."

Waverly looked at her family, feeling a surge of hope and anticipation. "Three days," she repeated softly. "We'll finally be home. Together."

Ridge clapped his hands together. "Sounds like a plan. Let's get to it, people!"

Lynx bounced on his feet, "I'm ready. Three days... I can't wait!"

As the family began to gather their thoughts, the weight of the journey ahead seemed lighter. For the first time in a long while, they could see the future clearly—their family would be complete again, their hearts whole. And with Elara's guidance, they would return to Earth.

51

The soft hum of energy filled the air, a deep, resonating pulse that seemed to vibrate through the very walls of Sage Manor. Gran Celia stood by the window, her eyes narrowed, listening intently to the sound. It had been quiet for so long, a lull in the chaos, but now—now, it was unmistakable. The portal was coming back to life.

"Francis, do you hear that?" Gran Celia asked, her voice thick with anticipation. Her heart began to race as the familiar hum intensified, the energy practically humming in the floorboards beneath her feet.

Francis, who had been quietly sitting in the parlor, her hands folded in her lap, rose to her feet. "Yes," she said softly, a smile tugging at the corner of her lips. "I think the time has finally come."

Gran Celia could feel it in her bones—the long wait was over. Her family, her entire world, was about to be reunited. She felt a surge of warmth and excitement flood through her chest as she turned toward the door of the parlor.

"We need to go," she said, her voice firm with urgency. "It's happening."

Together, they hurried out of the parlor, their steps echoing in the grand hall as they made their way outside to the gazebo and down the stone stairway into the chamber. As they entered the underground room, the hum was louder, more pronounced, almost like the pulse of a beating heart.

Gran Celia's heart skipped a beat when she saw the orb, the same orb that had once glowed faintly, now shining with vibrant energy. The room was alive, the energy swirling in the air like a storm about to break. But there was something else in the air—something different.

Elara's holographic form appeared in front of them, her ethereal presence glowing with a soft, otherworldly light. "Gran Celia, Francis," she said, her voice echoing with a soothing calmness. "You must leave the chamber. It's too dangerous for you to be here when the portal opens. The energies are unstable."

Gran Celia stood still for a moment, her eyes wide with disbelief. She had waited so long for this moment, to see her family again, to hold them close. "But... but my family is coming through, Elara. I need to see them."

Elara's gaze softened, and she nodded. "Your family is safe and well, Celia. They are coming home. But you must remain in the manor for now. The portal is a delicate thing, and it's best if you are away from it while everyone passes through."

Francis, her voice a little shaky with the weight of the moment, spoke up. "But when will they arrive? How much longer do we have to wait?"

Elara's holographic form flickered with a gentle pulse of light. "They are coming now. Stay inside Sage Manor, and I will bring them through. It won't be long."

Gran Celia felt a moment of hesitation, the desire to be close to her family, to reach out and hold them. But Elara was right. The portal was no longer something of mystery or fear—it was a bridge, a connection to the ones she loved. And she trusted that her family would be safe, that they would come through, whole and well.

"Very well," Gran Celia said, her voice steadying. "I'll wait in the manor."

With a final nod of reassurance from Elara, the holographic image of the spirit began to fade, and the portal, now activated, surged with a brilliant flash of light.

Gran Celia and Francis retreated to the parlor, the sounds of the portal's energy humming softly through the manor's walls. Gran Celia's pulse quickened, and she moved to the window, her eyes scanning the garden outside as if somehow she could sense her family's arrival. She knew that, any moment now, they would be home.

And then, there was a shift in the air.

The first figure to emerge from the glowing portal was Elara, her form stepping through with the grace of a being that had already seen countless worlds. Behind her, Ridge, Lincoln, Waverly, and Lynx emerged from the swirling light, each of them looking slightly dazed, but unmistakably alive. They were home.

After drinking the herbal mixtures that Elara brought for everyone, they quickly made their way up to the house and into the parlor.

Gran Celia's breath caught in her throat as she rushed forward, her arms outstretched. "My family… you're home," she whispered, her voice thick with emotion.

Lincoln was the first to step forward, his face softening into a smile as he embraced his mother. "We're home, mother. It's finally over."

Waverly, her face radiant with relief, joined them, her arms wrapping around Gran Celia in a tight hug. "We did it, Gran. We did it."

Lynx, ever energetic, bounced on his feet and ran forward to hug Gran Celia. "We're back! I can't believe it! We're home!"

Ridge smiled, his hand resting on his mother's shoulder. "It's good to be back."

Gran Celia stepped back, her eyes brimming with tears as she took in the sight of them all—her children, her family, whole again. It was more than she could have ever hoped for.

"You're all here," she said, her voice filled with awe. "You're safe."

Elara's voice, calm and gentle, broke through the quiet reunion. "I'm glad to see you're all together again," she said. "But I must leave now. Keelee will be arriving shortly with Bethany and the children. I'll leave you to your reunion, but remember—the portal will close soon, and I must return to Arcmyrin."

Gran Celia nodded, understanding the necessity. "Thank you, Elara," she said, her voice thick with gratitude. "Thank you for everything."

With a final smile, Elara left the parlor to return to the portal. Stepping back through, her figure faded from view as the light of the portal dimmed. It wasn't long before Keelee emerged, his tall form stepping through the glowing light, followed by Bethany and the two young children.

They left the chamber and walked up to the manor and into the parlor.

Gran Celia's eyes widened, a gasp escaping her as she took in the sight of them. Two children—young, with bright eyes and an undeniable spark of energy. She didn't know them, not yet, but they were part of her family, part of the legacy she had carried all these years.

Bethany, her face soft with relief and joy, stepped forward and embraced Gran Celia. "Celia," she whispered, her voice filled with emotion. "I'm so glad to be home."

Gran Celia stepped back, her eyes searching the faces of the children. "These... these are your children?" she asked, her voice barely above a whisper.

Bethany smiled, her eyes shining. "Yes. This is Maya and Maddox, our children born on Tanzlora. They've been waiting for the right time to come home."

Gran Celia felt a wave of emotion crash over her, her heart expanding with the sudden realization of just how much her family had grown. "Maya, Maddox," she said softly, reaching out to them. "Welcome home."

Maya, a bright-eyed girl with auburn hair, took Gran Celia's hand with a shy smile. "Thank you," she said softly.

Maddox, with a mischievous grin, reached up and hugged Gran Celia tightly. "Hello," he said.

Gran Celia's heart swelled as she embraced them, tears welling in her eyes. "I have more grandchildren," she whispered to herself, her voice full of wonder.

"It's time for me to go," Keelee said, his voice quiet but resolute. "The portal will close soon, and I must return to Tanzlora. The task is complete, and the balance has been restored. I leave you now, but know that you'll always have allies in Arcmyrin and Tanzlora."

Gran Celia nodded, her eyes filled with gratitude. "Thank you, Keelee, for everything."

Keelee left the parlor and returned to the chamber. He stepped back through the portal, his form disappearing into the light. The portal shimmered for a moment, the air still with energy before it slowly began to close, the hum dying down before it went completely dark.

The parlor was quiet for a moment, but it didn't feel empty. In fact, it felt fuller than ever before. The family was finally complete. The journey had brought them through struggles, sacrifices, and battles, but they had arrived—whole, united, and at peace.

Later that evening, the family gathered around the dining room table, the soft light of candles flickering in the center. The table was filled with food—simple, familiar dishes from Earth—but it didn't matter what was on the plates. What mattered was the people sitting around it.

As they ate, their laughter and conversation filled the room, the bonds of family stronger than ever.

And for the first time in a long while, Gran Celia felt the fullness of peace. The journey had been long, but it had brought them all home. Together.

TAKE A SNEAK PEEK AT

BOOK TWO

AVAILABLE FEBRUARY 1, 2025

Chapter 1

Beneath the twin suns of Tanzlora, the air shimmered with an ethereal glow, casting kaleidoscopic reflections across the endless canopy of the Lucidus Forest. The trees, towering like emerald spires, hummed with a subtle resonance, their translucent leaves catching light in a thousand colors. Rivers of liquid silver coursed through the land, weaving between crystalline cliffs that glistened like prisms. Every element of the planet pulsed with life, its vibrant energy unmistakable to those attuned to its rhythms.

At the heart of the forest, within a sacred grove untouched by time, Elder Sylvaris knelt. His tall form, draped in flowing robes spun from iridescent fibers, blended seamlessly with his surroundings. His blue-violet skin shimmered like polished opal, reflecting the radiant hues of the forest. Silver streaks in his hair framed his angular face, and his eyes, glowing like twin moons, were fixed on the ancient ceremonial pool before him.

The pool's surface, still as glass, held the secrets of Tanzlora's lifeblood. Sylvaris's long, graceful fingers hovered above it, and with a whispered incantation, the water began to ripple. Swirling images of the planet's energy web appeared, vibrant and whole. But as he continued the ritual, a dark tendril slithered across the vision, disrupting the harmony.

A deep, guttural hum reverberated through the grove, and Sylvaris's eyes widened. The tendril grew, morphing into a writhing mass of shadows that consumed the vibrant energy in its path. Trees blackened, rivers turned to ash, and the once-resonant hum of Tanzlora's life force fell silent.

"No," Sylvaris murmured, his voice trembling. The vision shifted violently, showing a massive, amorphous entity at the planet's core, its shadowy appendages reaching outward, spreading decay. It was not of Tanzlora—this was something ancient, malevolent, and unrelenting. The Umbralox.

With a sharp gasp, Sylvaris released his supernatural powers to counteract the evil vision. The pool's surface stilled, but the elder remained frozen, his breath uneven. The Lucidus Forest around him seemed to dim, as though it too had witnessed the devastation.

He rose to his full height, his robes billowing as if stirred by an unseen wind. The urgency in his movements betrayed the calm demeanor he usually carried. "The council must hear of this at once."

In the Tanzloran council chambers, a majestic amphitheater carved into a massive crystal formation, the other elders awaited Sylvaris's arrival. The room pulsed with faint light, the crystalline walls resonating softly as though amplifying the thoughts of those within. Each elder, tall and graceful, shared Sylvaris's shimmering blue-violet complexion, their features marked with the wisdom of countless cycles.

Sylvaris entered, his commanding presence silencing the low hum of discussion. He strode to the center of the chamber, placing a hand over his heart in the customary gesture of respect. "My friends, Tanzlora is in grave danger."

The air in the chamber grew heavy as Sylvaris recounted his vision. His words painted a picture of desolation, of a force that sought to consume the planet's essence. The elders listened in silence, their expressions grave. When he finished, murmurs rippled through the room, the crystalline walls echoing their concern.

Elder Brakar, the eldest and most revered among them, stood. Her voice, soft yet commanding, resonated like the chime of distant bells. "The Umbralox... we have not heard that name in eons. If it has returned, then the danger is greater than we feared."

"What do we do?" Elder Draven asked, his tone laced with urgency.

Brakar turned her luminous gaze to Sylvaris. "We must summon Keelee. He is our most capable envoy and the only one who can bridge the gap between Tanzlora and the Beaumonts. If there is any hope of survival, it lies with them."

Sylvaris nodded. "I will bring Keelee at once."

Keelee stood on the edge of a shimmering plateau, the Lucidis Forest stretching out below him like a sea of light. His form, tall and graceful, radiated strength. His blue-violet skin glistened under the twin suns, and his long hair, a cascade of shimmering silver, flowed in the breeze.

The summons came swiftly, a harmonic tone carried on the wind. Keelee turned, his sharp gaze meeting the Tanzloran messenger hovering nearby. Without hesitation, he stepped into a portal of cascading light, his heart steady yet heavy. The elders only summoned him for matters of utmost importance.

Moments later, he emerged in the council chambers. The solemn expressions of the elders confirmed his suspicions. He knelt before them, placing his hand over his heart. "What is your command, Elders?"

Brakar spoke first. "Keelee, Tanzlora faces a threat unlike any we have seen. The Umbralox has returned, and our very existence hangs in the balance. We must seek help from beyond our world."

Keelee's brows furrowed. "You mean the Earthlings? The Beaumonts?"

Sylvaris stepped forward. "Yes. They are uniquely positioned to aid us. Their legacy is intertwined with the Umbralox's history, though they may not yet realize it."

Keelee rose, determination glinting in his luminous eyes. "Then I will go to them. For Tanzlora, and for all we hold dear."

As the elders nodded in unison, a portal began to form at the chamber's center, its light reflecting the urgency of the mission. Without hesitation, Keelee stepped through, carrying the weight of his world on his shoulders.

Chapter 2

The gardens of Sage Manor were in full bloom, the late afternoon sun casting a golden glow over rows of vibrant roses, lilies, and wildflowers. A long table, adorned with pastel linens and bouquets, stretched beneath the shade of a grand oak tree. Balloons swayed gently in the breeze, and the sound of children's laughter mingled with the chirping of birds.

Maya and Maddox Beaumont, the youngest members of the family, were the center of attention, their wide smiles and sparkling eyes lighting up the gathering. Maya's curly auburn hair was adorned with flower clips, and Maddox, his blond locks slightly tousled, wore a crown of daisies he'd insisted on making himself.

"Happy birthday to you!" The family's voices harmonized as they gathered around a beautifully decorated cake, two sets of candles flickering atop it. The twins leaned forward, their small faces alight with excitement, and blew out the candles together.

Cheers erupted, and the twins laughed as bits of confetti rained down on them. Gran Celia clapped enthusiastically, her silver hair shining in the sunlight. "Perfect! Another year wiser for my little starlights."

Waverly handed out slices of cake, her movements graceful and precise. She smiled at the twins. "Six years old already. When did that happen?"

"Time moves differently when you're this close to the cosmos," Ridge said, smirking as he leaned against a nearby pillar. "These two are growing up faster than we can blink."

Bethany, the twins' mother, placed a gentle hand on their shoulders, her emerald eyes glowing with pride. "They've done so well since we came back to Earth. Better than I expected, really."

"It helps that they've got such a strong support system," Lincoln added, wrapping an arm around his wife. His deep voice carried warmth and admiration. "And a family that's a little too experienced with interplanetary adaptation."

Lynx, lounging on a blanket nearby, raised an eyebrow. "Still, you have to admit, they're not like other Earth kids. Not entirely."

"No," Bethany admitted, her gaze lingering on Maddox, who was giggling with Maya as they chased butterflies. "But they're finding their way. Tanzlora will always be part of them, but Earth is their home now."

As the celebration continued, Maddox suddenly broke away from the group, his playful demeanor replaced by an expression of confusion. He made his way to his father, tugging on Lincoln's sleeve. "Dad?"

Lincoln crouched down to Maddox's level. "What's up, buddy?"

Maddox hesitated, looking down at his shoes before meeting his father's eyes. "I feel... funny."

"Funny how?" Lincoln asked, concern creeping into his voice.

"My head," Maddox said, tapping his temple. "It's humming. And kind of... vibrating. Like there's music I can't hear, but I know it's there."

Lincoln frowned, his brows knitting together. "Does it hurt?"

Maddox shook his head. "No, it's just... weird."

Lincoln patted his son's shoulder reassuringly. "Okay, let's talk to Mom about this."

He guided Maddox back to Bethany, who was arranging a platter of fruit. "Beth, Maddox says his head's humming. Vibrating, even."

Bethany froze mid-motion, her face turning serious. "Humming? Vibrating?" She crouched down and took Maddox's hands in hers. "Sweetheart, when did this start?"

"A little while ago. It got stronger when we were singing," Maddox said. "I didn't want to tell everyone, but it's like there's something... trying to talk to me."

Bethany exchanged a sharp look with Lincoln, her voice lowering. "He's picking up on something. A higher consciousness entity. The vibrations aren't random."

Lincoln's face darkened. "You think it's connected to Tanzlora?"

"It could be," Bethany said. "Or it could be something else. Either way, we can't ignore it."

"Ridge!" Lincoln called, his tone urgent. Ridge, who had been laughing at one of Waverly's quips, immediately straightened and came over.

"What's going on?" Ridge asked, his relaxed demeanor replaced with alertness.

Bethany quickly explained Maddox's symptoms. "It's possible the portal has been activated, or something is trying to come through. You and Lincoln need to check the chamber."

Ridge nodded, his jaw tightening. "Let's go."

While the others tried to maintain the festive atmosphere for the twin's sake, Lincoln and Ridge slipped away, heading for the chamber underneath the gazebo. The chamber, an ancient, hidden part of the estate, housed the portal that connected Earth to its sister planets, Tanzlora and Arcmyrin—an interplanetary gateway to the cosmos.

The air grew colder as they stepped into the gazebo, the hum of energy faint but unmistakable. Lincoln and Ridge exchanged a wary glance before Ridge pushed the heavy stone door open. They quickly descended the narrow stone stairs.

Inside, the chamber was alive with faint light. The carvings on the stone walls pulsed faintly, resonating in rhythm with an invisible force. In the center, the portal shimmered faintly, a faint swirl of light and shadow stirring within its boundaries.

"It's active," Ridge said, his voice grim.

Lincoln stepped closer, his eyes narrowing as he studied the portal. "Something's trying to come through. We need to find out if it's a friend or a foe."

Ridge pulled a small device from his pocket, a Tanzloran scanner modified for Earth's energy signatures. The screen glowed, showing an erratic but distinct pattern. "It's not fully formed yet. But whatever it is, it's strong."

Lincoln's thoughts immediately went to his son. "Maddox could feel this before we even came down here. That's no coincidence."

Ridge nodded. "We should inform Bethany—and Waverly and Lynx, too. If this thing makes it through, we'll need all hands on deck."

As the portal pulsed brighter, the brothers turned and hurried back to the garden, their minds racing. The celebration was far from over, but they couldn't shake the feeling that something far greater had just begun.

ACKNOWLEDGMENTS

Thank you to all the readers who have journeyed with the Beaumont family - your presence made this story come alive. I'm so honored to share this story with you. I appreciate you for taking the time to read it.

Sincerely,

LG Rice

Check out all of my books at www.authorlgrice.com

Contact me: hello@authorlgrice.com

Follow me on Instagram and X: @authorlgrice

www.ingramcontent.com/pod-product-compliance
Lightning Source LLC
Chambersburg PA
CBHW021249131224
18930CB00042B/561